By JOHN INMAN

NOVELS
A Hard Winter Rain
Hobbled
Loving Hector
Shy

NOVELLAS
The Poodle Apocalypse

Published by DREAMSPINNER PRESS
http://www.dreamspinnerpress.com

HOBBLED

JOHN INMAN

Dreamspinner Press

Published by
Dreamspinner Press
5032 Capital Circle SW
Ste 2, PMB# 279
Tallahassee, FL 32305-7886
USA
http://www.dreamspinnerpress.com/

Hobbled

Cover Art by Paul Richmond
http://www.paulrichmondstudio.com

ISBN: 978-1-62380-855-6
Digital ISBN: 978-1-62380-856-3

Printed in the United States of America
First Edition
June 2013

For those who have tumbled into love with only a glance,
and in only a heartbeat. This book is for you.

CHAPTER ONE
HOUSEBOUND

SINCE his clothes usually hung all over him like a forty-foot flag on a twelve-foot pole, Danny Shay was one of those people who look a whole lot better *out* of clothes than they do *in* them. Unfortunately, Danny was so damned inexperienced and shy that not too many people had found that out yet. Almost none in fact. And they certainly wouldn't be finding it out for the next six weeks.

Or so he thought.

Danny sat in his upstairs bedroom, sprawled out with the recliner at full tilt, wearing nothing but a cast on his left leg that extended from just below his knee all the way down to his toes, and an electronic ankle monitor, courtesy of the San Diego Police Department, clamped snugly around the *other* leg, just above his right foot.

Smack in the middle of those two extremities lay his dick, and at the moment, it was looking pretty darned depressed and unhappy about the whole thing. It was looking red and exhausted, too, since Danny had just whacked off for the second time that day, for lack of anything better to do to pass the time. A splash of semen was splattered across his chest all the way up to his chin, and another puddle was drying in his belly button because he was too depressed to wipe it away. As the semen dried, he could feel it crisping on his skin.

The ankle monitor had a little green light that flashed continually. It looked totally high-tech and alien down there, wrapped around his ankle, three feet below his dick, like maybe some Venusian scientist from the Outer Nebulae had strapped it on him to track human migratory patterns. It felt heavy too. The cop who attached it to Danny's leg told him if it started flashing red instead of green, that meant he had gone farther from the house than allowed, and he would immediately find himself in some very deep shit. The way the cop explained it, every policeman from Los Angeles to Baja would converge on the property and haul his ass to jail pronto, and he would quite possibly never see the light of day again. Period.

Danny hadn't liked the sound of that, so he made up his mind then and there he would try to avoid making the damn contraption flash red at all costs.

But as horrible as it was, the ankle monitor was actually the least of his worries. It was not nearly as annoying and disheartening as the cast on the other leg. *That* was a miserably monstrous thing to have clamped around you, don't think it wasn't. It felt like it weighed fifty pounds, although it probably didn't. It was hot, it was hard, it smelled funny, and his leg was so itchy and sore way down inside it that sometimes Danny just lay there in the recliner and gnashed his teeth.

That was usually when he started beating off. Just to take his mind off the itchy, achy leg.

Danny Shay was eighteen years old. He had wavy brown hair down to his shoulders, big brown eyes like a puppy dog, and a spray of freckles across his nose. His aunt Edna said he was as cute as a cup of butterscotch pudding, whatever the hell that meant. Oy. Relatives.

By the way, Danny wasn't Jewish. He just liked to say "Oy."

Danny was tall and lanky, with hairy long legs, a lovely smooth chest with a sprinkling of hair around his belly button, and a beautiful circumcised cock that required a whole lot of attention, as most eighteen-year-old cocks do. Although he was gay, and he *knew* he was gay, he had never had sex with a man in his life, if you discounted the one time Larry Sullivan, back in the eighth grade, stayed at the house overnight and jacked him off.

Larry Sullivan was *really* gay. Danny sort of wished he had him here now. He bet good old Larry could take his mind off that fucking cast.

When his bedroom door rattled, Danny barely had time to yank his bathrobe off the floor and spread it over his come-splattered, naked body before his dad, Daniel Shay Sr., walked into the room.

"What's up, Son?"

If you'd walked in five minutes earlier, I would have shown you what's up. "Nothing, Pop. Jeez, can't you remember to knock? I could be doing *anything* in here."

His father actually blushed as he cast his eyes over Danny, lounging there in the recliner with his naked legs poking out from under the bathrobe he had so obviously just pulled over himself. Danny's dad decided to stare out the window for a while. He had been eighteen once. He knew what it was like, beating off every two minutes. Being ruled by your pecker. In fact, sometimes Danny's father thought, even at forty-two, he was still being ruled by his pecker. Maybe all men were, regardless of their age.

"Christ, Son, I'm sorry." He cleared his throat and looked even more uncomfortable than he had already. "So—just got off the phone with your mom."

"The bitch?"

"Now, Danny, I won't have you—well, yeah. The bitch." And they both chuckled.

Danny's chuckle was actually pretty perfunctory. He was wishing his dad would get the hell out so he could wipe the come off himself. It felt a little awkward, holding court with his old man while a puddle of come coagulated in his navel. He could feel it getting harder and harder and harder. Pretty soon he'd have to chip it out with a chisel. Or stick a firecracker in there and blast it out. Come on, Pop. Scram.

But his dad wasn't scramming. "I'm going to be going in a few minutes, Danny Boy. I just want to talk to you for a minute first."

Danny hated it when his father called him Danny Boy. It was like everybody should suddenly start singing in a high Celtic tenor and prancing around barefooted with fucking fiddles under their chins, like they did on PBS every Saturday night.

His pop was still rattling on, looking out the window. "I've left you some money in the kitchen in case you decide you can't live without having a pizza delivered." He gave a wry chuckle and turned away from the window to give Danny's ankle monitor a sly glance. "No pizza *pickups*, boyo. Delivery only. If you need groceries, call the number by the phone and the store will deliver. I left you a credit card for that. Don't be ordering a truckload of stuff off the Internet with that credit card either. It's strictly for food and emergencies. And no beer! Got it?"

"Got it."

"No trips to the mall, either. Guess you know *that*. And stay the hell away from your car. I parked it around the corner on the street so you won't be looking at it out front and getting all tempted to hop inside and take off for parts unknown. They've temporarily revoked your license, remember. If they catch you behind the wheel, they'll probably just take you out behind the police station and shoot you for being a pain in the ass. I'm taking the keys with me just in case you still get tempted. I think the cops left you enough leeway on your electronic leash to keep the grass mowed while I'm gone, and keep the hedges trimmed. I'll be back in exactly three weeks. If you know what's good for you, you'll make damn sure that little light stays green. The judge said he'd throw your ass in jail in a heartbeat if you don't pony up and do this thing right."

"I know, Pop. Sorry."

"I hate leaving you alone, but I don't have a choice. This business trip is important. The judge would probably throw *me* in jail if he knew I was leaving."

"I know, Pop."

"Your mom threw a conniption fit when I told her."

"The bitch."

His father gave a nod as if he couldn't have stated the facts better himself. "Bitch indeed. I'm sorry you share her DNA, Son. I was thinking with the little head at the time I porked her, not the big one." He glanced at the bathrobe Danny was tucked under. "Guess you know what that's like."

And finally, his father got the smile he was shooting for when Danny laughed. "Porking my mother, no. Being ruled by the little head, hell, yeah."

They grinned and giggled for about fifteen seconds; then suddenly his father started looking uncomfortable again. "Got the bill for the ice machine you destroyed when you threw your little tantrum at the burger joint. Care to know what it's going to cost?"

"I'll pay you back, Pop, I promise. As soon as I get out of this thing, I'll—"

"Nineteen hundred bucks."

Danny almost jumped out of the chair. If he hadn't been naked and splattered with come, he would have. "What! That's robbery!"

"No, Son. You're getting your felonies mixed up. That's destruction of property and vandalism. Robbery would be if you sneaked the thing out the back door of the restaurant and rolled it home. The owner said if I paid promptly, he would call off the lawsuit. So I paid."

"The peckerhead."

"Yes, well, be that as it may. We're pretty well strapped into doing whatever the guy wants. You did tear up his place of business pretty good."

"He was a dick."

"Yes, well, that's no excuse to—"

"He cheated me on my time card. We even proved it to the judge."

His father sighed. They had been through this a hundred times. "And the guy said it was a simple arithmetical mistake. And even if it *wasn't* a mistake, and the guy *had* tried to cheat you out of some of your wages, it was still no excuse for flipping over the ice machine and throwing all the hamburgers out the window, although I keep expecting a shitload of thank-you cards from all the homeless people in the neighborhood who got free sandwiches out of your little snit."

Danny laughed. "Yeah, that would be pretty funny." Then he spotted his father glowering down at him and decided maybe he shouldn't be laughing after all.

Although it was pretty funny.

"As soon as the monitor comes off, your anger management classes will commence."

"Fucking judge."

His father chose to ignore that. "It would have been nice if you had at least been smart enough not to slip in the ice and break your own leg after you were finished tearing up the restaurant. That cost another eighteen hundred dollars, as you know."

"Sorry."

"Sorry doesn't pay the bills, kid. And speaking of bills, there's also the matter of forking money over to the State of California for the privilege of keeping you out of jail. That ankle monitor is racking up charges even as we speak. It costs a pretty penny every single day you wear it. So please don't do anything to *lengthen* your period of house arrest. I don't think I'd be able to afford it."

"Sorry," Danny said again.

"And I don't think I'd be sitting there insulting the judge, either, if I were you. It's because of him you're not sitting in a cell counting off the days by scratching them on the wall with a spoon you stole from the jail cafeteria."

"Sorry," Danny said *again.*

His dad sighed. "Keep a low profile while I'm gone. Whatever you do, don't call the cops and get them over here. I'd rather they didn't know I left you on your own. They might not be too happy about that. If they come by to check on you, try not to say anything about me at all. That way, hopefully, they'll just think I'm at work. Got it?"

"Sorry. I mean, got it."

"The judge restricted your phone privileges but you can still use the Internet. I've got my laptop with me. If you want to contact me, shoot me an e-mail. As for the phone, I can call you, but you can't call me. Or anybody else for that matter. Okay?"

"Okay. Sir."

His father sucked in a deep breath of air, as if he had just swum up from the bottom of the pool in the backyard after having his toe stuck in the drain for five minutes. "Your mother wants you to move back to Indiana and live with her full time as soon as everything is completed to the judge's satisfaction. I told her you're an adult and you can do whatever you want."

He stared at Danny's face until Danny got the message and decided to be courteous enough to stare back and pay attention. As soon as their eyes connected, his father said, "I'd rather you stayed here, Danny. I want to make sure you know that. I know you weren't happy living with your mom and that dickhead she married, and only coming here to be with me during the summers. But that was how your custody panned out in the divorce, so we had to put up with it. Well, you're of age now, Son. You can do anything you want. Anything *legal,* I mean. When this house arrest business is all over, you stay here with me from now on in, okay? We'll find you another job, or maybe get you enrolled in a college where you can learn a trade. We'll get you squared away, and while you're doing all that, you can live here at the house. Rent free, till you're on your feet. Hell, even after you're on your feet, if you can still stand to be around me by then. What do you say? Is that a deal?"

Danny was touched. He really was. And the last thing he wanted to do was move back to Indiana with the cows and the chickens and his mother, who was a true pain in the ass, and her husband, the fucking farmer, who was *also* a pain in the ass, the putz, and that tiny one-stoplight town where he went to school all the way from first grade through high school graduation.

"Don't worry, Pop. I'll stay here. It's what I've wanted all along. And—thanks. I mean, well—thanks. I've always wanted to be here with you. I guess you know that."

Then, as if he were nine years old, Danny added, "I'll be good from now on. I promise."

His father looked touched, and he looked relieved on top of it. "I know you will, Danny. And I'm glad you're staying. Honest."

He clapped his hands together like people do when they're about to set off to search for the source of the Nile or something. "Now, then! Don't forget to feed Frederick."

They both looked up at Danny's bookcase by the window where Frederick the cat was eating the cover off of Danny's childhood edition of *Tom Sawyer*. He had been going back to it periodically for about a week now, gnawing at the binding, tearing through the pages with his claws. Really getting into the story. Danny figured the cat must have a thing for Mark Twain.

"I will, Pop. And I'll empty his litter box. Don't worry."

His father stared at Frederick for a moment as if maybe he had never seen a cat digesting Mark Twain before. *Literally* digesting it. Which was probably true. "He's humping the cat next door, you know. I'm seriously thinking of nailing the pet door shut. Or having his nuts removed. If somebody delivers a paternity suit with Frederick's name on it, just hold it until I get back. Then we'll ship Frederick off to your mother. Nuts and all."

Danny laughed. "Gotcha."

His father looked uncomfortable again, shuffling his feet and clearing his throat. Finally, he bit the bullet and leaned over Danny to give him a kiss on the forehead. "I'll be going now. Don't get up. That was a joke. I mean about getting up. Well, no it wasn't. *Don't get up.* I'll see you in three weeks."

"Have fun. And don't worry, Dad. Like I said. I'll be good. I promise."

His father nodded, as if he expected no less. He headed for the door, and just before opening it, turned back with a grin, and said, "When I'm back from my trip, maybe you might think about locking your door whenever you get the urge to pleasure yourself."

"Uh. Pleasure myself?"

His father laughed. "Yeah. In vulgar parlance I believe it's called pounding the pud. You know. Jerking the jackrabbit. Stroking the lizard. Spanking the monkey. Choking the chicken. Polishing the piccolo. Whatever you want to call it, just don't beat it to death. You may need it later in life, whether you think you will or not. So lock the door next time. Save us all a lot of embarrassment."

And now they were both blushing. "Okay, Pop. I'll try to remember."

His father nodded, gave him a wink, and eased himself out the door, latching it softly behind him, obviously glad that was over.

Danny just shook his head and grinned.

Spanking the monkey?

DANNY waited until he heard his father's footsteps descending the stairs. Then he waited until he heard the rattle of the front door as the old man juggled his luggage out onto the porch. *Then* Danny waited until he heard the slamming of the car door out in the driveway. Finally, with bated breath, he waited five seconds longer for the sound of his dad's car starting up and the sound of his dad's tires crunching their way down the gravel driveway and out onto the street.

As soon as Danny was hit by that feeling you get when you just *know* you're the only person left within spitting distance, he peeled the bathrobe off his body like Velcro. It made an audible *schleechking* sound, since it was by now pretty well glued to his skin with fossilized come. Naked, he clumsily struggled to his feet. Just getting out of a chair was a major undertaking, thanks to all the extra hardware he had strapped to his lower legs. He looked down at himself and made a face. "Ick." The dried come splattered across his body now looked like felt, thanks to the lint from the black bathrobe that was stuck all over it. "Jesus God," he said.

Ignoring the crutch leaning against the wall because he hated the damn thing, Danny headed to the bathroom, arms akimbo, legs stiff, broken leg thumping, walking like a zombie because he felt so damned *funky.* Once there, he looked at himself in the mirror, said, "Jesus God," again, and peeled off two trash bags from the roll now perched by the sink. He slipped his left leg with the cast on it into one bag and his right leg with the ankle monitor strapped to it into the other. Then he secured them both with rubber bands to make them watertight, and clomped his way into the shower like Frankenstein's monster.

While the water washed all the little dead babies away, he contemplated spending the next three weeks alone. His two best friends, *straight* friends, Spike and Tim, were back in Indiana where he had left them, so Danny was on his own. It was the start of a new life, or supposed to be. This was the summer he had planned to come out. Shed that "virgin" label once and for all. Get laid. Get laid by a *guy.* Come out to himself, out to his family, out to the world. Become the gay man he had always known he was meant to be.

But now, of course, his coming-out party would have to be put on hold for a while. He wouldn't be able to start a new life or turn over any new leaves for at least six more weeks. He'd have to get out of the house first, and that wouldn't be happening anytime soon, thanks to this piece of machinery screwed to his ankle and the six-week sentence of house arrest the judge had slapped him with. And the broken leg. He'd have to contend with that. Not that it much mattered. He didn't figure anyone would want to have sex with him, anyway, as long as he had an anchor strapped to each leg, weighing him down.

Actually his new life in California had gotten off to a stuttering start, what with the trouble at the restaurant and all, but Danny was determined to turn things around. He'd show his dad. He really would be good from here on in. He had arrived in San Diego barely a month ago, exactly two days after his high school graduation, determined to get as far away from the farm as he could get. It dawned on him that maybe he should consider this six-week period of house arrest as his last good vacation before a lifetime of adulthood drudgery began. He should take advantage of the fact he had nothing to do and be grateful for the fact he had six long weeks to do it in.

Geez, maybe this wouldn't be so bad after all. He had waited eighteen years to have sex with a guy. A few more weeks wouldn't kill him.

Lint-free and come-free, he clumsily clomped out of the shower, dripping and snorting, tugged the wet garbage bags off his legs, and patted himself down with a towel. He dabbed on some deodorant, gave his shoulder-length hair a good headbanging by way of styling it, and headed back to his room, where he pulled on a baggy pair of cargo shorts. He donned them commando because the leg holes of his underwear wouldn't fit over the cast. Then he slipped a T-shirt over his head. There. Clean and dressed for the day.

Now, then. What to do first? Ah, yes. Eat.

He clomped downstairs like Long John Silver, every other footstep echoing through the house like a gunshot. Fucking cast.

In the kitchen, he rummaged through the freezer until he found two TV dinners that looked promising, peeled off the wrappers, and tossed them in the microwave. He poured himself a tumbler full of milk, drank it down in four seconds flat, then poured himself another. He nibbled cookies while he waited for the dinners to cook. When the microwave beeped, he fished the things out, stripped off the cellophane, slid them onto the kitchen table, and dug right in.

It took him exactly four minutes to consume them both, right down to licking the tray clean like Frederick the cat might have done.

Satisfied for the moment, he moved to the living room, collapsed onto the sofa, and switched on the TV. He surfed his way from Channel 2 all the way back to Channel 2 *again* and couldn't find one damn thing that caught his fancy. It was all daytime crap. Dr. Oz. Ellen. Nate. Judge Judy. (Judge Judy was the *last* thing he wanted to watch. He'd had enough of judges to last him a lifetime.)

He finally switched the TV off, heaved himself up off the sofa, passed through the kitchen to grab a soda and what was left of the bag of cookies, and headed back up the stairs to his room, clunking up the steps one by one. Once there, he threw himself into his recliner, switched on his own TV and settled in with a video game he had been slogging away at for the past couple of weeks. It wasn't the best game in the world, but it was good enough.

He killed off his character about fifteen times trying to make one simple move and finally gave up. He wasn't in the mood. He switched off the game, laid the empty cookie bag aside, and stared morosely out his bedroom window until the afternoon sun began to dip behind the houses across the street.

As darkness fell, somewhere in the bowels of the city, someone pulled a lever or flicked a switch or slapped a button and streetlights began popping on all over town. Shortly after that, lights in the houses along Danny's street began to blink on as the darkness deepened: a kitchen light here, a porch light there. As the city started waking up for the night, portholes were illuminated into lives up and down Walnut Street. Being just about bored silly, Danny decided maybe he would do a little snooping.

He turned off his own bedroom light so no one could see what he was doing and snagged the binoculars off his desk. Since Danny's room, and the bathroom adjoining it, were actually a remodeled garret, and made up the entirety of the second floor, Danny had windows on three sides. These windows offered him a commanding view of the surrounding area. Positioning himself at the east window first, he scanned the street to see what was happening in the hood.

Not much apparently. Two little kids, one black and one white, were arguing over a basketball in the driveway four houses down. Danny didn't know why they were bothering. It would be too dark to shoot hoops in a minute anyway. In the house next to the two little kids, a woman was standing over the kitchen sink chopping onions. Danny suspected they were onions by the way the woman was holding her head and squinting her eyes and aiming her face off in another direction as if she was holding her breath. Danny figured she was either chopping onions or dissecting a skunk.

Farther down the street in the same direction he couldn't see much because of a tree. He moved to a side window and swept the binoculars in the other direction, sliding over the vacant house next door because nothing was happening there, obviously, since the lady who previously owned it had kicked the bucket and the place had been for sale for months, or so Danny's dad had told him the other night at dinner.

Danny focused on the houses across the street. Some old guy watching the news. Another old guy watching the news. Two kids playing *Tomb Raider* on their PlayStations while their mother set the dinner table and screamed at them to turn down the volume. Danny could actually hear the woman's strident voice from a block away. Oddly enough, it seemed her kids, who were less than eight feet from her flapping mouth, couldn't hear the woman at all. Poor things must be deaf.

Danny heard the clink of glass, and sweeping his binoculars around, he spotted Mrs. Trumball, three doors down. She was wearing her ever-present flowery pink housecoat and pink fuzzy slippers and sneaking gin bottles into the trash can by her kitchen door now that it was good and dark, just like she always did. You would think someone being that sneaky would take the trouble to turn off her porch light. But no. She might as well be on stage with a baby spot aimed right at her head. Her hair was in rollers, as usual. Danny had never seen her hair *out* of rollers, and he had known the woman since he was nine years old. Danny grinned. Mrs. Trumball had been hiding her gin bottles for a decade, at least. One would think she would be tired of sneaking around by now and would just lean out her kitchen window and scream to the neighbors, "Yes, I'm a drunk! So what! Mind your own business you goddamn pack of nosy-assed jackals!" Then Danny imagined her carefully scooting her African violets aside, tugging an Uzi out from under her housecoat, and spraying the neighborhood with bullets, all the while screaming, "Snoop on this, you miserable pack of poopheads!"

Danny giggled at the thought.

Moving to the south window that overlooked the pool at the rear of the house, Danny could peer over the back fence from his high vantage point. From there he could see the house that abutted his father's in the back. It faced the next street over. This house was ranch style. One story. It was stucco, painted in a Southwestern ochre, with Southwestern crap scattered around the yard. An old wagon wheel. About a thousand cacti. A couple of cow skulls. Artfully broken pots overflowing with lush succulents filled up the corners.

At that particular moment, the guy who owned the house was in his driveway by the open garage out back, working on his car. It looked like he was changing a headlight on his station wagon. He was wearing raggedy blue jeans with no shirt and no shoes, and Danny had to admit that for an old guy, he looked pretty darned good, with those slim hips and fuzzy chest and two little dimples just above his snugly blue-jeaned ass. Since Danny's cock had just given a little lurch inside his cargo shorts, Danny could only assume his pecker agreed the guy was indeed a looker. The man's name was Mike Something. Mike Childers, that was it.

Mr. Childers had lost his wife a couple of years earlier, and now he spent his time puttering around his property, keeping to himself, waving when he was waved to, but that was about all the socializing he did. Danny had to admit he really was a good-looking man, maybe around forty, which was old to Danny, and Danny didn't blame the guy one little bit for keeping his nose out of the neighborhood's business.

Actually, Danny should probably be following in the guy's footsteps and minding his own business, too, rather than standing here snooping on everybody, especially since they were all so damned boring anyway.

The fact was, Danny was starting to feel like a perv. Here he was in a darkened house staring out the windows with a pair of binoculars, spying on the neighbors from a room that *still* smelled like multiple squirts of jism. Next thing you know, he'd be whacking off in the bushes while he listened to Mr. and Mrs. Dinkens have marital relations in that Victorian monstrosity next door. This was not good. This was not healthy. Mr. Dinkens was a bean pole, and Mrs. Dinkens weighed about three hundred pounds. Danny didn't want to hear that.

Maybe now would be a good time to gauge the limits of his electronic leash. It would be good to know how far he could move in every direction just so he wouldn't be tripping the alarm every five minutes and bringing nine million cops down on his head. It was nice and dark outside, so none of the neighbors would be able to see what he was doing. He was sure they were all talking about him being under house arrest. It was probably the lead story on the neighborhood grapevine. They might very well be watching his every move, like he was watching theirs, just to make sure he didn't try any funny business, what with him being a bona fide criminal and all.

Hmm. Danny wondered if he should borrow Mrs. Trumball's Uzi. Give himself some cover fire. Nah. Too dramatic. He'd just sneak around and do what he had to do on the sly.

It was completely dark outside now, except for the streetlights out front, which cast enough light through the windows to let Danny see what he was doing. With all the house lights off, including the porch lights, Danny slid through the front door like a ninja, except for the damn noisy cast on his leg thumping all over the place. Hunched over to make a smaller target just in case anyone did happen to be watching, he moved down the front walk, plucking the solar night-lights out of the ground that bordered the walk as he went along, like some deranged flower picker. They were about a foot high, the night-lights. One end was pointy to stick in the ground and the other end had a tiny solar panel that powered a wee light bulb inside. They gave off just a speck of white light, not really enough to see anything by, but enough to be able to follow the sidewalk and not take off in the wrong direction and end up in Portland. The little lights were mostly just ornamental, but for what Danny wanted to use them for, they would be more than sufficient.

When he had his arms full of night-lights, he saw the flaw in his plans. Hell, *everybody* could see him now, with this bouquet of night-lights cradled in his arms like Miss America clutching a spray of radioactive roses. From a distance, he probably looked like he was glowing. He quickly scooted back through the front door and dumped the night-lights in the foyer. Then, carrying only one light stick this time, and shielding the white light at the tip of it with his hand, he set off down the front walk again, watching his electronic monitor with every step, waiting for the light to go from green to red.

At the very end of the walk, the ankle monitor flashed red. Danny's heart did a somersault, and he stepped hastily backward, hoping to God the light would go back to green before every cop in California descended on his ass. And it did. Thank God.

Danny stuck the night-light he was carrying into the ground right next to the last square in the sidewalk, then he did an aboutface and went to fetch another. With this one, he took off across the grass to the west, and just as he reached the hedge and picket fence that separated his property from the vacant house next door, the light flashed red. He stepped back, poked the night-light in the ground and headed back for another one.

It didn't take him long to realize that the police apparently knew what they were doing. Every time he reached the edge of his property, be it front yard, or side yards, the light flashed red just before he crossed the property line. It was only in the back, behind the pool at the six-foot-high fence that separated his backyard from Mr. Childers's backyard that the monitor did not flash red. And with Mr. Childers still working on his car in his driveway by the open garage just on the other side of the fence, Danny couldn't scale the fence to test the limits in that direction. He'd have to do it some other time. Or never. Chances are the light on his ankle monitor would flash red just a couple of feet past the fence line anyway, so maybe he wouldn't even worry about it.

He stuck the last light stick in the ground on his side of the back fence, and called it quits.

His reconnaissance hadn't really accomplished anything, but at least he had a clearer idea of where his prison walls were. He knew exactly where he was allowed to go during the next six weeks. He wouldn't be tripping the alarm by accident, at least.

Just before he clunked his way back to the house, Danny dared a brief peek through the back fence, thinking a closer look at Mr. Childers's naked chest would give him something to think about later if he found himself in need of a little sexual stimulation.

With his eye pressed to the wooden fence, right at the point where two boards didn't quite come together, Danny gave a little gasp when he realized Mr. Childers was only a few feet away. He was still putzing around with the front fender of his car, and he was still looking pretty darned good in those faded blue jeans and nothing else. The skin of his back was smooth and well-muscled, with a little patch of dark hair just over his ass that Danny found very attractive indeed. When he turned, Danny saw a nice bulge in the crotch of his neighbor's jeans. Danny swallowed, looking at it. God, it was beautiful.

Danny's heart did a little stuttering tap dance when Mr. Childers stopped what he was doing and turned, as if he could feel a pair of eyes on him. He looked around in every direction, his gaze sliding over the fence where Danny was crouched. After a minute, he seemed satisfied he wasn't being watched after all.

He turned his back to Danny once again, and returned to whatever the hell he was doing to the front end of his car.

Breathing a sigh of relief that he hadn't been caught snooping, Danny sneaked off through the grass, dragging the damn cast along with him, to the kitchen door, where he ducked inside.

Before turning on the house lights, he went around and closed all the drapes.

Finally, cocooned safely in his house with all the drapery closed and all the house lights switched back on, he wiped a patina of nervous sweat from his forehead. Yep. He really did feel like a perv.

No more peeping through windows and fences, he told himself. *No more snooping ever.*

Yeah, right. Like that was going to happen.

He went off in search of sustenance, trying his best to ignore his half-hard dick as it flopped around inside his shorts striving to get his attention, which it was managing to do quite well, thank you very much. Lord, he always did have trouble with boners when he went around without underwear staring at half-dressed men. Of course, there wasn't much he could do about finally coming out of the closet for the next six weeks. He'd just have to muddle through, bone hard and horny. And try to stay away from the back fence. Too much temptation in that direction.

Still trying to take his mind off sex and the hunky older next-door neighbor, Danny built a sandwich with every ingredient and condiment he could lay his hands on. Then he tore into a family-sized bag of potato chips. Two seconds later the phone rang.

It was his dad, wondering if everything was okay and telling Danny his flight had been on time and he had arrived at his destination all in one piece.

While they chatted, Danny made all the appropriate responses, but his mind was still on that little patch of hair over Mr. Childers's ass. It looked so—*welcoming.*

Gee, maybe he really *was* a pervert.

On top of being gay, of course. Which was a whole different ballgame.

A ballgame Danny was all too aware he had yet to play.

CHAPTER TWO
GRANGER AND LUKE

DANNY woke up on the second day of his house arrest feeling, of all things, lonesome. That was certainly a surprise. He had thought he might actually enjoy the novelty of being alone for a while, but apparently his brain had other ideas.

He ignored his morning hard-on and clambered out of bed awkwardly, thanks to all the extra crap strapped around his ankles. He rubbed the sleep from his eyes, grabbed the old curtain rod that he now kept on the nightstand and which had become his new best friend, and eased it down inside his cast as far as it would go. Then he started digging and poking and scrambling it around between his skin and the plaster. Scratching. Scratching. Jesus God, that felt good. Danny rolled his eyes and grunted and grimaced, and just before he thought he might actually pass out, or come, that's how good it felt, it started hurting, and he knew he had probably removed a layer or two of skin, so he thought he'd better stop.

His dick was still hard; nothing much ever seemed to affect *that*. So he went to pee, and by the time he brushed his teeth and gave his head a shake to get his hair out of his eyes and pulled on the same shorts and T-shirt he had worn the day before, his hard-on had slipped into sleep mode. It wouldn't take much to revive it, of course, but for now his dick was comfortably flaccid, being on hold and all, and he was able to walk around without looking like he was dowsing for water.

The house was so quiet. He missed the sound of his dad banging around in the kitchen getting their breakfasts ready. He missed the smell of his dad's coffee brewing. He missed the scent of his dad's aftershave wafting through the house. He missed his dad's cheerful voice screaming up the stairs, "Come eat your breakfast, kid, before I eat it myself!"

Face it, Danny told himself. *You miss your dad. Period.*

And he knew it was true.

Danny had waited his whole life to be here with his father on a permanent basis, and look how he had screwed it up already. Tearing up the restaurant, costing his dad money, making him worry, getting him in trouble with the bitch in Indiana. Well, he hadn't been blowing smoke up the old man's ass when Danny promised him yesterday he would be good from here on in. Danny meant it. And he would start by taking advantage of his time under house arrest to get a few things done around the place. Things his dad had been putting off because he was so busy with work. That would be a nice surprise for the old man when he got back from his trip.

But first things first. Breakfast.

Actually, even *before* breakfast, came Frederick. The cat. Danny clomped his way to the kitchen and just as he was about to go through the door, he stopped. His jaw fell open. What the hell? Frederick was crouched in the middle of the dining room table eating a bird. A *big* bird. Like a condor. Well, no. More like a crow. But there were feathers and blood and bird guts everywhere. It might as well have been a condor. Or an emu.

Frederick must have grown tired of snacking on the whimsical writings of Mark Twain, and thought he'd partake of something meatier.

Danny threw his arms in the air and screamed like his Aunt Mildred did that time she caught him when he was five years old peeing on the Boston fern in her parlor. "Aarrhggh!"

Then he yelled. "Holy Mother of God! Get that thing off the table!"

Frederick just glared at him and growled, dead bird clamped protectively in his jaws, its poor little head lolling, sightless eyes looking nowhere. Frederick's tail lashed back and forth, showing how pissed he was at having his fine dining experience interrupted. There was a bead of blood on his whiskers and a couple of bloody feathers dangled off his chin. Yuk.

"Git. Scram. Shoo. Beat it. And take that dead bird with you. Jesus, Mary, and Joseph Goebbels on a cross! What a mess. What a fucking mess!"

Tired of hearing Danny rant, Frederick finally stalked off, dripping bird blood everywhere and leaving a trail of sodden bloody feathers behind on the mahogany tabletop, all the while grumbling and growling and looking surly as hell. Nobody can look more pissed off than a pissed off cat. They've mastered the art of wounded dignity and elevated it to an art form. Like post impressionism, only angrier.

So Danny's first job of the day turned out to be scrubbing bird guts off the dining room table. Not a propitious beginning to *any* day. Although it did keep him from thinking about sex for a while.

He was still fuming about the cat when he finally sat down to eat his own breakfast. A soup tureen full of Cap'n Crunch's Crunch Berries. Just because a guy's an adult and thinks about sex all the time, well, that doesn't mean he has to eat like one. Danny figured Cap'n Crunch was good for him. It was practically gravel after all. It was so rock hard and crunchy it probably scraped all the tartar off his teeth like Milk-Bone biscuits do for a dog. And everyone knows that good oral care is essential to a healthy lifestyle.

Plus Cap'n Crunch's Crunch Berries tasted great, and he could get his required weekly allowance of sugar in three minutes flat. Saved time.

While he shoveled in the cereal with a serving spoon, he stared at the little portable TV perched on the kitchen counter by the sink. Too lazy to get up and change the channel, he was stuck watching a news report.

The Middle East was a seething hotbed of unrest, as usual. In Washington, the Republican senators were throwing darts at the Democrat president, trying to piss him off. Also as usual. The economy was struggling. The oceans were polluted. The price of gas was up. Diane Sawyer needed a haircut. And closer to home, right here in San Diego, someone had taken it into his head to knock off a succession of young men, murdering them and leaving their massacred bodies scattered around the city like so much jetsam. Citizens were up in arms, demanding the police catch the killer, and the police were up in arms, telling the citizens to get off their ass, they were doing the best they could. So far the body count was at four.

Danny watched it all, unconcerned, mindlessly consuming his cereal, and when the last Crunch Berry had gone the way of the dodo, he lifted the soup tureen off the table and tilted it in front of his face like a wash tub to slurp down the remaining quart of pinkish-greenish-yellowish sludgy milk still lingering in the bottom.

Aah. Breakfast of champions.

Sated for the moment, he sipped at a cup of instant coffee to help get the mail moving, since everyone knows a good bowel movement is also essential to a healthy lifestyle. Then, after the mail was moved, he planned to get to work around the joint fulfilling the promise he had made to himself to help his dad out with some of the stuff he had been putting off.

Before he finished the coffee, however, the phone rang. Probably his dad, checking in.

Danny picked up the phone. It wasn't his dad. It was his mom. As soon as he heard her voice, he felt his heart sink into his lower colon like an anchor gurgling its way to the bottom of the ocean after being tossed over the side of a boat. Christ.

His mom was frantic. He wasn't sure why. Danny's crime had been committed a week ago, and the judge's proclamation had come down three days after that. It was a little late to get all riled up about it now.

"My poor baby! I knew I shouldn't have let you move away and live with that man in the city."

"You mean Dad?"

"Oh, don't call him that. Gerald is your father. You know that, baby."

Gerald was the putz she'd married. Danny hated Gerald. Gerald was an asshole. "No, I don't know that," Danny said, his voice turning to steel. "My dad is my dad. As far as I'm concerned, Gerald is nobody."

"Oh, you're breaking my heart, Danny!"

"Maybe it'll heal."

"Why are you being so mean? It's that man, isn't it? Leaving you all alone with that horrible thing strapped around your ankle. How could he do that? And how's your leg? Does it hurt, baby? Is it uncomfortable?"

"It's fine. What do you want?"

"I want you to come home. As soon as your house arrest is finished, I want you to come home."

"I'd rather set myself on fire."

"Oh, you're breaking my heart, Danny!"

"Yeah. You said that already."

"Gerald wants you home, too."

"He probably needs somebody to scoop cowshit out of the barn. He never wanted me for anything else. Unless he wanted a punching bag. He used me for that a couple of times."

"That's not true."

"It is, and you know it."

"He's sorry, Danny. But sometimes you would try the patience of Job, you're so headstrong and so—"

"I'm hanging up now. I'm not coming back to Indiana. Ever. I like it here with Dad. And Dad likes having me here. I'm an adult now. There's nothing you can do about it. So get off my ass, and get off Dad's ass, too. You're driving him nuts. Good-bye. Have a nice life. Or not. Tell Gerald to—"

And he hung up the phone, leaving it up to his mom's imagination to decide what Danny wanted her to tell Gerald to do. Whatever it was, she'd probably be smart enough to know it wasn't something genteel. More like cramming a fence post up his butt. Nothing genteel about that.

Danny resolutely ignored the pang of guilt he felt for speaking to his mother like that, although the bitch deserved it, and to push it out of his mind completely, he took a peek through the kitchen window toward the back fence. He remembered how those blue jeans had clung to Mr. Childers's ass the night before, and how that little patch of fuzz just above the swelling of the man's butt drew Danny in like a magnet. Jeez, it was sexy. Then he remembered Mr. Childers stopping what he was doing and looking around as if he thought maybe someone was watching him. Danny could feel the blood rushing to his face, thinking about it. Thank God the man hadn't spotted Danny snooping on him through the fence. Talk about embarrassing.

Danny made a vow to himself that he would never again peek through the back fence at Mr. Childers. It was just too dangerous and too potentially humiliating. Nope. The next time he wanted to take a gander at the next-door neighbor's delectable forty-year-old ass and fuzzy chest, Danny would do it from his upstairs window with the binoculars. In the dark. He could see better from up there anyway.

With that resolution out of the way, Danny set out to do some actual work. It was a beautiful Southern California day. Sunny. Not too hot. A perfect day for some manly yard work.

He slipped a sneaker on his right foot, a plastic bag over the cast on his left leg, and then as an afterthought, he slipped another plastic bag over the right foot as well, sneaker and all, so as to protect the ankle monitor from grass cuttings. After securing the garbage bags with rubber bands, he stared down at himself. Lord, he looked like a fool.

Well, maybe the neighbors weren't up yet. Or maybe they had all gone to work. Or maybe no one would notice him. Or maybe there would be a total eclipse of the sun and it would be so dark outside no one would be able to see any farther than the nose on their face and therefore wouldn't notice the weirdass guy mowing the lawn and trimming the hedge wearing trash bags on his feet.

Or maybe he'd simply have to abide looking like a fool. Period.

It was just too bad his dad had bought *pink* trash bags.

Regardless of all that, it actually felt good to be doing physical labor. The last thing he had done lately that was truly strenuous was flip over that frigging ice machine. Those things are heavy. Danny thought he might have even pulled something in his back when he did it, but there never seemed to be a good time to complain about that. People seemed more concerned with the damage to the ice machine. And the fact that he had actually broken his leg during the commission of his crime. As the judge had pointed out, Danny was not only inconsiderate and hot-headed, but clumsy on top of it. Then the judge had snickered and shaken his head and wiped a couple of happy tears out of his eyes, which still brought a blush of shame to Danny's cheeks when he thought about it.

Damn judge.

Danny had plenty of time to think about stuff while he mowed the grass and trimmed the hedges. It was while he was edging the sidewalk that a couple of kids went by on skateboards and one of them screamed out, "Ooh, I like your pink leg warmers!" referring to the garbage bags Danny had strapped around his feet.

Being an adult now, Danny did the only mature thing he could do under the circumstances. He gave the kid the finger. The boys roared on past on their skateboards, hooting with laughter, both of them shooting a finger back in return. Ah, youth.

Danny saw a couple of faces poke around curtains in nearby windows, but he ignored them. He went about his work, trying to be as thorough as he could. He wanted his dad to be pleased with the way the yard looked. He was very, very careful not to pass the nightlights he had poked around the perimeter of the lawn the night before, delineating his green-light zone. The last thing he wanted was for the neighbors to enjoy the sight of twenty squad cars screaming up to the house and a shitload of cops hauling Danny off to the hoosegow, kicking and screaming, just because he had overstepped the limits on his ankle monitor.

While he was thinking about that, Danny had another thought. He suddenly realized his dad wouldn't be back for three weeks. Three weeks! The grass would be all grown back by then. Even the hedges would look ratty again in three weeks' time. Danny would have to do the work all over again for his dad to see the results of his labor.

Well, poop. He stopped what he was doing immediately.

Danny gathered up all his equipment—lawn mower, edger, shears—and stored it back in the basement. He peeled off his grass-splattered garbage bags on the back stoop and tossed them in the trash. He went inside, showered, did another round of headbanging to style his hair after climbing out of the shower, swiped another streak of deodorant across his armpits, and donned a clean pair of shorts and a clean shirt. He ignored the urge to beat off and ate lunch instead. Frederick sat at the other end of the table, watching him. The cat had cleaned the blood and feathers off himself since the last time Danny saw him. Danny supposed he would be running across a desiccated pile of bird bones and feathers sometime soon since he didn't know where the cat had finished devouring the poor beast, but Danny would cross that bridge when he came to it. In the meantime, he accepted the uneasy truce between himself and Frederick and even gave the cat a little smile and a finger waggle of greeting when he saw it watching him.

The cat yawned and walked away. Hmm. Maybe all wasn't quite as forgiven as Danny thought.

Danny cleaned up his mess from lunch, parked himself in the recliner in his room, and after digging around inside his cast for five minutes with the curtain rod trying to appease an itch that was apparently unappeasable, he finally conked out and slept the rest of the afternoon.

It wasn't until later, when the day was long over and the moon was high and most of the city was sound asleep, that things got interesting.

Danny couldn't know it at the time, but his life was about to change. For better *and* for worse.

The "better" part would be great. Phenomenal. Better than he could ever have imagined.

The "worse" part would suck. Big time.

IT WAS two in the morning when headlights swept across Danny's bedroom walls, jarring him awake. It must be Mr. Childers. Sometimes the man stayed out late, maybe because of a night job; Danny wasn't sure. Mr. Childers's driveway was situated so the headlights of his car were aimed right into Danny's bedroom. Especially if Mr. Childers backed into his garage like he usually did.

But the headlights were on the wrong wall for it to be Mr. Childers. Mr. Childers of the nice ass. Mr. Childers of the nice patch of fuzzy hair situated at the base of his nicely muscled back between the two butt dimples on *top* of the nice ass.

Danny struggled out of bed when he heard the roar of a truck engine. Then the headlights swept across the room in the opposite direction and he heard the beep-beep-beep of a truck backing up.

Danny ignored his itching leg and clomped naked to the west window. Once there, he pushed the curtain aside with one hand while rubbing sleep from his eyes with the other. Stifling a yawn, he looked down into the driveway of the vacant house next door.

Danny couldn't believe it. There was a moving van just pulling up to the side of the house. It was a rental van. One of the big ones. While Danny watched, the motor was shut off and the engine rumbled down to silence. The driver's door squeaked open with a rattle and a bang and out stepped a young guy not much older than Danny.

And holy shit, he was cute! He had blondish-red hair with ear buds dangling from his ears and wires from the ear buds trailing down around his neck and disappearing into his shirt pocket where an iPod must be tucked. He was wearing sandals and shorts and a polo shirt with the long sleeves rolled up over his elbows. He was kind of a little guy but well put together. Danny wasn't sure, but he thought he could hear the guy humming along to whatever the song was he was listening to on the iPod.

He had a bounce in his step that Danny found very, very attractive. And the guy was wearing glasses. Glasses with heavy black frames. On anyone else those glasses would have looked geeky. On this guy, they looked sexy as hell.

Danny fumbled around in the dark for his binoculars, damn near breaking his neck. He accidentally kicked a basketball, which went bouncing across the room making a racket and scaring the cat, who took off like a bat out of hell, thundering down the stairs. After a couple of minutes of blind searching, Danny finally found the binoculars under a bag of tortilla chips. He raced back to the window and once again squinted down at the driveway next door as he adjusted the binoculars to get a better look at the young cute guy who had shown up out of the blue.

The guy was gone. At least the truck was still there, so Danny knew he wasn't nuts. Then Danny heard another door squeak, a house door this time, and a light switched on in what was probably the kitchen of the vacant house. Then the back porch light went on. Then another light farther inside the house. Then another. And pretty soon every light in the place was burning brightly. Danny had never seen the vacant house lit up before, and he had been looking down at it from this bedroom window ever since he arrived in town.

Danny supposed he would have to stop calling it the vacant house. Didn't seem to be vacant any longer. No sirree. Danny had a new neighbor, and he was cuter than crap. Woo hoo!

Listening to his own thoughts, Danny just shook his head. God, he was pathetic. He really had to get laid. He really, really, really had to solve this virginity problem and come out as a proud gay man and *simply get laid.* His dad would be surprised he was gay, he supposed, and his mom would throw a conniption fit, of course, but sometimes a guy just has to do what a guy has to do, and Danny's dick was screaming at him to *just get the job done already.*

Danny wondered if he could get the job done with the cute new guy next door, but even he had to admit the odds of that happening were pretty slim. First of all, the guy would have to find Danny attractive. And Danny would have to not make a fool of himself the first time they met. And then they'd probably have to get a friendship going, and Danny always had a problem with friendships, he was so damned shy and all. And then, of course, the guy would have to be willing to overlook the cast on Danny's leg and the ankle monitor courtesy of the San Diego Police Department on the other leg. And then he'd have to overlook the fact that Danny was a criminal. And on top of all that, the guy would also have to be gay. Duh. Jeez, the longer Danny thought about it, the slimmer the odds became of getting it on with his new next-door neighbor at all. And wasn't *that* a depressing realization.

Danny was pulled out of his reverie by the sound of barking. A dog poked his head through the truck window like maybe he had just woken up. It was a big dog. The dog had reddish-blond hair, just like the guy. It was a golden retriever. Beautiful. Also just like the guy.

The dog leapt through the open truck window and bounded through the back door of the house, which the guy had left open. Danny trailed his binoculars from one window to the next until he found one that seemed to look into a parlor, or a den, although it was hard to tell since there wasn't any furniture in the house yet. There, Danny saw the guy down on his knees, giving the dog a hug. The dog was eating it up too. Tail wagging, tongue lolling, butt swinging back and forth.

Danny supposed his tail would be wagging, too, if the guy was down on his knees in front of *him* and petting and cuddling *him* like crazy.

Danny wasn't sure, but he thought maybe he heard music all of a sudden. Like, you know, a love song. Playing somewhere in the back of his head. God, that guy was hot!

And while Danny was thinking about love songs and being petted and all, his dick, unencumbered by clothes, woke up and lifted its little head to see what was going on. As it looked around, the little head got bigger and bigger.

Not knowing what else to do, Danny took a firm grip on his cock with one hand, continued to watch the cute guy through the binoculars, which he held with his other hand, and before he knew it, his knees were shaking. Of course, once a guy has a hard-on and his dick's in his hand and his knees start shaking, that's about it. Danny suddenly found himself groaning and shooting a torrent of come across his bedroom window like a fire hose.

Lord, it hadn't taken two minutes.

When his heart stopped hammering and his dick stopped squirting, he went to fetch the Windex.

Oy. What a pervert he truly was.

But at least the music stopped.

THE next morning at the crack of dawn, Danny was up and about, bright-eyed and bushy-tailed, so to speak. He showered so long he began to prune, and afterward he styled his hair properly, with gel and blow-dryer, taking infinite care in placing each hair exactly where he wanted. Then he headbanged and tossed it around to add volume and messed it all up again. Perfect. He used cotton swabs on his ears, brushed his teeth until he foamed up like a rabid dog, gargled three times, and even flossed between his toes with the towel on the one foot that wasn't entombed in concrete. On the other foot, where his toes barely stuck out beneath the cast, Danny swabbed those toes with a washcloth liberally splashed with alcohol. After that, he clipped his toenails and fingernails with the nail clippers. He even trimmed the hair inside his nose with a tiny pair of scissors his dad used for the same thing. Then he smeared an itty-bitty dab of zit cream on a spot on his neck that looked like it was thinking about blossoming into a full-fledged fucking pimple and topped it off with just a speck of concealer.

Nothing gay about that, he reassured himself. Every teenage boy in America had a bottle of concealer stashed away somewhere for moments like this. They might not admit it, but they do. Cover Girl wasn't just for chicks. Uh-uh.

Danny applied deodorant to his armpits twice because he forgot he had already done it once, then he tugged on a sexy pair of gym shorts and a muscle shirt that (he hoped) showed off his pecs and biceps, what little there was of them, since he was so damned skinny. And lastly, because he flat-out refused to wrap his legs in pink trash bags on this all-important morning, he dressed up his one foot that was available for public viewing with the right half of his best pair of sneakers and a brand new ankle sock.

There wasn't much Danny could do about the ankle monitor or the cast. They would just have to be taken at face value. Hopefully, his new neighbor wouldn't be hypercritical in the matter of broken bones and/or electronic detention as it applied to the criminal justice system.

Danny decided to skip breakfast because he was so nervous he figured he would probably throw it back up if he ate anything. He studied his reflection for five full minutes in the bathroom mirror to make sure everything was copacetic, and even he had to admit, he looked pretty darned good. He prayed to God the guy next door would think so too.

As soon as the sun crested the rooftops across the street, Danny was positioned at the westernmost edge of his property, clippers in hand, trimming, yet again, the hedge he had just trimmed the day before. This time he trimmed it like a neurosurgeon removing scar tissue from a damaged, but still living, brain. Carefully. Very, very carefully. Leaf by leaf and stem by stem. Once in a while, he would step back and study what he had just done, like an artist examining his latest brushstrokes on canvas. Then Danny would trim a little more. Snip snip—snip.

Danny trimmed and retrimmed the hedge so many times he began to wonder if there would be a hedge left by the time the guy showed up.

Of course, what Danny was really doing was killing time, waiting for the gorgeous guy who just moved in next door to step outside his house to either walk the dog or start unloading his truck. Danny had the whole "accidental introduction" scenario down pat inside his head. In fact, his bravery in the matter pretty much astounded even him. He must be truly smitten to be so determined to meet this guy. Good grief, the truck had been driven into the driveway barely five hours earlier. Danny supposed this was what his father would call "thinking with the little head."

And yep, he had to admit, that's pretty much what it was. If he hadn't been under house arrest and unable to leave the property, Danny would have probably baked the guy a cake and delivered it to his door like Beaver Cleaver's mom working for the Welcome Wagon. Of course, Danny would have to learn how to bake first. And then he'd have to somehow trick himself into not eating the cake himself.

Still, there was no getting around it. Danny was determined to come out. Coming out required having sex. Gay sex. And if he had his druthers, he'd like to come out with the new guy next door as his first conquest. If Danny could shoot sperm all over the bedroom window just by looking at the man from thirty yards away, what might happen if they actually came into physical contact with each other?

God. Danny blushed and suffered a flurry of heart palpitations just thinking about it.

Something cold touched the back of his leg. The clippers flew out of his hand and he squealed like a toddler. Whirling around, he saw a golden retriever. *The* golden retriever.

And behind the golden retriever, a guy.

The guy.

He was holding Danny's clippers in his hand and grinning. Danny wasn't sure, but he thought maybe the dog was grinning, too.

"Caught these in midair," the guy said. "We should start a circus act."

Danny touched the back of his leg. "Was that…?"

The guy looked fondly down at his dog. "Yeah. That was Granger. His nose is cold, isn't it? He likes saying hello like that. Does it to me in the bed every morning, pressing that coldass nose to some body part or other. I don't usually squeal though. Nice touch, that." And the guy grinned even wider. There might even have been a chuckle or two in there somewhere, trying to get out.

Danny was still imagining what it would be like to press a cold nose to a few of the guy's body parts. Jesus, that was one lucky dog.

Up close and personal, the guy was even cuter than he was the night before. While Danny floundered around trying to think of something intelligent to say, Danny checked the guy out, all the while trying not to *look* like he was checking the guy out.

The young man's hair was ginger in the morning light. Redder than how it had looked in the moonlight the night before. It was cut shorter than Danny's, and it was curlier. Thick, lush, and sexy. Danny hadn't even known he liked redheads until he saw this one. Boy, he sure liked redheads now.

The redhead's face was a collection of clean, crisp lines. Sharp handsome nose, lightly sprinkled with freckles, neat jawline, firm little chin with the hint of a cleft in it, and finely delineated lips that seemed to smile an *awful* lot. There were two tiny commas at either side of his mouth. Dimples. And between the dimples was a beautiful array of small white teeth. At the moment, since the guy was grinning, those teeth were on brilliant display. Behind the heavy black glasses, which on this guy somehow managed to look chic instead of geeky, his eyes were cornflower blue. They were surrounded by long pale lashes that seemed to catch the light when the sun glinted across them just right. In the middle of the cornflower-blue irises, there were tiny streaks of gold. Like sunbursts.

The face, over all, was open, friendly, amused, and cuter than hell.

While the guy was shorter than Danny, he was better muscled. And since he was dressed almost exactly like Danny, in shorts and a muscle shirt, Danny had a bird's-eye view of nicely constructed arms and legs, all four of the little devils sprinkled with a pelt of reddish-blond hair that almost took Danny's breath away, he so wanted to run his fingers over it. Or his tongue.

There was just a hint of blond chest hair peeking out of the top of the guy's muscle shirt, and Danny could see his nipples poking up against the fabric.

Casting his eyes a little lower, not that he thought he should, but because he didn't know how to stop himself, he detected a promising bulge in the front of the guy's running shorts. That gave Danny food for thought; don't think it didn't.

And looking ever *farther* south, Danny saw the young man was standing on Danny's lawn barefoot. Even his feet were cute. Strong, pale, competent looking. They were wet from the dew and speckled green with freshly mown grass clippings.

With a start, Danny realized that the guy was on the same side of the hedge as Danny was. Danny had been hoping that on their first meeting, the hedge would hide some of the hardware strapped around his legs, at least long enough to let Danny explain it all first. He guessed that wasn't going to happen now. Although, if the guy *had* spotted Danny's cast and ankle monitor, it didn't seem to bother him much.

Besides Danny's clippers, the young man was also holding a plastic bag full of dog poop, which explained everything. In one motion, he handed Danny the clippers back and flung the bag of dog poop over the hedge and into the yard next door. His yard.

"So," the redhead said, sticking out his hand, "I'm Luke Jamison."

"Nice to meet you," Danny stammered, taking the hand and holding onto it for way too long because he really, really liked the way it felt. Then he came to his senses and realized how long he was holding onto Luke's hand, which made him drop it like a live grenade. And that made him blush. He could feel the blood infusing his head all the way up to his cowlick. Christ, he hated that feeling.

Luke seemed to enjoy it. He blinked back a laugh. "Nervous?"

No, just head over heels in lust, Danny wanted to say, but of course he didn't. Instead, he started jabbering. And once he started, he couldn't seem to stop. He became more horrified as the seconds passed and he just kept blathering on and on and on, but still he couldn't seem to make himself shut up.

"You're probably wondering about my ankle monitor and the cast and everything. It's like this, see. My boss pissed me off, so I flipped the ice machine over to get back at him, and then I wasn't watching what I was doing because I was busy throwing all the hamburgers out the drive-thru window and I slipped in the ice and broke my leg and the judge thought it was pretty funny but he didn't think it was funny enough to let me off the hook scot-free so once my dad talked him out of making me go to jail, the judge slapped this monitor on my ankle and told me I have to wear it for six weeks and since this is just the second day I've still got nearly six weeks to go before it comes off but I'm not dangerous or anything so you don't have to worry about living next to me and even if I was dangerous I can't leave the yard or the red light comes on and then ten thousand cops will come and beat me to death with night sticks so you'd be safe anyway."

Danny finally managed to force his mouth shut by sheer willpower, sort of like closing a rusty gate. Then he said, conversationally, sanely, nonchalantly, and as if he hadn't been mindlessly jabbering for the last forty-five seconds like a lunatic, "And how about you? Moving in, huh?"

Luke gave a little headshake. "Wow. That was a whole lot of information there."

He stared at Danny for a minute and finally seemed to come to the conclusion that Danny was normal. Danny couldn't imagine why.

Without answering Danny's question, Luke dropped to his knees and took a closer look at the monitor around Danny's ankle. Him and the dog both checked it out. While he was checking it out, Luke cupped Danny's calf in his hand and lifted the foot up closer to his face to get a better look.

Danny gasped at the feel of Luke's hand on the skin of his leg, then he gasped again because he started to lose his balance, and when he started to lose his balance, he dropped the hedge clippers and reached out for the only thing available to brace himself against, which happened to be Luke's head.

With his hand in Luke's hair, and Luke's hand on his bare leg, Danny thought he had died and gone to heaven. When Luke looked up at him with his face no more than a foot away from Danny's crotch Danny figured this was a major improvement on heaven. Heck, heaven was probably *nothing* compared to this. Heaven was probably *Newark* compared to this.

Luke smiled up at Danny. He seemed to be inordinately amused by Danny's wide, wide eyes looking down at him. "You're enjoying yourself, aren't you?"

Danny could only nod.

Luke stroked the back of Danny's leg. He didn't seem to be shy about it either. "So do you have a name or are you just known as the criminal mastermind of the neighborhood?"

That made Danny laugh. "Danny," he sputtered, still engrossed with the feel of Luke's hair between his fingers and Luke's fingers on the back of his leg. "My name is Danny."

Luke patted Danny's calf and gave it a couple of strokes before releasing it and hauling himself to his feet.

"Well, this is going to be fun, Danny. Let's get to know each other, what do you say?"

Luke looked down at the monitor on Danny's right foot. He cocked his head to the side and stared at it for about five heartbeats, like he was thinking things over. Then he looked like he had thought things over long enough and had finally come to a decision.

"Your place it is then," Luke finally said. "My place seems to be out of your, shall we say, comfort zone. Plus it doesn't have any furniture in it. Plus they haven't turned the water on yet." Luke took Danny's hand and pulled Danny in the direction of his front door.

Tail wagging, tongue lolling, Granger padded along beside them.

Two minutes later, they were drinking Cokes at Danny's kitchen table. Except for Granger. Granger was having water and a bowl of cat food. It was the only pet food Danny had in the house.

Frederick was hissing from the top of the fridge at the fucking dog because the fucking dog was eating his fucking food and drinking out of his fucking dish. Frederick wasn't big on sharing. Canine intolerant. That was Frederick.

Both Danny and Luke thought the cat's reaction to Granger was pretty funny. Granger didn't seem to care one way or the other. He was too busy scarfing up the cat's Meow Mix to worry about the cat.

By the time Danny and Luke had drunk their first Cokes and scrambled around in the fridge for seconds, they were friends. Sometimes friendship just happens that way, Danny figured. Then he wondered if people ever fall in love that fast.

While trying to make sensible conversation and trying not to say anything stupid, and also trying not to get lost in Luke's cornflower-blue eyes, which was a constant hazard, Danny was too busy and too inexperienced to know love sometimes does indeed happen that fast. In fact, it had already happened to him. He was just too untested in the ways of love to know it yet. When he did figure it out, it would either make him the happiest guy on the planet, or it would break his fucking heart.

Danny was also too inexperienced to understand *that* universal truth.

CHAPTER THREE
CHATTING

LUKE was sitting at the kitchen table next to Danny, looking down at Danny's cast. "So does that thing hurt?"

It did hurt a little, but Danny thought he would make more points by being stoic. "Nah. Itches though. Itches like crazy."

Luke scooted his chair around until he was in a position to pick up Danny's leg, the one with the cast on it, and place it in his lap.

"Gosh, it's heavy," Luke said. "Must be a bitch dragging this thing around all day."

"No kidding," Danny said, still shooting for stoic, with just a hint of heroic forbearance thrown in to make it more manly. Or so he hoped.

Danny was practically holding his breath by this time, wondering what was going to happen next. Under his shorts he was still commando, after all. Anything could pop up without warning. He couldn't help wondering how fast his new neighbor would run out of the house if Danny's dick suddenly poked its head out of the bottom of his shorts to say hello.

Blithely unaware of the thoughts running through Danny's head, for which Danny was truly grateful, Luke gently slid his finger inside the top edge of Danny's cast, just far enough in to make it snug. While he talked, he left it there. Oddly enough, that cool finger stuck inside his cast, made Danny's itch go away. That one *particular* itch, anyway.

Unfortunately, it made the other itch worse.

Danny jumped when he felt his cock stir. To head it off at the pass, so to speak, he once again started talking without really thinking about what he was saying. Happily, this time he made a little sense.

"So you bought the house next door. It's been vacant a long time. Hope you like the place. It'll be nice to have neighbors again! Aren't you a little young to buy a house? Or maybe I shouldn't ask that. Sounds nosy."

Luke smiled. He seemed to know Danny was uneasy, although Danny prayed to God Luke didn't know *why*. With his index finger still tucked inside the top of Danny's cast just below Danny's knee, Luke placed his drink back on the table. While the fingers of his other hand were still cold from holding the soda, he started massaging the toes sticking out from the bottom of Danny's cast. Danny actually had to close his eyes, it felt so good.

"My dad rented it with the option to buy," Luke said, paying particular attention to Danny's littlest piggy. Massaging it, flexing it, making it grunt with happiness like all happy little piggies do when they're having the time of their lives. "My dad's gay," Luke added. "We moved here so he can be closer to his boyfriend. I don't know if they're going to move in together or not. I think Dad wants to be sure they are absolutely right for each other before he takes that final step."

"Wow," was all Danny could say to that. Then he said it again. "Wow."

Still massaging the little piggy, Luke leaned forward and gazed deep into Danny's eyes. "You aren't homophobic, are you?"

"Who, me?" God, Luke's eyes were blue. Oh, wait. *What* was he talking about? Danny did a rewind on the last few seconds and tried to forget about Luke's eyes and catch up on the conversation.

Luke laughed. "Well, you looked a little stunned there for a second. I thought maybe—"

"No, I—wait. Your dad must already know the two of them are right for each other or he wouldn't have packed up and moved here. By the way, where'd you move from?"

"Tucson."

"That's weird. My dad goes to Tucson a lot on business. He's there now, as a matter of fact."

"Small world."

"So where's your mom?"

"She died," Luke said. "Long time ago. I was little."

"Oh. I'm sorry. My mom lives in Indiana. She's a bitch."

"Oh," Luke said. "*I'm* sorry."

"So you're still living with your dad, then," Danny said. "Me, too. At least until I get on my feet."

"You mean *both* feet," Luke said, patting Danny's cast.

And Danny laughed. "Yeah. *Both* feet."

"It's pretty much the same story with me. Pop and I are close. He didn't want to move away from Tucson unless I came, too. I think he felt like he would be abandoning me if he did, although I am old enough to take care of myself."

"Of course you are," Danny said. "So am I, for that matter. So how old *are* you, if you don't mind my asking."

"I'll be twenty." Luke said.

"Oh." He was older than Danny thought.

Luke plucked at Danny's toe, as if to say "gotcha." "In a year and a half, that is."

Danny blinked. Then he got the joke. For some reason, Danny felt immense relief knowing the guy wasn't actually older, although he wasn't really sure why he felt that way. Maybe Danny simply felt safer knowing he and Luke were on a more even footing age wise. "Oh! Well, that's cool. So am I. I'll be twenty in a year and a half, too."

"Well, aren't we a pair." Luke grinned, and Danny grinned right back.

Luke moved along to the second toe. Figured he would spread around the happiness, Danny supposed. And if that was really what he was doing, then he was succeeding admirably. Danny was happy as a clam. Oddly enough, Luke seemed to be enjoying it too.

They fell into a companionable silence, with Danny staring at Luke as if he simply couldn't get enough, and Luke staring back at Danny through his bigass glasses with a gentle smile on his face. And when their eyes seemed to be a little *too* hooked into each other, Luke gazed about the room.

His eyes fell on a picture hanging on the wall by the window. It was a blown-up snapshot of Danny with his dad's arm draped across his shoulder. They were standing in front of the polar bear tank at the San Diego Zoo. A polar bear was grinning behind them like it knew it was having its picture taken.

Luke laughed. "Cute bear. Is that your dad?"

Danny followed Luke's eyes to see what he was looking at. "Oh. Yeah. That's us at the zoo last summer."

"Wow," Luke said. "Your dad is hot."

"I'm sorry. What?"

"No, really," Luke said. "Look at him. He's really hot."

"Shut up!"

Luke laughed. He reached out and tucked his finger under Danny's chin. Then he tilted Danny's head until he was sure Danny was staring at the same picture he was. "Your dad looks like an actor or a model or something. Don't tell me you never noticed it before."

And now, truly looking at the picture for maybe the very first time in his life, Danny realized Luke was right. His dad really was a hottie.

"Gee. I honest-to-God never knew."

Luke giggled. "I'll bet."

Danny was getting a little embarrassed talking about his dad like this, so to change the subject, sort of, he asked, "What does *your* dad look like?"

Luke shrugged. "Looks like me, I guess. Reddish hair. Kind of short. Also like me. I guess he's good-looking enough."

"If he looks like you," Danny said, unable to stop himself, "then I don't imagine he had much trouble finding a boyfriend."

Luke gave Danny a searching look, as if maybe what Danny had just said made him wonder something. And Danny was afraid he knew what it was. So to cover his tracks, Danny blurted out, "So have you met the guy? The boyfriend? Did your dad introduce him to you?"

Luke appeared to set aside any questions he might have about what Danny said about his dad finding a boyfriend. He was on the third toe now, and that toe was just as giddily happy to be the center of attention as the other two toes had been.

"Nope," Luke said. "I wasn't even sure he was gay until a couple of months ago, when he told me we were moving."

"Gee. Were you shocked? About him being gay, I mean?"

Luke thought about that. "Not so much. I, well, I know some gay people. They're just like you and me, you know."

Like me, certainly, Danny thought.

Luke left Danny's third toe screaming in protest when Luke moved along to the next toe too damn fast. Luke was too busy thinking about Danny's last question to notice. "I think I was just glad Dad had finally found somebody he loved. I knew he was seeing somebody. I just didn't know it was a guy. Not until he told me. But I don't have a problem with it." His eyes bored into Danny's once more. "Would you?"

Danny blinked. "Uh, no. I don't think I would. I mean, it would be a shock and all, what with it being my dad, but, uh, no. No problem."

Danny couldn't help wondering if that were really true. How *would* he react?

On the other hand, Danny was a wee bit more worried about how his father would react when Danny finally got around to telling him *he* was gay.

But that was a speculation Danny was always trying to avoid. Now was no exception. He steered the conversation to another heading.

"So where's your dad now, Luke? Closing up the house in Tucson?"

"Yeah. I came early to bring the van and maybe get this house arranged a little bit. Dad won't be here for a couple more weeks. He had to train his replacement at the bank. Talk to a Realtor. Shit like that. I didn't want to hang around in a torn-up house, so I talked Dad into letting me bring the van early." He released Danny's toes and patted Danny's knee instead. After he finished patting it, he let his hand lie there. "I'm glad I did."

Danny swallowed, looking down at that warm hand resting on his knee. He studied the hair on the arm the hand was attached to. Then he gazed a little farther south to study the hairy legs of the boy cradling Danny's left foot in his lap.

God, Luke was beautiful from one end to the other.

Danny's dick stirred again, making him jump. Jeez, he wished it would stop doing that.

"So am I!" he blurted out. He blushed, then toned it down a bit. "I mean, well, so am I. Glad you came early, I mean."

Luke grinned and gave him a wink. "I think you and I are going to get along just fine."

"Yeah," Danny said, still blushing but finding his own smile as well. "So do I."

Danny had almost built up the nerve to reach down and pat the hand that was patting his knee, but before he could get around to it, a car horn made them both jump.

"Crap!" Luke said. "Must be the peons Pop hired to empty the truck. Good thing he did though, huh? If *you* tried to help me they'd drag you to the state pen for breaking parole. Or jumping ship. Or crossing the thirty-yard line. Or whatever the hell they call it."

"They call it the quickest way to find my ass in jail and break my father's heart," Danny said. He didn't even try to *fake* a smile after he said it. The thought was too depressing.

Luke looked at him, his cornflower-blue eyes wide, full of sympathy. He reached out and touched Danny's cheek. Just the lightest touch imaginable. But to Danny, the touch burned all the way down to the bone.

"Then we won't let it happen," Luke said. "And for what it's worth, I think you did the right thing flipping over that fucking ice machine. Sometimes a guy has to do what a guy has to do."

"Thanks," Danny said.

Before anything else could be said by either of them, the car horn blasted again, making Granger bark and making the cat spit and hiss at Granger for barking. It also got Luke moving toward the door.

"Later, buddy," Luke said.

And Danny nodded. "Later."

Danny's heart was going a mile a minute.

He didn't know it, but so was Luke's.

DANNY stood at the kitchen window and watched Luke hop the hedge with ease and speak to the two guys waiting for him in the driveway next door. Once again Luke's ginger hair was set ablaze by the morning sun. Danny had never seen anything so gorgeous in his life. Luke was smiling and gesticulating to the two workers, pointing to the truck, then the house, bending to pet Granger's head, and once, he faced Danny's kitchen window and gave Danny a wave. Danny was so startled, Luke had turned away before he thought to wave back.

Wow. The past thirty minutes had been the most erotic thirty minutes of Danny's young life. He could still feel Luke's warm fingers touching him. *Touching* him. He could feel the timbre of Luke's voice still flowing across his skin like a sweep of silk.

Danny actually had to close his eyes when he remembered Luke reaching out to brush his cheek just before he left the house. His fingers were so gentle. His eyes so kind.

His body so sexy.

Holy shit. The guy had to be gay. He *had* to be. But what if he wasn't? What if he was just really, really friendly? Danny knew if he made the first move on Luke, and Luke backed away, or worse, *ran* away, Danny would be crushed. He would be so humiliated, it would probably set back Danny's little coming-out party for another decade. Or longer. Or forever.

Danny let the kitchen curtain fall closed, and he clumped his way back to the kitchen table, where he collapsed into the chair he had been sitting in earlier.

Torn somewhere between despondent and exhilarated, he reached out and touched the seat of the chair Luke had been sitting in.

It was still warm.

Danny sighed. He really had to get laid. Please, God, just once.

CHAPTER FOUR
DINNER

SINCE his erotically charged *tête–à–tête* with Luke earlier that morning, erotically charged from Danny's perspective at any rate, Danny had been alone the entire day. Playing video games. Playing *more* video games. Facebooking with people he didn't really know or ever want to meet. Eating. Eating again. Then eating maybe a couple more times. He could have clomped his way to the hedge and struck up a conversation with Luke, but the guy and his two helpmates were busy unloading a huge truckload of furniture, and Danny didn't want to bother them. Instead, Danny had tried twice to strike up a conversation with the cat, but to no avail. The cat wasn't talking. Still pissed about the bird, he supposed.

Danny wasn't used to all the seclusion, or to the restrictions this house arrest business was making on his ability to move around and function like a normal human being. It pretty much killed that ability dead, is what it did. Danny hadn't appreciated what a wonderful thing it was to be able to just hop in his car and go somewhere when he had a mind to, or to simply pick up a phone and call somebody when he felt like talking. No wonder people go on and on and on about the importance of freedom. It is one of those things you don't miss until you don't have it any more. Like sex. Of course, in Danny's case he had never had sex to *begin with,* except with himself, so you'd think maybe he shouldn't be missing it so much *now.*

If Danny was going this crazy being restricted to the house and yard, without access to his car and unable to use the telephone to call out, what would it have been like to spend these six weeks in a jail cell? No wonder his dad pleaded with the judge to let Danny serve his sentence under house arrest. Funny it was only now Danny really appreciated what an act of kindness that had been on his father's part. And it was costing his dad a small fortune, too, because the cost of leasing the ankle monitor was accruing daily. Since a prisoner under house arrest saves the city over $150 a day in jail costs, you would think the city would be paying *them*, rather than the other way around.

But apparently the city didn't see it that way. The pricks.

On top of all the loneliness and the restrictions on his movements and the frustration of having a cast on one leg and a damn flashing light on the other one, Danny was also trying to understand his feelings about Luke. Not that they were really that hard to understand. Danny wanted to get into the guy's pants and he wanted the guy to get into *his*. Pretty basic stuff there. You'd think it wouldn't be so confusing for him to figure it all out.

Lord, virginity sucks dick. Or was that an oxymoron?

Late in the afternoon, Danny's father called. When Danny grabbed the phone on the first ring and heard his father's voice on the other end of the line, the first words out of his mouth were, "I love you, Pop."

There was silence on the line for a couple of heartbeats, then his father replied, "I love you, too, Son. Feeling lonely, are we?"

Danny gave him a wry chuckle. "How'd you guess?"

"Don't worry. You'll make it through. I'm just sorry I had to leave you to face the music alone."

"It's okay, Dad. You can't put your life on hold for me all the time. You have to do stuff for yourself once in a while."

"Wow. Who is this level-headed guy I'm talking to and where's my crazy son who takes his frustrations out on ice-cube-making machinery?"

Danny laughed. "Maybe he's growing up. I miss you, Dad."

And Danny thought he could feel his father smiling at him over the phone line. "I miss you, too, Danny. Anyway, I assume everything is okay."

"Yep. Just fine. Somebody's moving into the house next door. Did you know?"

His father hesitated for a second. "Actually, yeah, I did hear that was going to happen. Have you met anyone yet?"

"Just the son. He's over there now, unloading a bunch of furniture. Nice guy. His name is Luke."

"Same age as you?"

"Yeah," Danny said. "How'd you know?"

"I heard he might be. Maybe you can strike up a friendship with him and then you won't be so lonely. I know you left all your real friends back in Indiana, and you really haven't been in California long enough to make new ones. Outside of the penal system, I mean."

Danny groaned. "Stop it."

"Sorry."

His father cleared his throat. "I'm serious, Danny. Make friends with the new boy next door. It'll help get you through the next six weeks. You need an ally. Someone you can talk to. And he's new in town too. Don't forget that. I'm sure he needs a friend to talk to as much as you do."

"I'm talking to you."

"It's not the same as a friend, kid."

"I talked to Mom."

"Oh, God."

"Yeah. She wants me to come back to Indiana the minute I get this hardware off my leg."

"What'd you tell her?"

"I told her hell no."

His father chuckled. "Bet she loved that. I'll probably be getting a call from her myself any minute now. Sure looking forward to that. We have *wonderful* little chats, your mother and I. She's quite a woman."

"She's a bitch."

"I'm trying to think of an argument to that."

"Don't waste your time."

"Okay, I won't."

A comfortable silence settled over the line. The silence didn't bother Danny at all. He was just happy knowing his dad was on the other end. He could almost feel him there. Like he was in the same room.

When his father spoke, Danny listened. That's how much he loved him.

"Danny. I've been watching the news. That creep that's killing young guys in San Diego has made national news. There was another one last night, you know. Have you been watching the news?"

"Not since yesterday," Danny said. "He killed four people."

"Well, now he's killed five. There was another announcement on the news this morning."

"Wow."

"Yeah. Wow. I have to tell you, Danny, I'm sort of glad you're under house arrest and not running around the city while this guy is still on the loose. I feel a lot happier knowing where you are every minute of the day. Still, I'm going to try to cut this trip short and get back there as soon as I can. He's killing guys in your age group, you know. They think he's—well, they think he's raping them, too."

"Jeez," Danny breathed. He didn't know which was more shocking. The fact the guy was doing that, or the fact his dad felt compelled to talk to Danny about it.

"So be careful, Danny. Okay?"

"You know I will." He meant it, too. Meant it with every fiber of his being.

Another comfortable silence descended on the conversation. Danny knew what his father was doing. He was trying to think of something to say so as to extend the phone call because he knew Danny was lonely. It was exactly the sort of thing his father *would* do, and Danny loved him for it. He really did. Especially now.

"So are you getting all your work done?" Danny asked. "You must be, if you think you can get back early."

"I am," his dad said. Danny thought he sounded a little nervous all of a sudden. A little hesitant. "And Danny, I want us to sit down and have a talk when I get back. We need to get some things out in the open between us."

Danny's voice shot up an octave, and he clutched the phone tighter to his ear. He jerked himself upright so quickly in the kitchen chair he was sitting on that his cast hit the floor with a thud, jarring his broken leg. "Ouch!" he said. "I *told* you I'd be good, Pop. I won't be getting into any more trouble, I swear. I don't want you to send me back to Mom's. I'm never going back there. I want to stay with—"

"Hush, Danny. Hush." His father cooed into the phone like he used to do when Danny was little and couldn't sleep. "I'm not talking about you, Danny. I'm talking about me. I want you to stay with me too. I've waited years to have you with me. So don't ever think I'll send you away. It's something else, Danny. There are things I need to tell you about. Things we need to discuss. I'm not worried about you at all, kid. And I don't want you worrying about me worrying about you. That would worry me."

"Shitty couple of sentences there, Pop."

"Thanks."

"Can you give me a hint?" Danny wheedled, like a little kid shaking a Christmas present.

The wheedle didn't work, but he could hear a smile in his father's voice. "No. I want to talk to you face-to-face. You'll just have to wait. And don't be trying to imagine what it is. Or worrying about it. It's not a bad thing. It's just something that needs to be talked about. Okay?"

"Christ. I'm imagining things already. And none of them are good."

His father chuckled. "I thought you might be."

This time the silence that fell between them was slightly awkward. Slightly *too* silent, and lasting a little *too* long.

"You're wanting to hang up, aren't you?" Danny asked.

Danny could hear the reluctance in his dad's voice when he said, "Yes. I need to get back to work. That okay? You going to be able to manage on your own?"

"I'll be fine. And don't worry about the killer coming after me. If I need help, all I have to do is stick one toe outside the yard and every cop in Christendom will be beating a path to our door. Sirens wailing, pistols blazing, attack dogs attacking, stun guns stunning."

His father groaned. "That's what I'm afraid of. Take care, Danny. I'll call again tomorrow."

"Bye, Pop." And Danny hung up the phone.

Two seconds later the doorbell rang.

Danny clomped his way across the hardwood floor to the front door. On the off chance it was Luke, he looked down and checked himself out to make sure his fly wasn't open and he didn't have any food on his shirt or anything else of a humiliating nature stuck to his person before he opened the door.

When he finally *did* open the door, after taking a couple of deep breaths to calm himself down, he was happy to see it really *was* Luke. And here he thought prayers were never answered. Just goes to show how wrong you can be. Thank you, God.

Luke stood on Danny's front porch soaked in sweat. He was still wearing the shorts and muscle shirt he had been wearing that morning, but now his clothes looked like they had been dragged through a coal mine behind a runaway tram. Apparently, emptying out a bigass truck full of furniture is dirty work. There was even a good-size tear in the shirt just above Luke's belly button, and through the tear, Danny caught a glimpse of a beautiful flat tummy with a sprinkling of red hair scattered across it. It was the most intriguing thing Danny had seen all day. It took a burst of fortitude to prevent him from actually licking his lips at the sight.

Luke's cheeks were flushed from being out in the sun all day. There was a smudge of dirt on his cheek, his ginger-colored hair was sticking straight up off the top of his head like he had walked into an electric fence, he had a scrape on one knee, and he was *still* gorgeous.

There was a clean change of clothes and a neatly folded towel tucked under his arm like a football.

Granger was sitting at Luke's feet, sweeping the porch with his tail, looking hopeful.

"Well, hello," Danny said, after checking Luke over from head to toe, and probably lingering in the equatorial regions a little longer than necessary. "You look like crap. Just fall out of a plane?"

Luke laughed. "Worse than that. I've been working. Working sucks. I came to that conclusion about two o'clock. Oddly enough I was carrying a Panasonic TV at the time, one of the old fat ones, that must have weighed four hundred pounds. Before I could set it down, my life flashed before my eyes, and I knew then and there that me and work do not get along, and likely never *will* get along. It was an epiphany of sorts."

"Gee." Danny smiled. "I wish I had epiphanies."

"No, you don't." Luke tugged the clean clothes and fresh towel out from under his armpit. Laying them in his arms like an offering, he thrust them in Danny's face. "I need help. Whichever moron from the water company was supposed to turn on our water, didn't. I've been waiting for it to come on all day. Not only am I begging you to let me use your shower, but I also need to borrow a few buckets of water to throw in my downstairs toilet where me and the two Neanderthals my dad hired to help unload the truck have been peeing and pooping all day. It needs to be flushed before the paint starts peeling off the walls and the EPA gets wind of it. *Literally* gets wind of it. I know it's asking a lot, but I'm desperate. What do you say? Neighbor."

If Danny thought not having any water in the new house would get Luke over here to shower in *his* house, Danny would have turned the guy's water off himself. He would have chopped into Luke's water main with an axe if he thought it would accomplish the feat. As if he wasn't already under house arrest for vandalism and destruction of property. It was nice to know sometimes fate takes care of things you don't think of taking care of for yourself. Who knew the world could be so prescient?

"No problem," Danny heard himself say. He wasn't sure, but he thought those two little words might be the understatement of the century. "Come on in."

After Luke stepped inside, with Granger padding along beside him, Danny looked through the door to see if there was anyone else he should be ushering in, but the two Neanderthal furniture movers Luke's dad had hired seemed to have headed back to their cave. Luke and Granger were alone. Another blessing from the fates.

Danny closed the door and tried to ignore the hammering of his heart. "Use my bathroom. It's got the walk-in shower. Top of the stairs to the right. Ignore the room next to it that looks like it was hit with a Tomahawk missile and then bombarded with hand grenades. That's my room. It always looks like that. I'll go find a bucket."

"Thanks," Luke said and headed for the stairs. Danny watched the back of his strong, bare legs as Luke ascended the steps. The muscles in Luke's hairy calves seemed to roll around with a mind of their own underneath their luscious reddish-blond pelt. God, they were beautiful. The thighs above the calves were even more beautiful. Danny closed his eyes before he got to Luke's ass. He was afraid his hormones would ignite and he would go up in flames like a dried-up Christmas tree if he took a gander at *that* going up the stairs.

Danny suddenly seemed to be infused with an avalanche of nervous energy. He couldn't sit still. While Luke cleaned up in Danny's bathroom, Danny went about the house like he had never been there before. Looking at stuff, touching this, rearranging that, adjusting a curtain, fluffing a throw pillow.

Then he realized what he was really doing. He was trying not to think about what was going on in that stream of shower spray he could hear thrumming overhead. He was trying not to think of Luke stepping out of his clothes. He was trying not to think of the warm water sluicing down Luke's naked body as he stepped beneath the spray. Trying not to think of the soapsuds gathering in Luke's pubic hair and in his armpits and trying not to think of Luke rubbing his soapy hands over his bare wet chest and sliding his soapy fingers between those two gorgeous butt cheeks Danny had been afraid to look at when the guy was climbing the stairs. Did the warm water feel so good Luke couldn't stop his own dick from standing up and saying hello? Was Luke soaping himself down now, fully erect? Was he sliding his frothy hand up and down that erection and were Luke's knees beginning to tremble like Danny's did just before he came?

Jesus. Danny was hard now too. His imagination was getting way out of hand. Nothing new there, of course. Still, sometimes it was disconcerting as hell.

He gave a little jump when the water turned off upstairs. He looked down at his dick, standing straight up like a tent pole underneath the fabric of his shorts, and knew he had to do something to make the damn thing go down before Luke saw it, so he set about gathering some food together and setting the kitchen table for the two of them. Luke obviously couldn't do much cooking if there was no water in his house, so Danny would give him dinner. Luke must be hungry after moving all that furniture.

But most importantly, setting the table and dragging the food out of the fridge gave Danny something to do that would take his mind off that damn erection he was sporting. He was trying to be neighborly here. He didn't want to be waving his dick in Luke's face when he came prancing down the stairs all clean and refreshed from his shower.

Well, actually Danny *did* want to be waving his dick in Luke's face—there was nothing he wanted *more*. Just not right *now*. And it would probably never happen anyway. Danny wasn't that lucky.

Luke appeared in the kitchen doorway like a sunrise, bright and beaming. Danny couldn't stop himself from glancing down at his own crotch to see what state it was in. Happily, his pecker had deflated to a sociable size: still on red alert but not fully deployed. And through his baggy shorts, it hardly showed at all.

Luke watched Danny glance down at his own crotch, so he glanced down at it too. He had a quizzical expression on his face with a little smile tickling the corners of his mouth. Danny had the horrible impression Luke knew exactly what he was doing.

Danny blushed. And oddly enough, Luke blushed too.

A silence fell between the two of them. The silence was both awkward and comfortable. Both friendly and positively teeming with testosterone. One of *those* silences. Danny wasn't sure, but he thought he could hear their heartbeats thumping away in the middle of it.

Their eyes met, and Luke's smile widened. He motioned to the table loaded with food. "Is this all for me?"

Danny's blush deepened to a magnificent magenta, two shades short of a stroke. "Well, yeah, I thought you might be hungry after working all day. But, you know, if you have other stuff to do, I won't keep you. I just thought maybe—"

"I'd love to. Thanks."

Luke dropped the ball of dirty clothes and the wet towel he was holding in his hand. Just dropped it right there in the doorway. He was in clean shorts and another tank top, just like Danny. It seemed to be the perennial uniform of the day for both of them. Except for the cast on his left leg, Danny was barefoot. So was Luke.

When Luke brushed past him to get to the table, Danny could smell Luke's clean skin and the Ivory soap the guy had showered with and the shampoo he had used to wash his hair. Danny's shampoo. The combination of the three scents made for such a sexy smell that for a second Danny thought he might topple over just sniffing it. God, Danny wanted to reach out and stop Luke in his tracks, pull him into his arms, run his fingers across Luke's clean smooth skin, nuzzle his neck to smell him all the better.

But, of course, he didn't. Danny sighed, and let Luke pass on by like a lost opportunity.

They heard a horrible scream in some other part of the house. Sounded like a banshee.

Luke grinned. "I guess my dog is pestering your cat. Sorry."

Danny shrugged. "Don't be. That cat's a cunt."

They laughed.

Luke's hair was still damp. Wet like that, it was really red, Danny noticed. Much more so than it was when it was dry. Danny watched as Luke swung a bare leg over the back of the kitchen chair and plopped himself down. He arranged his silverware neatly beside his plate, since Danny had just sort of tossed it on the table, not caring where it all went. Then while Danny still stood there watching him, Luke reached across the table and arranged Danny's silverware too.

When he was finished, Luke motioned to the opposite chair. "Sit," he said. "Eat. I'm starved."

And Danny finally expelled the breath of air he had been holding for the longest time. He sank into the chair, happy to get off his wobbly legs, and they both started loading their plates with all kinds of stuff. Potato salad, ham, pickles, bread, coleslaw, cold pizza left over from a couple of days ago, cold green beans that had been in the fridge for God knows how long but didn't stink yet so they must be okay. They ate as eighteen-year-olds always eat. With tons of enthusiasm and not a speck of conversation.

Chomping away at a mouthful of food, Luke tugged his chair in a little closer, and their knees bumped into each other underneath the table. Luke acted like he hadn't noticed, so Danny did the same, but for the next ten minutes Danny did not taste one single bite of food he put in his mouth. All his senses were centered on the brush of Luke's hard, hairy knees against his own and the easy, gentle pressure that kept them there. Danny wondered what would happen if he simply crawled across the table, swept the food onto the floor with a crash like they do in the movies, and ripped Luke's clothes off his body right then and there. He imagined them writhing around naked in the potato salad, a slice of ham dangling off Danny's ear, a green bean stuck in his nose, Luke's balls pressed against his chin.

And uh-oh. He had a hard-on again.

To take his mind off of it, Danny started talking, even while he kept shoveling food in his mouth. It wasn't like he couldn't talk and eat at the same time, after all. It wasn't a crime or anything. Like, say, flipping an ice machine onto its back and flinging two hundred dollars' worth of hamburgers out into the street because your boss was a greedy dipshit.

"It'll be nice to have people in the vacant house for a change. Sometimes I look down at it from my room upstairs, and it always seems sort of sad. You know? Being empty and all. If you see a crazy old lady ghost with a chrome walker and a poodle at her feet, that was the woman who lived there for about a thousand years. Lydia. That was the poodle's name. I forget the woman's. Old Miss Something-or-other."

Luke nodded around a mouthful of cold pizza. "I'll watch for her."

"I'm terrible with names," Danny said.

"You remembered her dog."

"Well, yeah."

Luke dropped his fork onto his plate with a clang and extended his hand across the table. "And I'm Luke, just in case you forgot."

Danny laughed. He took the hand, though, and gave it a friendly shake. He wasn't about to pass up *that* opportunity. "Don't worry," he said. "*You*, I remember."

And again, Luke sort of cocked his head to the side and gazed at Danny as if trying to decipher exactly what it was he meant by that. In the end, he must have worked it out to be a compliment, because a gentle smile spread across his face. He gave Danny's hand a tiny squeeze before letting it go. Danny wasn't sure, but he thought maybe the pressure that kept their knees together might have just gotten a little stronger. Danny certainly had no problem with that. No problem at all.

They resumed eating. Danny got the impression that something had just happened, but he wasn't exactly sure what it was. Seemed promising though. It was as if the air in the room had changed. Became a little warmer, maybe. A little closer. Like maybe the house had shrunk around them, drawing them closer together. And Luke was still smiling, even if he was pounding down the food again like he hadn't eaten in a week. That seemed promising, too.

While Danny stared at that intriguing new smile on Luke's face, even while trying not to *look* like he was staring at it, a wily glint appeared in Luke's eyes.

"So you can see into the house from your room, huh, Danny? I guess I'll have to be careful what I'm doing over there then. Wouldn't want you to catch me doing anything, you know, *inappropriate*."

Just the *thought* of Luke doing something inappropriate made Danny's cock twitch. And when his cock twitched, Danny jumped. He stammered out a hasty bit of reassurance, trying to appease both Luke and his own dick at the same time. Actually, what he stammered out was a hasty bit of bullshit. Nothing more, nothing less. "Oh, now that I know someone's living there, I won't be checking it out anymore. Don't worry. Heh heh. You're inappropriate secrets are safe with me."

Boy, was *that* a lie. And the way Luke shot one eyebrow up into his hairline, even he seemed to know it.

Danny then proceeded to make matters worse by asking, "So which room is yours? I'll take special care not to look through *those* windows. No, sir. Wouldn't want to see anything inappropriate. Not me. Uh-uh."

Luke smiled a smile that made Danny blush from his kneecaps all the way up to his ears. There was a lot of knowledge in that smile. And it was sexy as hell. "My room will be the one with all the curtains open," Luke said.

"Ah," Danny said, and his dick gave another jerk. And while that was happening, the air in the room changed *again*. Wow. This was the most testosterone-laden meal Danny had ever eaten. It even topped the breakfast they had shared that morning.

The testosterone meter climbed yet *again* when Luke's two knees came together and squeezed one of Danny's.

Danny gave a tiny gasp, but Luke acted like he didn't hear it. Or at least Danny *thought* Luke was acting like he didn't hear it. What the hell was going on here?

"Good pizza," Luke said, and Danny lost his train of thought. Luke's two knees relaxed around his own, but Danny could still feel the pressure of them. Could still feel the hair on Luke's legs scraping against the hair on his own. Lord, that felt good.

Two minutes later, they had resumed stuffing themselves, and one would think there had never been any testosterone in the room at all. Danny was almost relieved. Well, no, he wasn't.

Suddenly, the house began to shake, and what sounded like a herd of buffalo came stampeding down the staircase, across the foyer, and through the living room. Something crashed to the floor just outside the kitchen door, and Danny was pretty sure it was the crappy ceramic statue his dad loved so much of the fat little Buddha holding his hands above his head. Damn. His dad would have a fit.

On the heels of the crashing Buddha, Frederick came flying through the kitchen door like he had been shot from a cannon. His hair was all puffed up, making him the size of three Fredericks instead of one. Granger flew through the door right behind him, snapping, snarling, and obviously having the time of his life. His front end looked positively homicidal, but his tail end was wagging happily, making him look schizophrenic as hell. Or at least of two minds concerning his current enterprise of tormenting the cat.

The cat wasn't of two minds at all. He hated every minute of it. And where the hell did this goddamn dog come from anyway?

Neither Danny nor Luke moved as the two creatures thundered past. They simply sat there, chewing, as the battle went screaming by.

No doubt about it, Granger, schizo or not, seemed to be winning. Frederick was in full retreat.

Forty toenails clattered across the kitchen floor as the animals hurled themselves across the room and flung themselves through the back door, hissing, spitting, growling, and snapping. As soon as they were gone, Luke and Danny calmly resumed eating as if nothing had happened.

"So do you have a car?" Luke asked, when the racket of Granger and Frederick's epic battle had faded in the distance.

Danny nodded. Again he blushed. "Yeah. A Gremlin. Don't ask."

Luke laughed. "Don't be embarrassed. I've got a Pinto. Neither one of us is exactly driving Motor Trend's Car of the Year. My dad bought me mine. You?"

"Yeah. But it's off limits right now."

"Because of the thing?" Luke asked, indicating the ankle monitor blinking green at their feet.

"Yeah," Danny said. "Because of the thing."

Luke gave a commiserating nod. "My car's back in Tucson. Dad's going to tow it out with him when he comes. Right now all I have to drive is that gigantic fucking truck in the driveway. Imagine going out for hamburgers in *that* thing. Probably won't even fit in a drive-thru lane."

"So what are you going to do for two weeks then? Just hang around the house? Arrange the furniture? Do inappropriate shit in your room?"

And they both laughed. But while they were laughing, Luke gave Danny another long, searing look. There was a happy sparkle in his eyes. The two little commas at the corners of his mouth were bigger now, more like parentheses. Deep ones. He was grinning. "Probably," he said. "since there's nothing I like better than doing inappropriate shit in my room."

"Me, too," Danny said, before he could stop himself. There was no doubt in his mind they were both talking about the same thing. Spanking the monkey.

And Danny's dick gave another lurch.

They stared at each other for a second, both seeming to know exactly what the other was thinking. But reality intervened.

Looking reluctant, but determined, Luke pushed his plate away. "I'm stuffed. Listen, my dad's supposed to be calling me pretty soon, so if you don't mind I think I'll scoot off home. I wonder if I could trouble you for that bucket of water we talked about earlier."

Danny nodded. "Sure. And I'll hook up the hose and leave the end of it by the hedge so you can get more water anytime you want."

"Then I won't be bothering you," Luke said.

"That's not what I meant."

A look of such wounded misery crossed Danny's face that Luke reached across the table and patted his arm. After he finished patting, he left his hand laying there, comfortably nestled in the hair on Danny's forearm. Danny looked down at it.

"I was kidding," Luke said.

And Danny nodded. "Oh."

"See you tomorrow?" Luke asked.

"Sure," Danny answered. "See you tomorrow." And he dredged up a smile. "I'll look forward to it."

"Me too."

And with that, Luke was gone. Danny heard him yelling for Granger to stop tormenting the cat and come on home. Then Danny heard Granger give a happy yip.

Danny clumped around the kitchen in the already too-silent house, cleaning up the mess he and Luke had left after eating everything in the fridge. Pretty soon Frederick came stalking through the back door. He looked like he had been groomed with an electric mixer. To say he wasn't happy would have been understating things considerably. He was royally pissed off, is what he was.

Frederick gave Danny a hateful look, then cast a surly glare at his cat dish, which the damn dog had been eating from and which now had dog cooties all over it. At least that was what Frederick *looked* like he was thinking.

When Danny grinned at him, it was the last straw. Frederick spat, then marched through the kitchen door and headed for the stairs, tail high, flashing his ass in Danny's face. He was off to lick his wounds. And probably plot revenge.

"Lighten up!" Danny screamed, as Frederick disappeared through the door. Then to himself, he muttered, "Stupid cat."

EXACTLY four hours later, Danny stood in his darkened bedroom with a raging hard-on. He had a firm grip on that hard-on with one hand, while the other hand had a firm grip on the binoculars he was holding to his eyes. He was so turned on, his legs were shaking.

Across the yard, and over the top of the moving van parked in the driveway next door, Danny watched as Luke peeled off his clothes and flung them across what was apparently his brand-new room. A newly erected bed sat in the middle of the room, sheetless, the mattress new, still wrapped in plastic. There were curtains on Luke's window but they were the curtains that had always been there, even when the house was vacant. They were pushed wide open now, the room well lit.

Naked as a jaybird, Luke was the most beautiful thing Danny had ever seen. Danny held his breath when Luke stepped around the edge of the bed and moved closer to the window. He walked like a god, Danny thought. His limbs were pale and perfectly formed. His body strong. As

Luke moved, his cock swayed gently in the patch of reddish pubic hair it nestled in. There was a grace to the way Luke crossed the room and to the way his cock swayed as he walked that made Danny's heart ache. Flaccid, as it was now, Luke's cock was beautiful. Unthreatening. Danny longed to see it hard. Hard and hungry. He wondered how unthreatening it would be then.

Watching, and thinking these thoughts, Danny gave his cock a gentle stroking. He shivered when the head of his dick brushed the cool window glass.

Danny was so rapt by the beauty of what he was watching, he failed to notice when Luke stopped directly in front of his bedroom window and peered outside. It was only when Luke cupped his hands around the side of his face and leaned in toward the glass to better see through the darkness that Danny realized his peril.

Could Luke see him?

Quickly, Danny stepped back away from the window, moving deeper into the shadows of his unlit room. When he finally got the nerve to take another peek in Luke's direction, he was surprised to find Luke was gone.

Luke's room was empty.

Danny looked down and realized his hands were shaking.

CHAPTER FIVE
SEX AT LAST—THANK GOD ALMIGHTY, SEX AT LAST

LESS than a minute later, Danny's doorbell rang.

Danny tugged on his shorts, then grabbed a baggy dress shirt out of his closet and pulled that on too. He had to do something to camouflage the hard-on making his shorts balloon out in front like a pup tent. What if it was old Mrs. Trumball asking to borrow a cup of gin? Wouldn't want to scare her to death.

Danny awkwardly plodded down the stairs to the front door, making an unholy racket on the stairs with his cast. He expected to open the door to find some jackass Jehovah's Witness spouting Bible verses, or some Girl Scout maybe, looking all hopeful and trying to unload a trunkful of Lemon Snickereens, or whatever the fuck they were. Although it was a little late in the evening for Girl Scouts to be roaming around trying to earn merit badges. A little late for Jehovah's Witnesses too. But Danny wasn't exactly thinking straight, since all the blood that usually sloshed around in his brainpan had pretty much migrated south to his pecker. He supposed it was a miracle he could think at all.

When he pulled open the front door, the last thing Danny expected to see standing on his front porch was Luke. But there he was. Oddly enough, he was once again wearing the clothes Danny had just watched him remove not more than five minutes earlier.

Luke's beautiful grin was back, and he was aiming it directly at Danny's startled face.

"If you want to watch me undress," Luke said. "We can do it a lot closer than from one house to the next."

Danny's heart gave a jump. "I—I—"

"Mind if I come in?" Luke asked with an easy grin.

"I—I—"

Luke gave his head a little nod, as if he wasn't surprised by Danny's stammering. Disappointed maybe, but not surprised.

"In that case," he said, "I'll just undress right here." And with that, Luke pulled his muscle shirt over his head and dropped it at his feet.

When Luke hooked his thumbs in the waistband of his shorts and prepared to push them downward, all the while staring directly into Danny's widening eyes, Danny finally got a grasp on what the hell was going on. Without thinking too much about what he was doing, he reached out and grabbed Luke's arm to yank him through the doorway and out of view of any neighbors who might be snooping around, eyeballing his front porch. "Are you nuts?"

Luke giggled as Danny closed the front door behind them. "Are *you*?" Luke asked. "I'm not the one with the binoculars. Spying on the new guy next door and all."

Danny could feel his ears burning like maybe they were going to burst into flames. It was all he could do to get the words out, but he finally did. "You—you saw me?"

"Clear as day," Luke smiled. And oddly enough it was a pretty normal smile. The guy didn't seem mad or anything. Just maybe... *amused.* "The streetlight is aimed right at the side of your house, you know. I even saw your hard-on." Luke gazed down at Danny's crotch, hidden now under the baggy shirt.

Most of the blood had left Danny's crotch, by this time, and was making a beeline north, traveling back to his head. He could feel it surging into his cheeks. "You did?"

"Yep," Luke said, dragging his eyes back up to Danny's face. "I liked seeing it too."

Again, Danny said, "You did?" His voice was softer this time, soft and breathless, even though his heart was banging away beneath his ribs as if a blacksmith were pounding on it with a ten-pound hammer. As shocked and embarrassed as he was, Danny could still not stop his eyes from sliding away from Luke's handsome face to contemplate that heavenly body below. And with Luke's shirt crumpled on the floor at their feet, Danny had an excellent view.

He gazed at Luke's wide, pale shoulders. At the sprinkling of blond hair scattered across Luke's chest between those two perfect nipples. Danny stared appreciatively at the shadows of a pretty good six-pack delineating Luke's abs. It was all he could do not to sigh as he studied another patch of blond hair, just verging on red, which trailed its way down from Luke's tight little belly button and disappeared beneath the waistband of his shorts. Those shorts were bright yellow and looked to be a couple of sizes too big. They were hanging on Luke's hips by the skin of their teeth. Beneath the baggy yellow shorts, Luke's legs were bare. They were as fuzzy and beautiful as they had been that afternoon when Danny first laid eyes on them. They were without a doubt the sexiest legs Danny had ever seen in his life. Luke wasn't even wearing flip-flops, Danny noticed. He seemed to enjoy going barefoot. Just like Danny did.

And if what Luke said was true, he seemed to enjoy looking at other naked guys just as much as Danny did, too. Danny had to take a minute to wrap his head around that thought. But when he did, a smile began to creep across his face.

"Did you say you liked seeing me?" Danny asked, forcing his eyes back to Luke's face.

"Yeah. I did." Luke's hand was mindlessly stroking the hair on his own chest. His eyes were locked on Danny's, and for a moment, Danny felt like the air was being sucked out of the room. "You're beautiful," Luke added in a whisper.

"No, *you're* beautiful."

"You have a beautiful dick."

"No, *you*—" But Danny couldn't say it. Not yet. Although he sure as hell wanted to. After all, Luke *did* have a beautiful dick, whether he said it or not. In fact, since he'd gotten a glimpse of Luke's dick in the binoculars earlier, it was about the only thing taking up space in Danny's head. That and the fact he was about as embarrassed as he had ever been in his life, but even that didn't bother him much. Not compared to the memory of Luke's dick.

Luke smirked, but it wasn't a mean smirk. More of a *resigned* smirk. Like maybe he was wondering what Danny was thinking. "I figure we've both got it bad."

"Got what?" Danny asked. Then he knew. "Oh."

Luke reached out and touched Danny's cheek. Danny could feel that simple touch burn all the way down to his jawbone.

"Tell me, Danny. Just tell me. Be upfront. Do you want me?"

Danny's heart could be heard all over the house, or he imagined it could. Talk about tell-tale hearts. "Yeah, Luke, I do. I want you more than anything. But—"

"But?"

And Danny let go. Eighteen years of frustration and longing and uncertainty came pouring out. He couldn't have stopped it if he wanted to. His mouth was a runaway train barreling down the tracks. And even Danny knew it was heading for a cliff. There was no happy destination on this particular rail line. At least he didn't think there was. It only went to hell and back. Or so he thought.

"I've never done anything like this before in my life, Luke. I've never been with a guy, you know, *that* way. I've got all these big plans about coming out and declaring to the world that I'm gay but I keep chickening out when it comes to doing something about it. It was hard back in Indiana in that little farming community I grew up in. You should hear the way they talk about gay people. Like they are pond scum. Perverts. Creepoids who'll steal your kids and have their way with them. I never once heard the word 'gay'. They don't call people like me gay back there. They call people like me queers and cocksuckers and faggots and homos and, and, a million other names. And it's not even the words they use that're so terrible, it's the way they use them. The way they *say* them. And it's because of those words that I've spent my whole life hiding from what I really am. Even hiding it from myself, I guess. Scared to death I'd find myself in exactly the position I find myself in right now. And now that I'm here, now that I'm in that position and the truth is out, the only thing I want to do is—is—"

Danny stumbled to a halt, stunned to find he had tears burning his eyes. They hadn't fallen yet, but they were about to. Jesus, that wasn't supposed to happen. He hadn't meant to let *everything* go like that. He actually felt drained. Drained, but good.

Luke stepped closer. So close Danny could smell the mouthwash on his breath.

"Is what, Danny? What is it you want to do?"

Danny sucked up a big blob of snot that was threatening to dribble out of his nose. After just spilling his guts like that, the last thing he wanted to do was cry. That would sure be the icing on the cake, wouldn't it? Luke must already think he was a whiny, immature moron.

But he wasn't *looking* like he thought that, Danny noticed. He was looking—*concerned.* Wonder of wonders, Luke was looking like he actually understood.

Danny gasped when Luke took another step closer and folded him in his arms. Gently. Comfortingly. There was nothing sexual about it. Nothing—*intense.* It was merely something a friend would do. A friend doing what he could to make another friend feel better. It was a *good* thing to do. A *kind* thing.

Danny closed his eyes when he felt Luke's bare arms slide around him, when he felt Luke's hands pressed softly to his back. Bending his head, Danny lowered his face into the crook of Luke's neck. He inhaled Luke's clean scent and gave a tiny shudder to feel the simple warmth of the man this close. Luke was making a shushing sound as he held him, and Danny closed his eyes, still embarrassed, but comforted too. And he found himself accepting the comforting. It was as if he had waited for it so long, *needed* it so long, and suddenly, here it was. Offered. Just like that.

And it was wonderful.

Without Danny even thinking about it, his arms came up to return Luke's embrace. The feel of Luke's naked back beneath his hands was so astonishingly *electric*, Danny had to close his eyes for a minute and just *think* about how it felt. The heat of Luke's bare torso seeping through Danny's shirt, warming Danny's chest. The flow and ebb of muscles underneath Luke's satin skin.

Luke seemed to happily accept Danny's hug. He seemed to enjoy the feel of Danny's arms around him. Edging just a little closer, and being almost a head shorter than Danny, Luke rested his head on Danny's chest. The top couple of buttons on the dress shirt Danny had thrown on were unbuttoned, and Luke burrowed his face into the opening to press his cheek to Danny's bare skin.

Danny pressed his face to Luke's hair and inhaled the clean scent of it. He could feel Luke's pale eyelashes sweeping across the hollow in his throat. Could feel the gentle scrape of Luke's young stubble on his skin. Luke must not have shaved for a couple of days. It felt wonderful.

Danny's arms tightened around him, holding him close.

Luke's words were muffled because his mouth was against Danny's chest now. Danny could feel Luke's lips move on his skin when he spoke. It was the most erotic thing Danny had ever felt in his life. His dick began to move. Danny couldn't have stopped it if he wanted to.

But it was Luke's words that filled Danny's mind at that moment, not the fear of his lengthening dick being discovered. Not yet.

"Danny. I had a hard time coming out, too. My dad's not the only one in my family who's gay. I guess you know that already. I'm gay too. I haven't had much experience, you know, *sexually,* but I do know I'm gay. I think you are, too. And I think you're a virgin. And I think maybe you don't want to be a virgin anymore." Then he chuckled. "God knows *I* don't want you to be a virgin any more either."

Danny laughed. "Really?"

"Shit, yeah."

And ever so gently, Luke tilted his head back and touched his lips to Danny's. Mouths closed, barely making contact, the kiss was pristine. Pure and sinless. It was the kiss of two children. Two innocents. But still, it made Danny's heart start hammering again.

Luke lifted his lips from Danny's and looked him in the eye. "Let me stay with you tonight, Danny. Let me sleep in the same bed with you. Please. We won't do anything you aren't ready to do. In fact we don't have to do anything at all, if you don't want. I just want to be next to you. Can we do that?"

Danny couldn't speak. The circuitry that led from his mouth to his brain seemed to be malfunctioning, and he didn't know the number for tech support. So he simply nodded.

Hand in hand, they climbed the stairs together. Luke's footsteps were silent on the carpeted steps. Danny's weren't. In fact, all Danny could hear was the pounding of his own heart and the clomping of his plaster cast on the risers.

There was a smile blossoming on Danny's face. He could feel it there, stretching his cheeks apart.

Casting a shy look at Luke, Danny saw another smile blossoming to life. This one was on Luke's face.

When their eyes met, Luke lifted Danny's hand and pressed it to his lips.

Because he couldn't seem to stop himself, Danny leaned in and brushed his lips against Luke's ear as they continued to climb the stairs. To his own amazement, he felt his shyness simply deconstruct. Poof! It evaporated from his mind like morning mist hit by a red-hot rising sun. Of course, as soon as his shyness went away his hard-on came back. And it came back with a vengeance. In three seconds flat, Danny's cock was so hard inside his shorts, he had to fight the urge to touch it. Then he began to tremble.

"I want you so much," Danny breathed, and Luke pulled him through the bedroom door, smiling.

"Then let's do something about it," Luke said. "Let's do something *now*."

TO DANNY, it seemed he and Luke were not simply the only ones in the house, they were the only ones in the *world*. Nothing existed anywhere in the whole frigging universe except the two of them. At least it felt that way inside his head. Consequently, Danny was a little surprised when Luke quickly marched from one bedroom window to the next, closing all the drapes. In just a few seconds, Luke managed to shut out the neighbors and the night and the streetlights and the stars, and seal the two of them into a heavenly cocoon of comforting, blissful shadow. The only light spilling into the room came through the doorway leading out to the stairs. When Luke closed that door, the room was pitch-black. It was so dark and silent, Danny could hear their breathing.

Then Luke stripped away the darkness by switching on the lights. All of them. The ceiling light, the desk lamp in the corner, the stupid little lava lamp on the bookcase, and lastly, the bathroom light, which cast a long golden beam of light across Danny's bedroom floor like a river of magma pouring out of the john. By the time Luke was finished, the comforting shadows were chased away for good, and Danny's bedroom looked like a Broadway stage with every spotlight burning and every footlight glowing.

When he was satisfied that he had flicked on every light there was, Luke smiled at Danny across the room. "I don't want to miss anything."

"I guess you don't." Danny grinned. While he was proud of himself for being nonchalant enough to offer Luke that grin, Danny still had to admit it probably wasn't the most easygoing grin he had ever come up with. He was a little nervous. Well, no. He was pretty much scared to death. And just when he thought his shyness had taken a hike, too.

Luke gazed at him with his head tilted to the side. Luke was still wearing nothing but gym shorts, and as Danny stared at him across the room, he felt himself grow breathless with need. He took one step forward, then stopped. Unsure of what to do. Uncertain how to proceed.

Luke saw Danny's hesitation and quickly closed the distance between them.

"Relax." Luke smiled. "This won't hurt at all."

Danny started to laugh, but the laughter died in his throat when Luke reached up and began slowly unbuttoning Danny's shirt. While he worked at the buttons, Luke's eyes never left Danny's face. Not until he reached the bottom button. Then, looking down, Luke's eyes opened wide as he spread Danny's shirt apart and pushed it back off his shoulders. The shirt slid to the floor at Danny's heels in a crumpled mess.

Danny felt a tremor go through his body when Luke laid his hands atop Danny's smooth chest. Luke slid his warm palms across Danny's skin, brushing his nipples, then running his fingertips along Danny's collarbone. From there he stroked Danny's arms from his shoulders to his hands, then slid his fingertips upward again, grazing the hair on Danny's arms until finally bringing his hands to rest at either side of Danny's neck.

When Luke leaned in to brush his lips over Danny's gaping mouth, he dropped his hands to clutch Danny's sides, just above the waistband of his shorts.

Luke swept his fingers inward over Danny's stomach, and as he did, Luke pulled his lips from Danny's and lowered himself to his knees.

Danny tried not to gasp when he felt Luke's breath against his stomach. Then he tried not to gasp *again* when he felt Luke's lips brush across his belly button. Luke's tongue probed his navel, and Danny's knees began to shake. Luke reached down to feel them. Bending lower he pressed his lips first to one hairy thigh, and then to the other. As he did, his fingertips slid beneath the leg holes of Danny's shorts. They played across the skin of his legs, never quite reaching high enough to touch Danny's balls. But they were close. Very close.

Luke pressed his mouth to the front of Danny's shorts, pushing against the firmness he found there: the firmness of Danny's rock hard cock, begging to be released. Luke moved his hands to Danny's waist to brace himself. With his teeth, he nipped at the tab on Danny's zipper and oh, so slowly tugged it downward. If it was release Danny wanted, then Luke was more than happy to give it to him.

Danny's legs were shaking so badly he was afraid he was going to fall on his face, so he placed his hands on either side of Luke's face and felt the warmth of Luke's skin against his palms.

As Luke pulled at Danny's zipper with his teeth, Danny closed his eyes and cupped the back of Luke's head with one hand, caressing his red hair, pulling him closer. With the other hand he stroked Luke's cheek. His hips pushed forward of their own accord, and Danny felt himself smashing his crotch against Luke's face. He wasn't sure, but he thought he felt Luke smile when he did it.

When the zipper tab was as far down as it would go, Luke slid his hands across Danny's stomach and converged on the button of his shorts. With a simple flick of finger and thumb, Luke popped it open, and Danny's shorts slipped off his hips and hit the floor.

Danny's breath was ragged, and he looked down the length of his naked body to see Luke looking up. Danny's stone cock was standing rigid against Luke's cheek. He could see moisture glistening at its tip, and as he watched, Luke turned his face toward it and licked the moisture away.

Danny gasped. And even as he gasped, he directed the head of his cock to Luke's smiling lips, begging to be taken in.

With his eyes centered on Danny's face hovering above him, Luke pressed a kiss to the tender skin beneath Danny's glans. Then he slid his lips all the way down the underside of Danny's long shaft until his mouth and nose were buried in Danny's balls.

"God—" Danny breathed.

Luke took that as a sign Danny wasn't exactly complaining or anything, so he cupped Danny's fat, heavy balls in his fingertips and slid his lips back up the shaft of Danny's cock. Once again, he licked the moisture away at the tip, probing the tiny slit with his tongue when he did, but he stopped short of taking Danny into his mouth.

Danny grabbed Luke's arms and pulled him to his feet. Pressing his lips to Luke's mouth and tasting his own precome in the kiss, Danny breathed, "My turn." And still shaking all over, he dropped to his knees at Luke's feet. Clutching Luke's hips with his strong hands, he pulled Luke close against him.

While Luke played his fingers through Danny's long hair, Danny let his hands roam over the body standing before him. From Luke's ankles, along the hairy calves and thighs of Luke's gorgeous, strong legs, Danny pushed his trembling hands upward until they crossed Luke's flat stomach to the sprinkling of hair across his chest.

While he explored with his hands, Danny pressed his lips to Luke's belly button. He wanted to watch everything he did, but the soft heat of Luke's stomach against his mouth was such a beautiful sensation, he had to close his eyes to experience it.

He only opened them again when he felt his fingertips, as though acting with a mind of their own, dig beneath the waistband of Luke's running shorts and tug them downward off his hips. As they slid away, Luke's cock sprang up and pressed itself to Danny's face.

Danny couldn't believe the heat of it. Or the hardness. He had felt his own cock a million times, but this was different. This was— *amazing.*

He rocked back on his heels to see Luke's cock better. He cradled it in his hand, and Luke's hips surged forward, begging for Danny to stroke it. So Danny did. Slowly. Gently.

Luke's cock was pink and perfectly shaped. It was almost as big as Danny's, and just as with Danny's earlier, there was a crystal drop of precome trembling at the tip, ready to fall.

Hesitantly, but not so hesitantly, either, Danny reached out with his tongue and licked the glistening drop away. The precome was sweet in his mouth. He closed his eyes to relish the flavor of it. And with one hand pressed flat to Luke's stomach, Danny used his other hand to gently stroke Luke's cock until another glistening drop formed.

This drop he kissed away with both lips. And just as Luke's hands came down to caress the sides of Danny's face, Danny let all hesitation fall away. He knew beyond any doubt whatsoever that what he was doing, right now, at this very moment, was what he had been born to do.

This was absolutely who he was.

So parting his lips, he smoothly and eagerly encompassed Luke's cock, drawing it in. Danny closed his eyes at the sensation of that hard, hot cock sliding into his mouth. God, he had wanted this for so long. And to make it even better, it was happening with Luke. Although he had never sucked a cock before, it took Danny exactly one and a half seconds to figure out exactly what to do.

And when he did, it was Luke's turn to gasp. It was Luke's turn to feel his own knees shake.

Danny's mouth around his dick felt wonderful. Too wonderful. Luke was going to come in about three heartbeats if Danny didn't stop right now.

He pushed Danny away and wrestled him to his feet. Taking his hand, Luke dragged Danny toward the bed. Once there, they endured a moment of giggling confusion while Danny hurriedly cleared the bed of a shitload of rumpled clothes and books and other crap to make enough room for them to lie down. But once the bed was cleared, they wasted no time falling into it, arms and legs entwined, lips pressed together, heartbeats pounding a mile a minute. The feel of their young, hard cocks grinding together caused both of them to moan.

Twisting around to face in opposite directions, they settled into a sixty-nine position, and without one moment of hesitation, each took the other's cock into his mouth as if he had been waiting for this moment forever.

It wasn't as if the two of them had just met. It was as if they had known and wanted each other for years.

And the want had consumed them.

When Danny came, seconds later, it was the first time the lips of another had brought him to orgasm. And it was the most fabulous experience of his young life.

As Danny cried out, shooting load after load of spurting come into Luke's eager, hungry mouth, Luke suddenly cried out himself.

And with his eyes wide open and the sound of his own orgasmic heartbeat thundering in his ears, Danny felt Luke's hips push upward as his sperm came skyrocketing out of that beautiful, beautiful cock. It poured over Danny's face, splashed across his lips, shot up into his hairline.

Danny groped at Luke's ass and pulled Luke's dick as deep into his mouth as he could get it. With Luke's balls pressed against his nose, Danny inhaled their heavenly scent as he sucked the last drops of come from Luke's cock. When the spurting finally stopped, Danny still did not release him. Nor did Luke release Danny.

As they sucked away each final drop of the other's come, their cocks slowly softened inside the other's hungry mouth. And as they were gently drained, the two men, who were really little more than boys, pulled each other close and savored every sensation. With naked bodies pressed tight, and the smell of their hot come still permeating their senses and making them smile, they luxuriated in the feel of each other's skin. They listened to each other's heartbeats pounding down to a calmer cadence as they melted into each other's cradling arms, angelic smiles twisting their lips, both of them as contented as they had ever been in their lives.

It was the taste of come that Danny remembered last, just before sleep overtook him.

God, it was wonderful. *Luke* was wonderful.

Burrowing his face into Luke's velvet stomach, even as Luke did the same to him, the two young men closed their eyes and dreamed of only one thing, although they would not remember in the morning what their dreams had been about.

They would dream of each other, and they would be smiling as they dreamed.

And when they awoke in the middle of the night, they would once again be consumed with hunger. They would reach out for each other before their eyes were fully open.

CHAPTER SIX
ROUND TWO

TRYING not to move, Danny took a peek at the clock on his desk. It was a little after four in the morning. The lights were still on, just the way they'd left them. His cheek was pressed to Luke's thigh, and they were still lying side by side in opposite directions on the bed. Just like they were when they nodded off.

Carefully, Danny raised himself up onto his elbow to better study the man lying next to him. God, Luke was beautiful.

Ever so gently, Danny brushed his palms along the blond hair on Luke's strong legs. He pressed his lips to Luke's thigh to feel the heat of his skin. Luke's cock was sleeping, resting snugly atop his plump balls, which were only inches from Danny's face. Unlike the hair on Luke's legs, and the spattering of hair across his chest, which was all blond, Luke's pubic hair was ginger. Almost red, but not quite. Moving as gently as he could so as not to waken Luke, Danny pressed his lips to those ginger covered balls and inhaled Luke's scent. His own cock immediately stirred.

Then so did Luke's. Danny watched as it languidly yawned itself awake, lengthening and thickening until it slid sideways and stretched itself out in all its glory to lie hard against Luke's stomach. Suddenly, there was nothing languid about it at all. Danny watched, enthralled, as that stiffening cock gave a tiny jerk with every beat of Luke's heart.

Luke's eyes were still closed. Ever so carefully, Danny took Luke's cock between his fingertips and stood it upright. He admired the perfect shape of it; the plump glans, beautifully formed; the firm ridge of the corona encircling the glans; the bulging veins climbing along the shaft, pumping in the blood even as Danny watched. Slowly, Danny traversed the corona with his tongue, savoring the salty taste of sweat and spent come that still lingered there. Then he slipped his lips around the entire head of it, and when he had taken it completely into his mouth, Luke's hand came down and stroked his cheek.

"That feels good," Luke whispered, eyes still closed.

Danny slid his lips away and pressed them into Luke's balls, once again inhaling Luke's scent. He was smiling. He couldn't seem to *stop* smiling.

"I didn't mean to wake you," Danny whispered, which was a lie.

"Yes, you did," Luke said.

And Danny laughed. "Okay. I did."

Luke twisted his body around just enough to bury his face in Danny's crotch, just as Danny had done to him. He wasn't surprised to see Danny's gorgeous cock standing straight up. He slipped it into his mouth to say good morning.

Danny shuddered and gave a tiny groan. Luke's mouth felt wonderful.

As they quietly talked of unimportant things, each of them calmly pleasured the other. It was without a doubt the most sensual experience of Danny's young life. Danny was happy to note that Luke's mouth on his cock felt just as fabulous this morning as it had the night before. And Luke's cock in his own mouth tasted even *better* than it had the night before.

Luke released Danny's cock long enough to slide his lips down Danny's leg. He seemed to enjoy the heat of Danny's thigh pressed against his face, the bristle of Danny's leg hair tickling his nose.

Danny enjoyed it, too.

Luke kissed his way down one leg until he came to Danny's cast, then he shifted over to the other leg. Danny suddenly squealed like a little kid when Luke took one of his toes into his mouth.

"That tickles!"

Luke didn't seem to care. He just kept sucking on it, ignoring Danny writhing around on the bed and laughing like a hyena. Finally, Luke said, "Your light's still green."

"Thank God," Danny gasped, catching his breath. "I'd hate to see a bunch of cops storm into the bedroom right now."

And it was Luke's turn to laugh. "No kidding."

Danny's dick was as stiff as a poker and aimed directly at his nose. If it was a compass it would have shown true north. As stiff as it was, Luke still managed to get it aimed in a different direction, namely down his throat, and suddenly Danny found himself thrashing around again. But this time he wasn't laughing. This time he was enjoying the shit out of every fucking moment.

When Luke flipped Danny over onto his stomach and knelt on the bed between his legs to massage his shoulders and slide his hands over the back of Danny's long legs, Danny started shaking, it felt so good. He was also a little nervous, not quite knowing what Luke had in mind.

But he needn't have worried. Beginning at the nape of Danny's neck, Luke kissed his way down along his spine, over the rise of his ass, down the length of his long, hairy legs, dragging his tongue through Danny's leg hair, tasting his flesh, feeling his heat. Then he started kissing his way back up.

And when he came to Danny's ass, Luke gently parted Danny's ass cheeks and laid his tongue to Danny's opening. Taken by surprise, Danny almost flew off the bed.

Luke giggled and pushed Danny back down. Again, he gently spread Danny's ass cheeks wide and pressed his lips to his hole. Luke circled the puckered opening with his tongue until Danny was chewing on a pillow, it felt so good. Danny was trembling like he had been struck with a horrific case of malaria. Jesus, get the quinine! Never in Danny's wildest dreams had he ever imagined a sensation like this.

Now Luke's tongue lapped at Danny's ass like an ice cream cone. He wasn't being shy about it at all. Danny pushed himself up onto his elbows and knees to give Luke all the help he could. He never wanted Luke to stop. Never.

When Luke pulled his lips away, and said, "Do me," Danny collapsed onto the bed with a smile. Then he rolled over, raised himself up to his knees like Luke had done, and watched as Luke sprawled out before him on his stomach, legs wide, ass lifted high off the bed, aimed directly at him.

Danny pressed his palms to either side of Luke's ass and relished the feel of it. There was a sprinkling of ginger hair across the top of Danny ass at the base of his spine. Danny started there, pressing his mouth to that little patch of fuzz, letting it tickle his lips, his nose.

Stroking and kneading that heavenly ass, Danny slid his tongue across the firm cheeks, gave each cheek a gentle nip with his teeth, gradually working his way inward. Grabbing Luke's thighs, he lifted Luke's ass completely off the bed and buried his face in it, inhaling the manly scent of need and desire and passion. Luke trembled and thrashed around when Danny carefully laid his tongue atop Luke's sphincter, but he wasn't trying to get away. He was just enjoying the hell out of every single second of the attention Danny was giving him.

Luke's reaction spurred Danny to experiment. He pressed his tongue to Luke's hole and slid it in as far as he could. Luke cried out, and reached behind him to take a handful of Danny's hair and hold him in place.

Holding Luke's thighs in his strong hands, Danny pulled Luke's ass to his face and slipped it on like a Halloween mask. He lapped and tongued and laughed, and when he reached below to cup Luke's balls and feel Luke's concrete cock flopping around in midair, Danny couldn't wait any longer. He flipped Luke over onto his back and sucked that beautiful cock down his throat as if he had been sucking cock for centuries.

Luke gave a loud moan, and the come shot out before he could stop it. It filled Danny's mouth and oozed down his throat, and when Danny finally had to pull away to take a breath, the come continued to shoot across his face and over his lips.

When Luke was drained, Danny pushed him down onto the mattress yet again. Danny straddled him and perched his ass atop Luke's chest. He took his long cock in his hand and pressed it to Luke's lips, smearing the precome coating the head of it across Luke's face.

Luke tried to catch it with his tongue, tried to take the cock into his mouth, but Danny stroked it with his own hand until he knew he could wait no more.

Rising up onto one knee, awkwardly because of the cast, Danny pressed his cock to Luke's lips again, and this time Luke's mouth opened wide just at the exact moment when Danny's sperm tore out of him like buckshot.

Luke roughly pushed Danny's hand aside and took control, gripping Danny's hard, fat cock as his orgasm made Danny sob, it felt so good. Luke squeezed Danny's cock to get every last drop into his mouth and Danny shivered and bucked and helped him get it.

When Danny was as drained as Luke, they collapsed onto the bed side by side. They had barely enough energy left to hold each other close.

"Don't go home yet," Danny said, his face pressed to Luke's chest.

"Don't worry. I won't," Luke answered, still savoring the taste of Danny's come in his mouth, and longing, even now, for more.

Five minutes later, they were asleep again.

WHEN they woke the second time, the sun was just beginning to rise across the city. Danny could hear birds chirping up a storm in the palm trees outside his bedroom window. He climbed out of bed and flung open the drapes to let in the light. He gazed down at the pool in the backyard. The water looked cool and delicious, and not for the first time, Danny regretted the fact that as long as he had a cast on one leg and a fucking police monitor on the other, the pool was off-limits. He sadly turned away, and as he passed the bookcase by the window, he reached up to scratch Frederick's chin. The cat was once again in the process of shredding Mark Twain's literary efforts. He seemed to be on a different volume now. It looked like *Huck Finn*. He must have grown tired of mutilating *Tom Sawyer*.

Even if he was a pain in the ass, Danny was glad to see Frederick had found his way back inside after having been chased out of the house by Granger the night before. He didn't look mad any longer. Now he just looked—contemplative. Danny wondered if he was ripping that book to shreds just to have something to do while he plotted his revenge against his new neighbor, the fucking dog next door. It wouldn't have surprised Danny a bit. Cats are sneaky. And Frederick was sneakier than most.

While Danny was up, he limped around on his cast switching off the lights. When he was finished, he jumped back into bed and snuggled up next to Luke, who had been watching him all the time he was roaming around the room.

"The cat's back," Danny said. "Where's the dog?"

Luke yawned and stretched his arms above his head, which gave Danny the perfect opportunity to bury his face in Luke's furry armpit. He really liked doing that. He wasn't sure if Luke liked it or not, although it did make him giggle.

Luke's voice was gravelly with sleep. "I left Granger locked in the house last night when I came over to rape you. I'll have to go let him out soon or he'll poop all over the place."

"I liked being raped," Danny said around a smile.

Luke tapped Danny's smile with a fingertip, and said, "I know you did."

They spent a few quiet minutes just enjoying the fact they were lying in each other's arms, sated and naked and happy, and knowing full well there was nowhere in the world they would really rather be.

"I thought about you when I used your shower yesterday," Luke said.

Danny slipped Luke's nipple into his mouth and ever so gently tweaked it with his teeth. "Oh, yeah? What were you thinking?"

"I was thinking I wished you'd take off your clothes and join me for a bath."

"I wish I had," Danny said, releasing Luke's nipple and propping himself up on one elbow to peer down into Luke's handsome face. He planted a tiny kiss on the tip of Luke's nose. "I really, really wish I had."

Luke lifted his head just enough to brush his lips across Danny's mouth, then he fell back on the pillow. "Well," he said. "You're not a virgin anymore."

Danny grinned. "That's true. I'm not. So what am I now?"

Luke pressed his face to the hollow of Danny's throat and inhaled his scent. "Delicious. That's what you are. And I have to say, I've never seen anybody come the way you do. I mean, you *really* come."

Danny twiddled with the scattering of hair across Luke's chest. His dick was getting hard again. Christ, would he ever get enough? "Just how knowledgeable on the subject are you?"

"Say what?"

"How many guys have you been with to compare me to?" Danny asked. And as soon as he asked, he had a feeling he was going to be sorry he had. The last thing he wanted to think about was Luke having sex with someone else.

But Luke only smiled. "Maybe three or four. Why? Did you think I had screwed my way across Tucson?"

"No, I—"

"I don't have much more experience than you do, Danny. And the experiences I *have* had were scary and clumsy and not much fun. None of them came even close to comparing with last night. Not even close. Last night was perfect. At least for me. You enjoyed it, too, right?"

Still propped up on one elbow, Danny smiled down at Luke's upturned face. He watched his hand slide down Luke's chest to stroke the hair around Luke's belly button. He slid it downward a little more, and fingered the ginger pubic hair surrounding Luke's growing cock. Then he moved it even farther down and cupped Luke's plump balls in the palm of his hand. He loved the way they felt there, resting in his hand. Heavy and warm and soft. By the glint of light that suddenly flashed in Luke's cornflower-blue eyes, Danny was pretty sure Luke liked the way they felt there too.

"Jesus, Luke. How can you ask that question? Wasn't it obvious? Last night, with you, was the most incredible experience of my life. I'm not afraid of who I am any more. I'm not afraid of what I know I've always been. The only thing I'm afraid of is that maybe last night I hit my peak and it's never going to be that good again. Oh, hell, actually even *that* doesn't scare me much. At least I'll still have the memory of what we did together. You're something else, Luke. You really are. You're the sexiest guy I've ever known. Bar none."

Danny was surprised to see a blush creep across Luke's face. Luke knew he was blushing, too, and that seemed to embarrass him more. He turned to his side and pressed his face to Danny's chest so Danny couldn't see how red he was getting. His arms slid around Danny's back and pulled him close.

When he spoke, his lips brushed Danny's skin and his voice was muffled by Danny's chest pressed against his face. "To tell you the truth, what little experience I've had with sex was all pretty disappointing. I honestly never knew it could be like it was with you last night. That was—phenomenal. I really love your body, Danny. I love everything about it. I'm glad I worked up the courage to come over."

"So am I," Danny said, and meant it. "If you'd left it up to me, we probably never would have gotten together."

"Boy, I sure would have hated that," Luke said.

"Me too." Danny had never spoken two truer words in his life.

He let his mind do a Nascar victory lap while he held Luke tightly and thought about the words Luke had just spoken. Strangely, they were the exact same words Danny would have used to describe how he felt about the hours he'd spent with Luke. If nothing else, they seemed to be on the same page as far as each other's bodies went.

Suddenly, a thought exploded in Danny's mind. It was the memory of Luke climbing to orgasm, his slim hips lifting off the bed, his legs shaking, fingers clawing at the sheets, while Danny's mouth brought him closer and closer to the point of no return. Danny could hear again Luke crying out as the semen surged from his straining cock, filling Danny's mouth, making Danny gasp.

Making Danny smile.

Danny closed his eyes, hopefully locking that perfect memory inside his head forever where he could pull it out every now and then and relive one of the greatest moments of his young life.

He prayed to God Luke felt the same as he did.

Danny pushed his lips into Luke's hair. "Does your dad know you're gay? Have you told him yet?"

Luke gave an almost imperceptible shake of the head. "Not yet. I think he suspects, though. Takes one to know one, you know. I get the feeling Dad was hoping I wouldn't be. I don't know why. It's just an impression I've had for a long time. I hope he won't be disappointed. My dad is really a good guy. I don't want to hurt him."

"Mine too," Danny said. "I don't know what he's going to say when I tell him. But like you said, I just hope he isn't too disappointed. I've caused him enough trouble already. I'd hate to cause him any more."

Luke grinned. "Yeah, it must be a real trial having you for a son."

"Well, happily the trial is over. Now we're into the penal phase." Grunting, Danny lifted his right leg and tried to get in the right position to wave his ankle monitor in Luke's face. "See?"

Luke laughed, giving the monitor a friendly pat. Then his hand stroked the calf the monitor was attached to. He leaned in to kiss Danny's shin, once again closing his eyes at the incredible feel of Danny's hair and skin against his lips. Loving the smell of the guy. The lean, young strength of him. And god, the *beauty*. Danny thought he was a skinny geek. Luke thought he was gorgeous.

It was true what Luke had told Danny about him not having much sexual experience, but still he was wise enough in the ways of the world to know what he and Danny had going here was pretty extraordinary. It had been an incredible night. He and Danny had really connected. In every way possible.

Then he spotted the reflection of sunlight on water, shimmering across the ceiling.

"Hey," Luke said. "I just remembered."

Danny looked up to where Luke's eyes were aimed. "What?"

Luke pointed to the bright dabs of reflected light, shifting and sparkling above their heads. "You have a pool! I saw it from my bedroom window."

Danny thought he knew what Luke was getting at. "Oh. Yeah. You want to go for a swim?"

"I'd love it. Not right now. But maybe later. Okay?"

Danny laughed. "Sure. That's what it's there for. The only bad thing is, if you're swimming in the pool, it means you won't be in bed with me. I don't think I'm too crazy about *that* idea. Nope. Uh-uh. Don't like it at all."

Luke pulled Danny into his arms and touched his lips to the cute little pout Danny had made for his benefit. Luke's tongue shot out and wormed it's way inside, scraping across Danny's teeth, foraging around the roof of Danny's mouth.

Danny giggled, and did the same to Luke.

Then they both started laughing. Finally, Luke broke the kiss.

"Let me go get Granger before he recarpets the house with dog poop. We'll go for a swim later. Okay?"

Danny groaned. "You'll have to swim alone. With all the concrete and electronics strapped to my legs, I'd either sink like a rock or electrocute my sorry ass. I'll watch you, though. How's that?"

"Deal," Luke said and sprang out of bed.

Danny was thrilled by the sight of a naked Luke scooping his shorts off the floor and slipping them on. He wasn't thrilled knowing Luke was leaving, though. He wasn't thrilled about that at all.

When Luke saw Danny watching him, he came back to the bed and leaned down to give Danny another kiss. "Don't worry. We'll be back in bed before you know it. But I really do have to go get Granger. Unattended, he's a poop machine."

And then Luke was gone, thumping down the stairs and banging his way out the front door.

Danny climbed out of bed. For one of the few times in his life, he was smiling when he did it.

But his heart was aching just a little bit, too, having Luke out of his sight. Out of his arms.

Naked, wearing nothing but his ankle monitor and the fucking cast, Danny clomped his way across the bedroom floor, grabbed a couple of trash bags from the sink in the bathroom, and headed for the shower.

Frederick stopped shredding *Huckleberry Finn* long enough to watch Danny pull the trash bags over his feet. And all the time Frederick was watching, he was wondering where the hell his breakfast was.

Unfortunately for Frederick, the last thing on Danny's mind right then was feeding the cat. The smile that kept popping up on his face as he stood beneath the warm spray and soaped himself down, didn't get there because he was looking forward to opening a can of tuna or fondly remembering the last time he rattled a bag of Little Friskies.

Nope. That smile was there because he was wondering when he and Luke would get together again. And what they would do when they did. And how many times they would do it.

After all, for the first time in his life, it wasn't only his *own* come he was washing off his long, lean body, now *was* it?

And those thoughts were so delicious to contemplate, Danny broke into song. And he sang so loud, and it echoed so horrendously between the shower walls and out the bathroom door, that Frederick made a *chuffing* noise and stalked off down the stairs to get away from it.

Damned humans anyway.

CHAPTER SEVEN
DEVON AND BRADLEY

ONCE Danny was dried off and dressed in his customary shorts and T-shirt, he headbanged his hair into place while grabbing the binoculars to see what was going on next door. Luke had only been gone for twenty minutes, but already Danny missed him.

Aiming the binoculars at Luke's bedroom window without even *trying* to be sneaky about it, Danny saw Luke drying off with a towel as he meandered around his room stark naked with Granger padding along behind. The two of them seemed to be exploring their new domain, peeking into closets, switching lights on and off.

Danny grinned when Luke looked up and spotted Danny spying on him from across the way. Luke gave a sexy little striptease bump and grind for Danny's benefit, and still drying his hair with the towel, Luke slid the window all the way up and leaned out to yell, "The water's on! Yay!"

Danny laughed and gave him a thumbs-up. Then Danny stepped back from the window and grabbed his heart. Lord, that little bump and grind routine of Luke's had sent the blood rushing to Danny's groin like the levee in his diaphragm had burst. Suddenly Danny wasn't sure which was worse: wanting something you've never had, or wanting something *again* you've only had a couple of times. He was referring to sex, of course. Well, no. He was referring to sex with *Luke*.

Then Danny remembered the two of them, him and Luke, crying out like lunatics as they happily shot come all over each other's faces, and a bit of the blood that had just sluiced down to Danny's dick, sluiced back up again and burned his cheeks. The memory made his heart start hammering even louder. He decided on the spot it was his brand-new favorite memory, that one. None of his other memories even came close to that one for sheer stopping power because it really did stop him cold every time it entered his head.

Danny gave himself a shake and stepped back to the window to see what Luke was doing now. But Luke and Granger were gone. Off to begin their day, Danny supposed. With a sad little exhalation of breath, Danny decided he should do the same. And using every ounce of willpower he possessed, he turned away from the window, set the binoculars aside, and headed for the stairs.

Today, to do his dad a favor (and also to maybe take his mind off sex for a bit), Danny decided he would clean windows. Inside and out, upstairs and down. It was a job he and his dad both hated, which was all the more reason to do it. Danny sure as hell wasn't going to do anything now to get himself sent back to Indiana to live on the farm. Hell no! Unless Luke moved to Indiana, which seemed highly unlikely, Danny was staying right here. And the trick to staying here was to keep his father happy. Thus the windows.

But first—breakfast.

While Danny chomped his way through another humongous bowl of Cap'n Crunch's Crunch Berries, he pondered life. And the first thing he pondered about life was the fact that now he thought he was pretty sure why people were always talking about and obsessing about and dreaming about and reading books about and watching movies about—wait for it—*sex*.

Danny couldn't stop reliving every single moment of the night he had spent with Luke. At one point, he even caught himself just sitting there at the dining room table, spoon hanging forgotten in his hand, while he remembered the taste of Luke's lips. The heat and pressure of them. Luke's velvet tongue trying to worm its way inside Danny's mouth, and then Danny doing the same to Luke. Their arms drawing each other close, hands exploring, cocks rubbing together. Cornflower-blue eyes studying him—studying him—

Then Danny remembered Luke flipping him onto his stomach and touching him *there* with that heavenly mouth of his. Just the thought of it made Danny's hands tremble so badly he dropped his spoon in the cereal bowl, splashing milk halfway across the table.

Oy.

Danny made a concerted effort to eat the rest of his Crunch Berries without thinking any more about last night because he was never going to finish breakfast this way. Afterward, he slurped down his daily cup of coffee, *still* trying to block those memories from his mind, but without much success. Luke and his scrumptious body were everywhere inside Danny's head and there was just no getting away from it.

So with his poor besotted skull still filled with last night's wonders, Danny finally went to work. He gathered up rags, window cleaner, and a stepladder. And all the while he was lugging stuff to the front of the house, he was hoping he wouldn't break his neck trying to maneuver with the damn cast and ankle monitor hindering his movements. Frederick wasn't helping either, getting underfoot, winding in and out between Danny's legs, wanting his head petted, wanting to play.

Danny was in the mood to play all right, but not with the cat. It took him about twenty seconds to figure out that sidestepping a needy cat and lugging a clunky old stepladder across the yard while balancing a shitload of cleaning supplies and sporting a hard-on all at the very same time was a recipe for disaster. Something had to go before he broke his neck.

So he shooed away the cat and gave his dick a friendly pat on the head instead, after looking around to make sure no neighbors were watching. Then he girded his loins, so to speak, forced himself to ignore his erection from that point on, and went to work in earnest.

By the time the sun had climbed up toward noon, and the temperature had climbed up right along with it, Danny was finished with all the outside windows except for the ones in the back overlooking the pool.

He gathered together all his cleaning crap one last time, and dragged the ladder around the final corner of the house.

Then he stopped cold.

Behind the pool, in among the towering hibiscus plants that blossomed by the back fence, he saw a pair of legs sticking out along the ground. Little legs. They were wrapped in little ratty blue jeans, and the little feet sticking out the end of them were shod in little ratty tennis shoes.

Looking closer, Danny spotted another pair of legs a few feet over under *another* hibiscus plant, sprawled out in the *opposite* direction. They looked like book ends.

"Hey!" Danny bellowed, and all four legs jumped. Then all four legs wiggled into the shadows and disappeared.

A moment later, two young boys stepped sheepishly into the light, rattling the hibiscus blossoms and looking guilty as hell. They were the same boys Danny had seen arguing over the basketball in the driveway down the street two days earlier. They were also the same boys he had given the finger to after they ragged him about his pink plastic leg warmers that day they roared past on their skateboards.

Danny grinned when the two kids glanced at each other as if to say "Busted" then turned to face their fate. Danny bit back a chuckle. They looked like Danny was going to stand them up against the fence and call in the firing squad or something.

"You guys were going to sneak into the pool, weren't you?" Danny said, trying to look stern but not really pulling it off very well. The kids looked so guilty, it was actually pretty funny. Still, neighborhood kids trying to take a swim in Danny's dad's pool was a common enough problem, and one Danny's dad tried desperately to control. Nothing could wreck a guy's standing in the community like letting someone's kid drown in his backyard.

The two boys looked to be about eleven years old. One was black and the other was white, and they were both about as cute as they could be. Once they got a good look at Danny standing there with his cast and his ladder and his ankle monitor with the green light blinking over his right foot and the cleaning rags draped all over himself, they started looking a little less guilty and a little more defiant.

"What the hell are *you* supposed to be? A mummy?" the white kid asked.

"Yeah, man. What the hell are *you* supposed to be? A mummy?" the black kid echoed, and Danny watched as the two kids sort of giggled and snorted and nudged each other.

Danny propped the ladder against the side of the house to get it out of the way; then he dropped his cleaning supplies in the grass and tugged a dozen or so rags off of different parts of his body, glad to be rid of them. They were cramping his style. And probably *did* make him look like a mummy.

He tried to salvage his dignity by assuming the pose of a proper adult. Hands on hips, head cocked to the side. All that grown-up shit. Then he said, "I'm the guy who's going to keep you from drowning in this swimming pool because nobody's around to watch over your little asses when you sneak in for your sneaky little dip thinking you're cool."

"We weren't going in your pool," the black kid said.

"And we weren't sneaking," the white kid said.

Danny didn't believe either one of them. "So what are you doing in my backyard, then?"

And suddenly the two boys glanced at each other all shifty-eyed, looking guilty again.

"Well?" Danny prodded. "Out with it. What the heck are you doing? And don't tell me you weren't being sneaky. Good lord, you look sneaky right now."

From the other side of the back fence, just behind the two boys, Danny heard a car door slam. The kids obviously heard it too, because they both jumped about two feet into the air before whirling around to look behind themselves. Danny had never seen two kids look more startled in his life.

"It's just a car door," Danny said. "Nobody's shooting at you, you know. Don't be so nervous."

"We're not nervous," the black kid said, and Danny laughed.

"Kid, if they had a picture next to the word 'nervous' in the dictionary, it would be a snapshot of the two of you taken right this very minute."

"We're not nervous," the white kid said. "We're scared."

"Scared of what?" Danny asked. "Me?"

And there was a beat of silence before both boys laughed. It wasn't a very flattering laugh either.

"Man, you're about the last thing we'd be scared of," the black kid said, bending down and slapping his knee like some old guy laughing at his own joke.

And the white kid echoed him, bending down to slap *his* knee. "Yeah, man, you're about the *last* thing we'd be scared of."

"So what *are* you scared of then?" Danny was getting hot. And not just hot under the collar. *Physically* hot. It was broiling out here. Sweat was gathering inside his cast and his leg was itching like crazy. He wanted to finish the windows and get inside out of the sun and take a shower and dig around with his curtain rod for a while and hope to hell Luke would come back over and do that little strip tease of his again. Danny didn't want to spend the rest of his life talking to these two brats and melting in the sun. Actually, he sympathized with them completely for wanting to jump into the pool: the water was so damned inviting. Danny wanted to dive into it too. And if he hadn't had one leg encased in cement, he would have.

He jumped when a hand came down on his shoulder. It was his turn to whirl around, and when he did, he saw Luke standing there. Luke had a grin on his face that made his dimples really deep. And really cute.

It was all Danny could do to drag the word out of his mouth. "Hi." God, he was smitten.

Luke was staring at the two kids. To Danny's surprise, he broke into a pretty fair Irish brogue.

"What's with all the wee laddies? Leprechauns? Garden gnomes?"

Danny giggled. "Trolls. *Trespassing* trolls."

The black kid stuck an elbow in the white kid's ribcage. "So says the convicted felon under house arrest for vandalism and throwing a hissy fit in public."

"Not to mention assault and battery on two hundred cheeseburgers," the white kid added with a smirk.

Danny laughed. That was actually pretty funny. It also proved word of his escapades was indeed out on the street. If these two kids knew about his little meltdown at the hamburger joint, then everybody in the neighborhood did. Oh, well. Not much he could do about it now.

"What are your names?" he asked, not even trying to look serious any more.

Luke still had his hand resting on Danny's shoulder. He was standing real close to him, too, Danny noticed. Danny liked having Luke snuggled up next to him like that, but he was beginning to wonder what the kids might think of it. Obviously, Luke didn't care *what* the kids thought. And after Danny thought about it for a minute, neither did he.

"Yeah," Luke said, "what are your names? And what are you doing on my friend's property, if you don't mind my asking."

The white kid giggled. "More like *boy*friend."

Luke leaned forward and stuck his face two inches from the white kid's nose. "And that would matter *why?"*

The black kid broke up their little staring contest by stepping forward. "My name's DeVon." He aimed a thumb at his buddy standing next to him. "This is Bradley. He's white, but don't hold that against him. We don't care if you're gay. We've got other fish to fry."

"Who said we were gay?" Danny asked. He wasn't sure if he was bothered by the fact these brats thought they were gay or not. Basically, he just wanted to know *why* they thought it.

"Hey," the black kid groaned, "if you don't want us to think you're gay, then fine, we won't."

"Even though you are," the white kid added with a twisted little smile.

Danny was getting a headache thinking of them as the black kid and the white kid. He made it a point to try to think of them by their names. DeVon and Bradley. DeVon and Bradley.

DeVon decided to clear the air. "It's no skin off our noses if you like to chew the dingdong. Hell, I got an uncle that's queer. He chews on dingdongs, too. He gave me a bicycle last Christmas."

Whatever *that* had to do with it, Danny thought.

Bradley threw his two cents' worth into the pile. "Yeah, and I've got two aunts that chew dingdongs. And a gardener that does, too. The gardener's name is Raul."

DeVon turned to Bradley with a scathing grimace on his face. "If your two aunts chew on dingdongs that don't make them gay, you idiot. The gardener, yeah. But the aunts, no."

Bradley blinked and his ears turned red. "What does it make them then?"

"Sluts. To be gay they'd have to like licking pussies. That would make them lezbos. Which is Latin for gay."

"Oh, yeah. I knew that."

"No, you didn't. Anyway, eating pussy is a long way from chewing on a dingdong. Although I guess from a distance they look about the same."

Luke and Danny both laughed at that.

Danny decided to get back to the single statement in this entire conversation that he had actually found interesting. "What was it you boys said you were scared of?"

Both DeVon and Bradley cast nervous glances at the fence behind them. Suddenly they were speaking in whispers.

"Nothing," Bradley hissed.

"Nothing at all," DeVon added, barely audible. "Can we go now?"

Luke and Danny glanced at each other, then they stared down at the kids.

"Sure," Danny said. "But don't be sneaking around the pool any more. You could fall in and drown and I'd have to fish your smelly, lifeless black and white bodies out of the water, and then we'd probably have to drain the water and sterilize the fucking thing before we refilled it. Our water bill is high enough as it is."

"Yeah," Luke added. "And by the way. What was the name of your gardener again?"

Danny poked an elbow into Luke's gut to shut him up. He knew the guy was joking, but still, was that a pang of jealousy Danny felt? Good lord, he really did have it bad.

They watched as DeVon grabbed Bradley's shirttail and dragged him around the corner of the house where the two boys gave a hasty wave, called out, "See ya!" and finally disappeared altogether.

"Cute kids," Luke said, watching them go.

"Not as cute as you," Danny heard himself say.

Two minutes later, they were in Danny's room closing the drapes and pulling off their clothes. And a mere two minutes after *that*, DeVon and Bradley, and yes, even Raul the gardener, were forgotten completely.

Tumbling into each other's arms, they did not think to look out Danny's south window that overlooked the pool in the backyard. If they had, they might have seen their next door neighbor, Mr. Childers of the sexy (but older) ass and chest, pulling weeds on the other side of Danny's back fence. He looked hot and sweaty and kind of cranky, as if maybe he had been out there quite a while.

And even if Danny and Luke *had* spotted Mr. Childers by the back fence, slaving away under the burning California sun, they probably wouldn't have thought anything about it.

They were too busy to think of anything but themselves.

And rightly so, since they were both coming to some fairly astounding conclusions about how they felt when they were in each other's company.

And especially when they were in each other's company *naked.*

DANNY felt a little uncomfortable. "Let me shower. I've been working all morning."

But Luke was like the mailman. He would not be deterred from his appointed rounds. And at the moment, his appointed rounds centered on Danny's crotch.

"No," Luke said, without much finesse. He was too turned on for finesse. Didn't have time for it at all. "I want to smell your sweat." He lifted his lips from Danny's balls and gazed across the gorgeous flat plain of Danny's tummy and chest, still shiny with perspiration from his hours in the hot sun washing the fucking windows. Luke skated his hands across Danny's sweaty skin as if he loved the feel of it. "That doesn't make me weird or anything, does it?" Luke asked, looking remarkably young and innocent considering where he was positioned and all, with his chin resting lovingly against Danny's sweaty nuts. His cornflower-blue eyes were so bright with passion, Danny thought he might get lost in them forever and *never* find his way out. They were a hazard. Yes indeedy.

Danny had started trembling before Luke ever touched him. Now that Luke actually *was* touching him, and touching him *down there* no less, and with his *face,* and looking at him with those gorgeous blue eyes, Danny was trembling so hard he thought he might actually fall off the bed. And if he fell on his dick it would probably snap like a tree limb, that's how hard it was.

"Touch me then," Danny managed to say around a quaking intake of breath, and Luke smiled up at him as he obediently circled Danny's rigid cock with his hand.

Danny closed his eyes and sighed. Then he gasped when Luke slid his still-sweaty hand up the shaft of Danny's dick to gently enclose the head of it in his fist.

Conversationally, Luke said, "So I take it you're pretty happy about not being a virgin any longer."

"Fuck you," Danny stammered, feeling his cock pulsate in Luke's grasp. Every nerve ending in Danny's body seemed to have migrated to the head of his pecker. Jeez, he didn't know nerve endings could move around like that.

Again, Luke pressed his lips to Danny's balls, even while he continued to stroke Danny's dick. Slowly. Teasing the glans. Gently fingering the corona. Rubbing his thumb over the slit, dispersing the moisture leaking out like Danny was in dire need of a new gasket or something. Danny's hips rose and fell with every movement of Luke's hand, every twiddle of Luke's thumb. His legs opened wider to give Luke better access. Danny wasn't exactly sure where it was Luke planned to go, but wherever it was, Danny saw no harm in making his journey a smooth one. He reached down to brush his fingers through Luke's ginger hair when Luke took advantage of the better access he was offered to kiss the tender skin at the base of Danny's balls.

With his tongue sliding closer and closer to Danny's hole, and with Danny spreading his legs wider and wider to let him get there, Luke mumbled, "You want to be careful bandying words like "fuck" around. You never know where it might lead."

"You're right," Danny said, realizing what Luke meant. He was pretty sure he wasn't ready for *that.* "I'm sorry."

"Are you?"

Danny stammered. "Well, I—think I am."

And Luke laughed. "Yeah, right. You look about as sorry as I do."

Then he pushed Danny's long hairy legs high in the air, cast and all, and buried his face between Danny's ass cheeks. No warning. No heads up. Nothing. Just bam! There he was. He nibbled and slurped and foraged around Danny's opening until Danny, giggling and gasping and writhing like a crazy person, finally screamed for him to stop.

So Luke stopped. He stopped with his tongue resting lightly over Danny's hole. Unmoving. Hot. He left it there so long, exerting just the slightest pressure onto Danny's sphincter, that suddenly Danny didn't *want* him to stop any more, and started sliding his ass over Luke's face and tugging at Luke's hair until Luke got back in the ass-licking business. Which he did with gusto.

"Oh, Jesus—" Danny sputtered. He was so excited now, he was chewing on his *own* arm. "Sixty-nine, Luke. Please. Sixty-nine. Swing around and let me get at you before I come all by myself."

"Hardly all by yourself," Luke harrumphed, sounding hurt and possibly even emotionally scarred by such a callous statement coming from someone whose ass was at that very moment getting such a fine and thorough rim job. "I'm helping a little."

"You know what I mean."

Luke snorted a laugh, his lips still pressed to Danny's sphincter. "Well, since you insist." And so he did. As he wiggled his way around on the bed to face the other direction, he stopped long enough en route to give Danny a long probing kiss on the lips. Danny held Luke close, his tongue exploring the depths of Luke's mouth now that it had moved from one orifice to the other. He stroked Luke's warm velvet body from his neck to his ankles and back again. Danny had never felt anything so electrifying in his life. Luke's body was everything he had ever imagined another man's body to be. And he wanted all of it.

All of it.

It took a minute for Luke to get properly situated, but once he did, he and Danny found themselves in the very same position they had loved so much the night before. Face to crotch. The both of them. As he lowered his hungry mouth over Luke's rigid, beautiful cock, Danny figured this was about as close to heaven as he was ever going to get.

Luke reciprocated, and the next thing the two of them knew, they were clutching each other's asses and driving their dicks into each other's mouths and spraying come down each other's throats like a couple of horny fire hoses.

When their two hearts stopped bouncing around like a pair of basketballs and eventually settled down, they gazed across the long expanse of each other's naked bodies and allowed themselves a gentle smile of appreciation.

"Thank you," Luke said.

But Danny couldn't speak. Not yet. He pressed his face to Luke's thigh and felt the blond hair there scrape across his cheek. He laid his lips to the hard nub of Luke's knee and tasted it with his tongue. Inhaling Luke's scent, he closed his eyes when Luke's hand slid along Danny's stomach, softly caressing, obviously relishing the feel of his skin. Then Danny felt Luke's lips on his stomach.

They both shivered and smiled.

When Danny finally managed to speak, he said words he had no idea were coming. But once they were spoken, he knew they were exactly right.

"I really love being with you." And the moment he said them, his heart started hammering again. He wasn't exactly sure why.

But Danny calmed down when he felt Luke's smile brush against his pubic hair. Luke's breath tickled him there. He reached around to stroke Luke's back and pull Luke's body even closer. That way it tickled a little less.

"I know," Luke said, pulling Danny closer too. Snuggling in for all he was worth. Pushing his face into Danny's stomach. Inhaling Danny's scent, just like Danny had done to him. "I feel the same way."

"We've got a couple of weeks before our dads get back," Danny ventured. "Why don't you and Granger move in here until they do? I like it better when I can see you naked without using binoculars. Makes me feel like a perv doing that."

"Some people might say we're pervs just doing what we're doing right now."

"Screw 'em. What we're doing right now is the greatest thing that's ever happened to me. I don't care what people think about it. I only know what *I* think about it."

"And what's that, Danny?"

But Danny couldn't say what he truly felt. Not yet. Maybe not ever. So he simply stated the obvious, and let it go at that.

"I like it."

Luke turned around and scooched up in the bed, dragging his lips along Danny's belly and chest as he went. When the two of them were head to head, Luke pressed his lips to Danny's forehead, then he kissed Danny's eyelids, first the right one, then the left. And finally he gave Danny's nose a quick peck as he dragged his fingertips though Danny's shoulder-length hair.

"Profound," he said.

While his face was getting all the attention, Danny nibbled at Luke's neck. "Thanks."

Danny was still waiting for an answer to his suggestion about the two of them moving in together on a temporary basis. He had dredged up the courage to mention it once. He wasn't sure he could ever find the guts to mention it again. But he needn't have worried.

Luke seemed to be thinking out loud when he said, "Somewhere across the way, I've got a box packed full of telephone stuff. In that box are enough phone extension cords to drag our house phone halfway back to Tucson if we wanted. Shouldn't be anything to drag it through the hedge and across the yard over to here. That way when my dad calls, he won't know I'm here instead of there. Pretty smart, huh?"

Danny's heart did a flip-flop. "So you'll do it? You'll move in?"

Luke cradled Danny's face in his hands and scooted his lips down to press them against Danny's mouth. Then he pulled back to study Danny's expression. "Sure I'll do it. Did you think I'd say no?"

"Well, I—"

Luke glanced over to the bookcase by the window. Frederick's ass was hanging off the shelf. He was sound asleep.

Luke gave a tsk. "Your poor cat doesn't know what hell he's about to be in for. Granger will drive him nuts."

"Fuck the cat," Danny said. "Let's have sex again."

Luke propped himself up on one elbow and stared down into Danny's eager eyes. "What, already?"

Danny's hands slid south. One cupped Luke's balls, the other stroked Luke's fuzzy ass.

"Yes, please," Danny said.

And Luke grinned. "Well, as long as you say please." He felt Danny's dick twitch against his leg. He liked feeling it there. Luke thought Danny looked as if he pretty much liked feeling it there too. Luke grinned, getting caught up in Danny's enthusiasm. "Just give me a minute to catch up."

Danny grinned back, as happy as he had ever been in his life. "Take all the time you need."

CHAPTER EIGHT
ROOMIES

DANNY dragged half his clothes out of the closet and flung it all under the bed to make room for Luke's stuff. Luke didn't bring *everything* over to Danny's house, of course. Hell, he had just schlumped it all out of the moving van and stuffed it into his *own* house, so he didn't want to move it again. Besides, while he was staying with Danny, Luke figured he wouldn't need that many clothes anyway. At least he hoped he wouldn't. He and Danny seemed to get along just fine wearing nothing but a couple of smiles and maybe an occasional layer of sweat.

There was also the fact this was a temporary arrangement and they both knew it. Their dads would be arriving in a couple of weeks and that would pretty well throw a monkey wrench into the whole shebang.

Still, for two weeks, he and Danny would be on their own. And Luke was thrilled.

He was also beginning to wonder if maybe he wasn't falling a little bit in love. Danny was absolutely the best thing that had ever happened to Luke. And Danny's body was exactly the kind of body Luke found most attractive. Long, lean, responsive. Danny's sweetness was a big draw too. And his innocence, which Luke was doing everything he could to cure the guy of. Tee hee. The only drawback Luke could see to Danny at all was the cast on his left leg and the ankle monitor on his right. But even working around those impediments was kind of fun. Just took a little patience and ingenuity is all.

The most astonishing thing of all was the fact Luke was pretty sure Danny was falling in love with him too. Danny certainly got some loving looks in his eyes sometimes. And God, he was sexy when he got those looks.

Luke found the packing box with all the telephone stuff in it and hooked together one telephone extension cord after another until they stretched all the way across two lawns, from Luke's kitchen outlet to where they snaked up the side of Danny's house and through his bedroom window. Luke still had his cell phone, too, but he never knew if his dad would call on the cell or the landline, so having both phones available at Danny's house took care of that little problem. Now Luke's dad would never need to know Luke wasn't home at all. Of course, Luke would still be close. When he wasn't working on getting the house ready for his dad's return, he could easily keep an eye on the property from Danny's bedroom window at night. If he could drag his face out of Danny's crotch long enough.

So the days passed. And they were happy days.

He and Danny settled into a strange but ultimately satisfying routine. They each managed to accomplish everything they needed to do as far as their own chores went and still find plenty of time to be together. They took their meals together, spent each idle minute together, and found lots of time to lay by Danny's pool and sunbathe. Even if Danny couldn't go in the water, Luke certainly could. And he enjoyed the hell out of it. And Danny enjoyed the hell out of watching him.

They both loved the hours they spent by the pool. Eyeing each other's bodies as they lay together in the hot sun, and occasionally reaching out to share a touch, they found themselves talking for hours on end. On those lazy afternoons, with the summer sun pounding down on them and their tans quickly deepening, they talked about everything that popped into their heads. They talked so much they discovered just about everything there was to learn about each other. But it was the secrets they didn't mean to share, but eventually did, that were the real eye-openers.

They were astonished to learn they both enjoyed writing stories. After overcoming a certain reluctance about sharing their talents, they finally showed each other everything they had written from grade school on. They laughed over some of the plotlines and groaned over some of the really bad writing, which took another pair of eyes to spot.

They talked about the angst of being gay, and *knowing* you were gay, but being afraid to share that truth with the world and with the people who love you. Danny was still astounded that Luke, whose father was openly gay, had not had the courage to tell his dad about his *own* gayness. Even Luke couldn't really explain why that was.

One afternoon, Danny lay at the apron of the pool on the hot concrete, merely dragging his arms through the cool water because he knew if he actually dove in, he would sink like a rock, thanks to his fucking cast. Luke floated in front of him on the inflatable raft, flat on his back, eyes closed against the sun. Their hands came together in the water and they vowed to each other that the very day their two dads came back into town, they would sit them down and tell them the truth about their homosexuality.

Luke supposed his dad would be understanding about it. Why wouldn't he? He was gay himself. But Danny had no idea how his own father would react.

Still, it was something that had to be brought out in the open sooner or later. And now that Danny had spent time in Luke's arms, and he could honestly say his days of being a virgin were happily over, he knew he could never really be himself until his dad knew who he truly was. He wished, too, that he could tell his dad how nuts he was about Luke. But Danny hadn't even said those words to Luke yet, although the time was drawing near when he knew he probably would. They were on the tip of his tongue every day now. Soon they would come spilling out whether he wanted them to or not.

So swallowing back the words for now, both he and Luke fell a little more in love with every passing moment they spent together. Savoring the summer and the hours they shared, they relished every single day.

But, oh, the nights! The nights were *revelations!* Holding hands in front of the TV. Giggling through their dinners. Then reaching out to each other like two innocent children, leading each other up the stairs where their childish personas fell away and they became what they truly were. Men. Men driven by need and passion and consuming curiosity. Those hours in each other's arms were more fulfilling than anything either of them had ever expected to find in their young lives.

But they did find it. And they found themselves protecting those precious hours together above all else.

Small imaginings began to creep into their minds as they lay naked, sated, cuddling. Imaginings concerning what it might be like to *really* live together. To *really* commit to each other. Perhaps it was fear that kept the words from being spoken out loud. For neither could bear the thought of scaring the other away.

So the days went by. The sex got better and better. The longings grew exponentially. But still the words were left unsaid. It wasn't time yet, they both thought. They hadn't been together long enough. Hell, it hadn't even been a week since they first came face to face.

But still, Danny and Luke knew in their individual hearts that only one word could convey the way each of them felt about the other. That word was love. They just couldn't find the courage to say it out loud.

And while they waited for that courage to show itself, they still had to deal with real life.

It was a simple cry in the night that first lured their attention away from each other.

But it was Frederick the cat who finally brought reality crashing down upon their heads.

THEY lay spooning in the bed, watching the gibbous moon through Danny's bedroom window as it climbed ever so slowly up the star-spattered California sky. A nice breeze had come up and found its way through the darkness to cool the sweat on their skin as they lay in each other's arms. Cozy and contented, they listened to their pulses hammer down to normalcy after simultaneous orgasms had put their hearts into thundering hyperdrive about two minutes earlier.

Danny pushed his face into the back of Luke's ginger hair and breathed in his scent. It was a scent he knew as well as his own now. And it was a scent he was crazy about.

He could still taste Luke's come in his mouth, and he knew Luke could still taste his. While their lovemaking had in no way become rote, one unchanging pattern did seem to have come from the many times they had now explored each other's bodies. That was the cuddling they enjoyed afterward. The gentle stroking of the other's skin, the lazy kisses, the twining of fingers, the pulling together to hold each other close. Lying in each other's arms, they could barely restrain a tandem euphoric sigh.

Luke reached behind his head and laid a hand to Danny's cheek as Danny continued to nuzzle his nose into Luke's hair. Danny's breath was hot against Luke's scalp. Hot and comforting. Luke twisted his head around to kiss Danny's luscious bicep, which he was using for a pillow.

"I love the way you hold me," Luke whispered. He was too relaxed to raise his voice to anything higher than a contented murmur. If he were a cat, he would have been purring. "I love the way you do *everything*."

Danny smiled. "Except cook," he said.

"Well, yeah. That you suck at. And I mean not in a good way."

Again, Danny found himself fighting back the words he wanted to say more than anything in the world. Swallowing vows he wanted to make. Burying declarations of love beneath a mundane layer of mindless discourse that didn't really express the way he felt at all. "I love everything you do too," he said, and immediately felt guilty, as if those simple words were really a lie. But they weren't a lie. They just weren't the words he wanted to speak. They didn't even come close.

Luke squirmed and shifted around on the bed until they were lying face to face. Danny's face was lit by the moonlight streaming through the window, his long hair all over the place. Luke brushed his lips across Danny's mouth and pulled him tight when Danny kissed him back. Their thighs lay hot against each other's, their tummies firm and satiny. Their cocks, soft and sated, lay warm and contented next to each other just as Luke and Danny were lying. Their pulses beat slower now, thumping softly inside their heads. Luke and Danny felt lazy and comfortable and as happy as they could ever remember feeling.

"We've got about a week left before my dad gets back," Luke said. "I think if I have to start sleeping alone, I'm going to go crazy."

"Me too," Danny sighed, his lips still brushing Luke's. "What are we going to do?"

"What *can* we do?" Luke asked. "Sneak around, I guess. Maybe I can tiptoe over here in the middle of the night and climb up your rain gutter, if you have one."

"Yeah, right."

Danny took a deep breath and pulled back just enough to give Luke a searching look in the moonlight. Maybe the time had come to say the words. Maybe even if the time *hadn't* really come, he was ready to say them anyway. Maybe. "I think we have to tell our dads how we feel."

"And how *do* we feel?" Luke asked, suddenly shy. But not really afraid any more. Still, he couldn't bring himself to say the words first. He just couldn't. So he waited. And he didn't have to wait very long.

Danny had found his courage at last.

"I—I know exactly how *I* feel," Danny stammered, reaching up to lay his hand against Luke's neck, feeling Luke's pulse there, just below the skin. Needing his touch. Absorbing his heat. Savoring the sensation of Luke's life thrumming beneath his fingertips. "I—I just don't know how *you* feel."

Luke scraped the stubble on Danny's chin with his thumb. Enjoying the crispness of it. Enjoying the fact that Danny tilted his head down to kiss Luke's palm. "Tell you what, Danny. You tell me how you feel, and then I'll tell you how I feel. How's that?"

Danny took a deep shuddering breath. His heart was doing flip-flops. He was scared, but he was happy too. He *wanted* to say the words. He *needed* to say them. "Okay," he murmured, nervous yet determined.

But before he could speak the words of love he had been dying to say for so long, the oddest sound suddenly tore through the bedroom window from somewhere outside. It was a soft keening. Like a gentle wail. A *fearful* wail. And then it dwindled down to a stuttering moan. And then nothing. Silence.

It hadn't lasted more than three seconds.

They both turned to the window, and in the moonlight they could see Frederick, too, sitting alert on the bookcase where he usually rested. He was staring through the open curtains, peering out into the night. His tail was hanging straight down and the tip of it was flicking back and forth like it did when he was intrigued. Or agitated.

"What *was* that?" Danny whispered, feeling a cold chill crawl up his spine. "What was that creepy noise?"

Luke just shook his head, still listening, hoping to hear it again. But not really wanting to either.

Instead, a different sound came through the bedroom window. It was an unmistakable sound this time. Nothing mysterious about it. It was Granger. He was next door, where Luke had left him, locked inside Luke's house, and he was barking up a storm.

Luke swung his bare legs out of bed, and Danny did the same, awkwardly because of the cast. They hurried to the window and leaned outside. Granger was still barking like the mailman was coming down the chimney or something. Granger hated the mailman.

"I don't see a thing," Danny said, looking in both directions, his face next to Luke's, his chin digging into Luke's shoulder. Luke's naked ass was pressed comfortably against Danny's groin.

The street was quiet. A few porch lights were on, but that was about it. It was almost two in the morning. The neighborhood was asleep. Or most of it was, except for Granger and whatever or whomever had made that creepy-ass moan.

"I'd better go check the house before Granger wakes up the whole state," Luke said. He glanced down at the green light on Danny's ankle monitor. "You might want to stay here."

"Very funny," Danny snarled.

He stopped snarling when Luke dropped to his knees in front of him and gave his sleeping pecker a gentle kiss on the top of its little head. Needless to say, the head of Danny's dick didn't stay little very long. But Luke was back on his feet and tugging on a pair of shorts before Danny could insist Luke finish what he had started. Damn.

The sound of Danny's cast echoed through the house as he clumped over to the nightstand and grabbed his curtain rod. Then he clumped back to the window and stood there naked, half-hard, leaning out, all the while digging around inside his cast with the curtain rod trying to satisfy that ever-elusive itch. He watched Luke exit the back door down below. Danny grinned when Luke gasped as his bare feet touched the cold, dewy grass. He mumbled "Holy shit!" as he set out across Danny's yard.

Granger was really making a racket now. While Danny listened and watched Luke hop the hedge and duck through his own back door and disappear, he thought he heard another cry coming from somewhere out there in the darkness. But it was so fleeting, he couldn't be sure. Still, it was enough to make the hair on the back of his neck stand up. It was such a bizarre sound. And it was eerie the way Danny couldn't tell which direction it came from. It was like it came from every direction at once.

Danny stood there hunched over in the window, digging away at his itchy leg with the curtain rod as he watched every light in Luke's house go on, one after the other, then quickly go back off again. Danny figured Luke was going from room to room, giving the place the once-over to make sure no burglars were lurking around waiting to steal the family jewels.

Soon Danny saw Luke slide across his back porch with Granger next to him on a leash. There was a jangle of keys as Luke carefully locked his back door behind him, then he and Granger wended their way back to Danny's place. Rather than lift Granger over the hedge, Luke led the dog all the way down the driveway and around. Again, Danny could hear Luke gasp when his bare feet hit the cold, dewy grass in Danny's yard.

Danny giggled when Luke was forced to stand below, hopping from one foot to the other on the wet lawn while Granger took his sweet time peeing on the petunias under Danny's window. Luke looked up at the sound of Danny's laughter above him and stuck out his tongue. Then he gave Danny the finger, and Danny laughed even louder.

Five minutes later, Luke was back in bed, after drying off his feet with a towel from the bathroom. He and Danny were cuddling just like they had been before they were interrupted. And Granger was softly snoring by the side of the bed.

Frederick had apparently decided to take a hike. Probably all pissed off about the dog invading his territory yet again and storming off through his pet door to take it out on the neighbors' landscaping. Frederick loved to poop in flower beds. Especially flower beds other than his own. Or maybe he was off to see his girlfriend. Who the hell knew?

Luke and Danny had climbed back into bed and resumed their cuddling as if nothing had ever happened, but their conversation seemed to have been permanently derailed. It wasn't that they had forgotten the things they were about to confess to each other. It's just that the courage to confess them seemed to have bled away in the night because of that ominous cry of horror, or pain, or fear, or whatever it was, that had come tearing out of the shadows.

Subdued now, they simply held each other close. Danny mouthed the words "I love you" into Luke's ginger hair, but he was afraid to utter them out loud.

By the tiny smile that crossed Luke's face, as he snuggled there with his cheek once again atop Danny's hard and heavenly bicep, and his fingers all tangled up with Danny's, one might have thought he heard the words anyway.

A moment later, he silently mouthed the same three words as he pressed his lips to the inside of Danny's arm.

Later, when the cry came again to echo through the darkness, louder and more desperate this time than ever before, they were both asleep. They did not hear it.

Only Granger lifted his head and softly whimpered.

LUKE was across the way, unloading boxes and stuffing kitchen stuff into the cupboards. Pots, pans, plates, glasses, all the crap humans think they need to feed themselves properly. Luke knew differently. He would be perfectly happy to eat fast food out of bags for the rest of his life and never have to wash a thing. Bored and wanting to get back to Danny as soon as he could, Luke was just flinging it all into drawers

and onto shelves, not much caring where it landed. He knew his dad
would come along later and rearrange it anyway. After all, his dad's
middle name was Anal. As in anal picky, not anal sex. Of course,
considering that question, Luke really had no idea what sort of sexual
stuff his dad was into. Probably better *not* to know. He gave a shiver,
thinking of his dad having sex at all. Too creepy.

He picked up the last item in that particular box, a stack of
potholders and dish towels, and sailed them into the cupboard under the
sink. He kicked the empty box through the back door, where it landed
in a pile of other boxes scattered across the driveway. Then he reached
for another. There was no shortage to choose from. Boxes were
everywhere. Piles of boxes. Mountains of boxes.

Standing knee-deep in a sea of crumpled-up newsprint, which the
dishes and glasses had been individually wrapped in—like *that* was
really necessary—Luke sighed and tore open the lid on the new box.
No wonder the box was so heavy. It was electric crap. Electric grills,
electric coffee pots, electric can openers, electric nose-hair trimmers.
Just kidding. Damn. Electric stuff *flew* okay but it didn't *land* very
well. He'd have to be a little more careful with this lot.

While he worked and grumped and sweated, Luke wondered what
Danny was doing.

At that very same moment, Danny was wondering the same thing
about Luke.

What Danny was doing was standing awkwardly at the edge of
the swimming pool, reaching out with the long pool scooper to pick the
leaves and dead bugs off the water. Since it was nice and sunny and
warm, he was wearing only his swim trunks: big baggy ones that barely
hung on the curve of his pale ass and looked really, really sexy,
although Danny probably didn't know that. He wasn't exactly
enamored with his long, skinny body, even if Luke was. And thank God
Luke was, Danny thought with a smile.

He looked down at himself, at his long, hairy legs, his flat belly
with the tuft of hair around the belly button, at his pretty much
nonexistent pecs, and just shook his head. He felt like a troll next to
Luke. Luke was beautiful. And the moment he thought that thought, his

dick began to move. He stood in stasis for about five seconds, enjoying the sensation of his dick creeping around inside his shorts.

A tap on his shoulder stopped Danny's dick in its tracks. It pretty much stopped his heart too.

Danny jumped about two feet straight up in the air, then whirled around to find Mr. Childers standing behind him. Mr. Childers looked like he was trying not to laugh at the way Danny had jumped. Danny supposed he couldn't blame him.

"Hi," Danny said, making a concerted effort not to clutch his chest.

"Hi, son. Didn't mean to startle you there." Mr. Childers looked down at Danny's cast and ankle monitor. "You're looking a little hobbled."

Danny just shrugged. What could he say? "Yeah, well…."

Mr. Childers was wearing his blue jeans again. He was wearing tan work boots, and he had a shirt on this time, but it was unbuttoned all the way down the front, showing off the man's fuzzy chest and tummy. Danny had a really hard time keeping his eyes focused on Mr. Childers's face.

"Can I help you?" Danny asked.

Mr. Childers squatted at the edge of the pool and played his fingers through the water. He was practically at Danny's feet, so Danny stepped back, just to be polite.

"I'm not going to bite you, son."

Danny forced up a chuckle. "I know."

Mr. Childers stood and looked around Danny's yard. He seemed to know what he was looking for, even if Danny didn't. The man looked up at Danny's bedroom window and saw Frederick lying on the windowsill, soaking up the sun. Frederick was looking down at them like he was trying to hear what they were talking about. He had a torn book page crumpled up in his front paws. *Looks like Mark Twain has taken another hit*, Danny thought, trailing his eyes up to where Mr. Childers was looking.

"Haven't seen my cat, have you?" Childers asked. "An orange tabby. I think she got laid last night, since I seemed to remember hearing her yell about what a good time she was having. Haven't seen her since." He tilted his chin in Frederick's direction. "That's her boyfriend."

Danny laughed. "Dad said Fred was porking one of the neighbors' cats. I didn't know he meant yours. No. I haven't seen your tabby. In fact, I didn't know you had one."

"So you didn't hear the noises last night?" Childers asked, still kneeling at Danny's feet and casually splashing the water with his fingertips.

Then Danny remembered the eerie wail he and Luke had heard the night before. The creepy cry that made Granger go batshit and sounded like someone being tortured to within an inch of their life. Could that have been a cat? Danny wasn't sure. Cats made some pretty horrendous sounds sometimes. Especially when they were getting laid.

"I might have heard *something,*" Danny said. "Didn't really sound like a cat, though. Anyway, if I see your tabby, I'll grab her for you. You'll have to come and get her though, if I do. I'm kind of being held prisoner here. Well—not *kind* of. I *am* being held prisoner here."

Mr. Childers looked down at all the crap on Danny's lower legs. "So I see," he said around a smile. "Well, this too shall pass, son. Don't let it get you down."

"Okay," Danny said, knowing full well that if Childers had all this crap strapped to *his* legs, he wouldn't be so goddamn chipper about the whole thing. Sometimes adults were pretty stupid.

"And if you hear my cat again, just ignore it. I guess she'll come home when she's ready."

Mr. Childers gave Danny one last lingering look, from his feet all the way up to his face, then he stood, and turning on the heels of his work boots, headed for the front yard. He'd have to go all the way around the block to get back to his own house. There was no gate in their mutual back fence.

Danny watched him go. The guy was hotter than hell but a little too intense about his cat, Danny thought. But lord, the guy was sexy. Not as sexy as Luke, of course. Nobody was as sexy as Luke.

With Mr. Childers gone and with Luke back inside Danny's head, Danny's dick gave another twitch. It seemed to be a little aggravated by the interruption and was now happily getting back to business, opening up the floodgates, letting the blood surge in.

With some of last night's bedroom shenanigans rumbling around inside his memory banks, Danny's dick had enough time to give itself a pretty good stretch before it was interrupted once again. This time Danny actually had to drop the pool sweeper and hold his hands over his crotch, casually he hoped, to hide the swell of his erection from his new visitors.

His new visitors were DeVon and Bradley. They were peeking around the corner of the house like a couple of midget ninjas. They both had red licorice whips hanging out of their mouths and their eyes were as big as Ping-Pong balls. Danny almost laughed. He hoped to God they weren't gawking at his dick.

"What the hell are you guys up to?" he yelled. "I thought I told you yesterday to stop sneaking around. Trying to get in the pool again, aren't you?"

It was DeVon who stepped out first. "Man," he grumbled, "you gotta learn to trust people. Ever hear of a neighbor dropping by to chat?"

"Yeah," Bradley echoed, "ever hear of *that?* Neighbors *chatting?* Say. What's that in your pants? A hammer?*"* And he and DeVon roared with laughter.

Danny blushed so hard he thought his ears were going to ignite. Since the blood had all rushed to his face, it at least made his dick go down a bit. Thank God.

"What do you guys want? Can't you see I'm trying to work?"

Both DeVon and Bradley cranked their heads around to make sure there was no one eavesdropping. This time it was Bradley who took the reins of leadership. He looked so serious, and that serious look was so out of place on his cute-as-hell face with the freckles scattered across his nose and the red licorice whip hanging out of the side of his mouth like a skinny little tongue, that Danny had to smile. Then Danny started listening to what the kid was saying, and Danny's smile petered out pretty fast.

"Did you hear the guy scream last night?" Bradley was almost squeaking, he was so excited. "There's going to be another murder on the news tonight. Just you watch. You did hear the guy scream, right?"

"No," Danny said. "But I heard a cat getting laid. It was the neighbor's cat. The neighbor just told me."

"Well, your neighbor, whoever it is, is a fucking twit." It was DeVon this time. As he spoke, Danny could see his front teeth were coated with red licorice. He looked like someone had popped him one in the mouth. And with his nasty-ass vocabulary, maybe someone should. "That was no cat! Jesus H. McGillicuddy! People sure get some screwy ideas. By the way, where's your boyfriend?"

"He's over at his house unpacking. Hey, wait a minute! What do you mean, boyfriend? Who said we were boyfriends? You're not getting that rumor going around the neighborhood, are you?"

"Nah," Bradley groaned. "We don't care about where you're sticking your salami. We got other fish to fry. Don't be such a chickenshit, cupcake."

"You're making me hungry," DeVon growled to his friend. "Stop talking about food."

"Speaking of food," Danny ventured. "You wouldn't by any chance happen to have an extra red licorice whip on you, would you? Those things look pretty good."

"Sure," Bradley said. He dug around in his back pocket and pulled out a fat wad of them. They were all tangled up and out of their wrapper and covered with pocket lint. It looked like Bradley's mom had run them through the washer along with about three hundred towels. Maybe more than once.

"Uh. Never mind," Danny said, trying not to barf.

Bradley shrugged and stuffed the lint-covered candy back in his pocket. "Suit yourself."

Danny looked from one kid to the other. He had the strangest desire to either laugh his head off or slap the shit out of both of them. He couldn't decide which. "What in God's name would make you think that noise we heard last night was the sound of some guy getting murdered? I think you're letting your teensy-weensy imaginations run away with—"

"We heard noises like that the *last* time a guy was killed too," DeVon said. Once again his eyes were bulging out, and Danny had to admit the kid looked really scared. He had licked the licorice off his front teeth so he didn't look so stupid either. "The killer is right here in the burg. We know he is. We think we know who it is too."

"Oh, please. Who?"

Bradley opened his mouth to answer but DeVon slapped him in the back of the head, shutting him up.

"We can't be talking about this here. Too many ears." And he looked around like Hercule Poirot waiting for the murderer to come barreling out from behind a curtain.

Danny bit back a giggle. These guys were too much. "Look, kids, it's been fun, but I really do have work to do. So why don't you run along and play. I hear Seattle is nice this time of year. Why don't you go there?"

"Fuckhead," DeVon said.

"Dick breath," Bradley said.

"Deranged munchkins." Danny grinned.

DeVon poked a finger in Bradley's ribcage. "Come on. Let's go investigate you-know-who in the you-know-where."

Danny laughed. "And while you're there, stick the evidence up your you-know-what."

Grumbling, DeVon and Bradley stomped off and disappeared around the corner of the house.

Danny watched them go, shaking his head in a good-humored sort of way, and wondering if Luke would mind making a licorice run to the supermarket. Damn, those things really did look good. He'd make it worth Luke's while if he would.

Danny gave a lecherous little smile, imagining *how* he would make it worth Luke's while.

CHAPTER NINE
VOWS AND PROMISES

LUKE unlocked Danny's front door with his brand-new key. Frederick looked up from the back of the couch at the sound of the door opening. Seeing Granger padding along at Luke's feet, Frederick puffed up his fur and spit out a string of obscenities before sailing across the house and diving through the pet door with a clatter.

"Asshole cat," Luke muttered, relocking the door behind him.

He was earlier than he'd told Danny he would be, but he just couldn't bear to open one more box of crap. He missed Danny, and now that he was here, Luke planned to do something about it. He had showered back at the house; he was commando under his baggy cargo shorts and muscle tee; and Luke Junior was ready to rumble. A very sexy smile played at the corners of Luke's mouth as he brushed his young cock with his hand through the fabric of his shorts, simply because he couldn't bear not to.

The house was quiet. He hadn't seen Danny in the yard for the past couple of hours, or standing at the upstairs window spying on him with a hard-on, so Luke suspected he was taking a nap. It was Luke's every intention to wake him the fuck up.

Luke's dick flopped around in his shorts as he quietly climbed the stairs. By the time he reached the top step, his pecker was rock hard and begging for action.

Luke tiptoed down the hall and peeked through the door of Danny's bedroom, which was standing wide open. If he had been a praying man, Luke would have dropped to his knees and thanked God Almighty for the gift he had just bestowed upon him.

That gift was Danny, sound asleep, lying on his stomach on his bed stark naked. His legs were flung wide, one with the cast, and one with the electronic beeper silently flashing green, telling every cop in a twenty-mile radius that Danny was right where he was supposed to be.

And boy was Luke glad he was.

In one fluid motion, Luke walked quietly through the doorway and stepped out of his shorts, letting them fall at his feet. A second later, his T-shirt went sailing into a corner. Luke was now just as naked as Danny.

He stepped to the edge of the bed and looked down at Danny's naked form sprawled out beneath him. Danny's arms were flung wide, his face was aimed in Luke's direction, eyes closed, and he had a little trail of slobber dripping from his mouth. His long hair was tousled around his face and splayed out across the pillow. He was softly snoring.

Danny's long frame was so beautiful that Luke just stood there contemplating it, languidly stroking his own cock. Already, Luke was beginning to tremble.

Danny was thin, but he wasn't as skinny as he thought he was. He was actually very well proportioned, Luke thought. His legs were long and lean and coated with dark hair. The one calf muscle that wasn't covered with a cast was hard and pronounced, even in repose. Those gorgeous legs reached all the way up to one of the most beautiful asses Luke had ever seen. It was firm and round and absolutely exquisite. The elegant swell of Danny's ass was paler than the rest of his body, which was nicely tanned after the many hours he and Luke had spent by the pool this week. The cleft of Danny's ass was furred with dark hair, and with his legs spread wide, Luke thought he could see the merest glimpse of Danny's puckered opening. Luke longed to bury his tongue in it. Instead, he dragged his eyes farther north, still stroking his dick and trembling like a leaf, he was so turned on.

There was beauty *beneath* Danny's skin as well. Luke could clearly see the indentations of Danny's vertebrae and the wales of his ribcage, since his arms were spread wide and out of the way. Where Danny's shoulders bunched up, being flung wide like they were, Luke could see the corded muscles snuggling up against the skin of his back.

In clothes, Danny looked skinny. It was true. But naked, he was breathtaking.

Ever so gently, Luke reached down and eased a strand of hair from Danny's face. There was a wet towel on the floor at Luke's feet, so Danny had just showered too. Hmm. Good to know. Luke smiled.

Luke tugged his glasses off his face and laid them carefully on the nightstand. Where he was going they would just be in the way. Easing himself around to the foot of the bed, he laid his hands softly on either side of Danny's thighs. Sliding them over Danny's flesh, Luke relished the feel of Danny's leg hair scraping across his palms, the texture and heat of Danny's skin teasing his fingertips. Luke lowered himself down between Danny's legs and pressed his lips to the swell of Danny's ass.

Still Danny snored away.

Easing himself all the way down onto the bed, Luke laid his hands on either side of Danny's ass and spread that perfect mound apart until the furry cleft between Danny's ass cheeks opened wide like a flower. Danny's ass came up a fraction of an inch, as if eager to be worshipped. Luke obliged by sliding his tongue into the cleft and dragging it across Danny's sphincter.

"Do I know you?" Danny mumbled into his pillow. Then he started laughing and flipped over onto his back, grinning down at Luke, who was looking up at him along the scrumptious landscape of Danny's balls, dick, tummy, and chest. Danny's dick, by the way, was just as hard as Luke's, and judging by appearances, just as ready for a little action.

Luke smiled. "Playing possum, huh?" He shifted targets and slid his tongue between Danny's balls, tasting, inhaling. He scooped first one testicle into his mouth, then the other. Danny's hips rose up to meet his lips. Straining. Pleading. Danny's hand came down to grasp his own standing cock, which, from this angle, was one of the greatest natural splendors Luke had ever seen in his life. Like Mount Everest. It was there, and Luke was damned well determined to climb it.

Luke slapped Danny's hand away and said, "Let me do that."

So Danny did.

Luke wanted to tease Danny and make him beg to be sucked, but Luke couldn't seem to prevent his own desires from getting in the way. He squirmed up onto his knees between Danny's outflung legs. Hovering over Danny's crotch like a happy vulture, he scooped Danny's cock into his mouth without so much as a by-your-leave.

Danny watched him, chewing on his lower lip. He looked like he was trying to bite back a gasp, and Luke thought that was the sexiest thing he had ever seen in his life. Luke's eyes never left Danny's face as he went to work on that perfect hard-on. Luke wanted to see Danny tremble as much as *he* was trembling. He rolled the head of Danny's dick around in his mouth, teased the slit with his tongue, and periodically circled his fingers around Danny's glans as he sucked. If Luke had had a stopwatch handy he would have seen he'd succeeded in making Danny start trembling in fifteen seconds flat. Probably some sort of world record.

Luke was so happy about his accomplishment, and so damned turned on by now, that he slid one hand along Danny's stomach and chest and hooked a finger in Danny's mouth. Danny closed his lips around it, and while Luke sucked at Danny's cock, Danny sucked at Luke's finger. They both seemed to enjoy what they were doing, but Danny had a nagging feeling he was getting the short end of the stick. So he flipped around to face the opposite direction, and without asking permission or sending an RSVP or anything, he pushed his mouth over Luke's cock and sucked it all the way down his throat.

Luke didn't bother biting his lip to prevent a gasp. He simply gasped. It was a happy gasp, too, don't think it wasn't.

Moments later, Danny and Luke were both gasping and gulping for air. The bed was squeaking as if a flock of bats were trapped in the mattress. Both boys moaned and writhed around while Granger stood in the doorway with his head cocked sideways, wondering what the hell was going on.

Danny and Luke came within moments of each other, swallowing it down like ice cream and savoring every drop. When the shudders and groans and gasps and cries had finally quieted down between the two of them, they fell happily into each other's arms and pulled each other close.

Danny pressed his lips into Luke's ginger hair and the words he had been afraid to say just fell out into the air. He didn't even know they were coming.

"I love you, Luke. Jesus. I love you so much."

Luke tensed in his arms.

When Danny realized what he had said, his first reaction was to wonder why he didn't feel afraid that he had spoken the words. His second reaction was to wonder what Luke had thought of them. It was Luke's silence that suddenly made him a little worried. Good God, what had he done?

He gripped Luke's shoulders and pushed him far enough away to look into his eyes. What he saw there made Danny's heart do a somersault. It was a somersault of relief.

Luke's face was still flushed from sex. He had tears in his cornflower-blue eyes, but he was smiling at the same time. As Danny watched, one of those tears spilled out over Luke's strawberry-blond eyelashes and skittered down his freckled cheek.

Without thinking about it, Danny flicked out his tongue and licked the tear away. It was delicious.

Danny took a deep breath, and said, "If you don't say something in the next five seconds, I'm going to implode."

"Don't do that," Luke said.

"Why?"

"Because I love you too."

"You do?"

"Hell, yes."

"Why didn't you tell me?"

"I thought maybe you should say it first. After all, I was the one who seduced a virgin. I figured the second move was up to you. I think you just took it."

"I think I did. So what are we going to do about it?"

Luke gave that question about three seconds of thought time. "I think maybe what we have to do is figure out a way to stay together. Permanently. We have to tell our dads, lay it all out in the open, and then whatever they say, we stay together anyway. I'm not leaving you for nothing."

"A teacher once told me that double negatives are wrong. Just plain wrong," Danny said with a grin. "But everything else you just said was absolutely *right*. That's exactly what we'll do. So that means—what? We're lovers?"

"I ache just thinking about you, Danny. I don't think we can be anything *but* lovers."

"I ache thinking about you too."

"I love you, Danny."

"I love you too."

"I really love the way you come."

"I really love the way *you* come."

Luke grinned. "I'm glad DeVon and Bradley aren't around to hear us now, or they'd be puking on their tennis shoes."

They both laughed.

They quieted down and continued to stare into each other's eyes. Then Luke ducked his head to press his lips into the hollow of Danny's throat. His hands splayed out against Danny's warm back and pulled him close. They both smiled and closed their eyes, Luke's lips on Danny's throat, Danny's lips in Luke's hair.

"We can do this," Luke said, his voice muffled by the hard lump of Danny's Adam's apple bobbing around against his mouth. "I know we can. We're adults. Our dads will just have to accept it."

"They'll accept it. I know they will."

And as if the mere mention of their fathers set wheels in motion elsewhere in the world, at that very moment, their two telephones rang:

Danny's landline, and Luke's as well, the cord of which still trailed up the side of Danny's house and through Danny's bedroom window from the house next door.

"Well, shit," they said in unison.

Luke and Danny scrambled around to answer their respective phones. When they had the receivers in their hands, they sat on opposite sides of the bed, backs to each other, all hunched over.

Luke reached behind him and clasped Danny's hand.

That simple act made Danny's heart flutter happily.

Smiling a fearless smile, Danny said, "Hello. Pop?"

SURE enough, it was Danny's dad on the phone. Judging by snippets he could hear of Luke's conversation on the other side of the bed, it was *his* dad on the phone too. Wow, Danny thought. Was this a coincidence, or what, that they would both call at the very same moment? Their two fathers must be psychically connected.

Danny could sense his own dad smiling over the phone. It was another psychic connection, this one between father and son, and it always sort of surprised Danny when he felt it.

"Well, Danny, you sound more chipper every time we talk. I think you're getting used to living alone. Not missing your old dad so much anymore, are you?"

Danny laughed. "You're not so old. And I've been busy. But I miss you. When you coming home?" Danny tried to ignore the sinking feeling that invaded his gut when he asked that question. God forgive him, he didn't want his dad to come home at all. Not yet anyway. And thinking that thought, he grasped Luke's fingers a little tighter.

"It'll be another week," his dad said. "Think you can survive that long without me?"

"I'll manage," Danny said, before he could stop himself.

And his dad chortled. "I thought you might."

"I cleaned the pool," Danny said, unable to think of any other news flash with which to wow the man. Well, he *could* think of another news flash, but he was pretty sure his dad would shit bricks if Danny told him point blank he had just taken a lover, and that lover was a man, and they were bound and determined to live together whether their parents liked it or not. Seemed a little too intense for a casual phone conversation. Besides, it would probably get his dad on a plane for San Diego in five minutes flat, and that was the last thing Danny wanted.

"You been listening to the news?" his dad asked, suddenly serious.

"Sometimes," Danny said. "Why?"

"There was another murder last night. At least they think there was. Another young man is missing. They haven't found his body yet, but if they do, that'll be the sixth one. *Six.* I hope you're keeping the doors locked and all that."

"Sure, Pop. House is always locked up tighter than a drum." Danny looked across the room at his own naked reflection in the dresser mirror and rolled his eyes. That was a lie. Half the time, all the windows were wide open. It was a thousand degrees outside. Why wouldn't they be?

The lie seemed to appease his dad. "Well, good. Keep it that way. At least until they catch this guy. I don't want anything to happen to you."

"Don't worry," Danny said. "I'll be careful."

Somewhere just out of reach, an errant thought was jiggling Danny's brain. What the hell was it? Something to do with those damn kids. DeVon and Bradley. Then *that* thought was interrupted when Luke lay back, and with his own phone still to his ear, rested his face against Danny's bare hip. Danny looked down and stroked Luke's hair. They smiled at each other. While Luke was listening to whatever the heck his dad was talking about, he craned his neck around and kissed Danny's thigh.

Danny snapped back to the present. "I'm sorry, Dad. What did you say?"

"I asked how you're getting along with the new neighbor boy. What did you say his name was? Luke?"

Simply hearing Luke's name from a mouth other than his own made Danny's heart flutter. Holy smokes. If that wasn't love, what was?

"We're getting along great. It's just a shame I'm hog-tied to this frigging house. I could help him unpack all those boxes he brought with him if I could hop the hedge without summoning a SWAT team and a pack of German shepherd K-9 commandos and fourteen sharpshooters armed with flash grenades."

Luke made a thumbs-up sign and stuck it smack in Danny's face, indicating a little help *would* be nice. At the same time, Danny's dad gave a good-natured groan. "Yes. Well, we all know who's responsible for *that* little fly in the ointment."

Danny's groan sounded a lot like his dad's. Heredity at work. He good-naturedly slapped Luke's hand away, and said, "I know. I know. Is this my cue to apologize *again*?"

His dad laughed. "No, Son. I'm sorry. I promised myself I wouldn't nag you about that whole 'upended ice machine and broken leg and hamburgers flying out the window' episode of your life, but sometimes you make it too easy not to throw it back in your face. I'll try to do better."

"Good," Danny said, and meant it.

His dad tried to atone by dragging the conversation back to safer territory. "So it sounds like you and Luke are really hitting it off."

Danny looked down at Luke's fingers wrapped around his sleeping cock. "You might say that."

"That's good, Son. I'm glad. Everybody needs a friend."

Danny's mouth took off running before Danny could stop it. "Umm. Remember when you said you had something important we needed to talk about? Well, I might have something important to talk about with you too."

His dad sounded more leery than intrigued. "And what would that be?"

Danny grinned. "I'll wait until we're together. Once you've showed me your secret, then I'll show you mine."

"Well, that's cruel. You enjoy making me worry, don't you?"

Danny's grin widened. "I live for it."

His dad laughed. "Don't I know it. All right. The minute I get back to town, we'll sit down and shake out all our dirty laundry. Deal?"

"Deal."

One last time, before they said their good-byes, his dad reminded Danny to keep the doors and windows locked. "I know you're young and think nothing really bad can ever happen to you, but remember, all those other young guys probably thought the same thing. And now they're gone. So be careful."

And again something niggled Danny's memory banks. "I promise, Dad. Honest."

Softly, the phone went dead in Danny's hand. He set it in the cradle and laid back on the bed, pressing his face to Luke's thigh, just as Luke was still doing to him. He wrapped his arms around Luke's legs and buried his face in them. Luke's knees lay hard against his forehead. Danny kissed first one hairy thigh, then the other, while he listened to Luke's conversation with his own dad.

"Yeah, I miss my car," Luke was saying. "But that's okay. I'm finding other stuff to occupy my time."

You certainly are, Danny thought.

Danny could hear the drone of Luke's dad's voice carrying through the phone, but he couldn't make out the man's words. Idly, Danny wondered what Luke's dad looked like. Danny wondered if his own dad would make friends with the man after he found out he was gay. His dad had never been homophobic before, or never seemed to be anyway. Danny prayed to God he wouldn't start acting like a rabid, hate-spewing, Bible-thumping nitwit now. Especially with what Danny was about to tell him about himself.

Then that niggling thought that had been driving him nuts finally coalesced into a definitive memory in Danny's head. When it did, he bolted upright on the edge of the bed, causing Luke to give him a questioning look. But since he was still on the phone with his dad, Luke didn't say anything. He merely gave Danny's dick a reassuring squeeze, as if to calm him down.

Danny loved that little squeeze, but even that wasn't enough to take his mind off what he had just remembered.

"There's going to be another murder on the news tonight," Bradley had said. "Just you watch."

And according to Danny's dad—*damned if there wasn't.*

Again Danny stared across the room at his naked reflection in the dresser mirror. He was still sitting at the edge of his bed. Luke's naked body was still sprawled out beside him. Luke's warm, comforting hand still cradled Danny's dick. It seemed funny to Danny that everything in his head had suddenly changed, while here in the bedroom nothing had changed at all.

My God, Danny thought. Could those stupid kids actually know what they're talking about? And if Danny really thought they did, what should he do about it? Call the cops?

The minute Danny considered that option, he knew he couldn't do it. His dad might get into a world of trouble if the judge found out he had gone out of town and left Danny on his own. He remembered his dad reassuring the judge he would always be around to watch over Danny while he was under house arrest. Not two hours after that, his dad had learned he had to go out of town. Danny talked him into going anyway, promising he would do nothing to get the cops over here so they would find out his dad was gone. Reluctantly, his father agreed to go.

If Danny saw a dead body lying in his backyard, he might recant on that promise and call the cops. But for an idea as goofy as this one, he wasn't about to.

He did want to talk to those kids, though.

He looked through the bedroom window. The sky was darkening. The sun had dropped behind the rooftops across the street more than fifteen minutes ago. Night was setting in. He wouldn't see DeVon and Bradley until tomorrow, and only then if they actually dropped by on their own. He couldn't go looking for them because he was under house arrest and wasn't sure where they lived anyway. He couldn't look them up in the phone book because he didn't know their last names.

Well, so be it. He would just have to wait until tomorrow. Hopefully, they'd be around. They were always popping up when you least expected. Until they did, it would give Danny time to think about it all. To figure out what it was he wanted to do exactly. If anything.

He looked down at Luke lying there beside him, so beautiful, making Danny feel so loved. It seemed funny that somewhere just outside the walls surrounding them, people were actually dying at the hands of a killer. Inside these walls, life was perfect. *Luke* was perfect.

Danny wasn't exactly a religious person, but he did take a second to cast up a prayer of thanks for the fact Luke was now spending his nights with him. While Danny never once considered his own safety concerning the serial killer out there stalking the city, he *was* glad to know Luke was being watched over. Even if it was only Danny doing the watching.

Side by side, they would be happy, he and Luke. As long as one protected the other, they would be safe. No danger could ever touch them as long as they stayed together.

Later, Danny would remember thinking those words and wonder how he could have been so wrong.

So dead fucking wrong.

CHAPTER TEN
BODY PARTS

DINNER was pizza again. The fifth time in five days. And again, over Luke's objection, Danny paid with his dad's credit card. This time he started feeling really guilty about it, so he promised himself from now on he would either let Luke pay, or he and Luke would eat crap out of the freezer until his dad got back into town. Danny would give the credit card a rest. He had cost his dad enough money lately. Besides, cooking a few meals would give Danny practice for when he and Luke were living together.

He got goose bumps just thinking about that. Good goose bumps. *Happy* goose bumps.

"What are you smiling about?" Luke asked around a mouthful of pizza crust.

Danny had such a humongous wad of pizza in his own mouth, he had to chew for a good fifteen seconds before managing to gulp it down, just so he wouldn't choke to death while trying to talk. "Us living together. Where do you think it will be?"

"Don't know."

"When do you think we can start?"

"Don't know."

"How often do you think we'll have sex?"

Luke's cornflower-blue eyes flashed happily. "Every five minutes?"

And Danny grinned. "That's what *I* was thinking."

A news bulletin on the twelve-inch TV sitting on the kitchen counter drew their attention to the screen. Luke and Danny stopped chewing long enough to listen. The TV was always blasting away in the background, but rarely did they pay it any attention. For some reason, this time they did.

The anchorman looked like he had been sent to the TV station from Central Casting. Rattling off the news, he looked about as sincere as a three-dollar hooker. His perfectly coiffed hair was sprayed to within an inch of its life. He had blindingly white teeth that looked amazingly like Chiclets lined up inside his mouth. The guy's chin dimple was so perfectly placed it might have been punched there with a nail gun. And to top it all off, he had a butt-ugly tie tied in a perfect Windsor at his pale throat, which had considerably less makeup on it than his face did. The man was trying to look like he wasn't reading from a Teleprompter but any fool could see he was.

"The San Diego Police Department is asking for the public's help in locating a missing person."

The photo of a young guy flashed on the screen. It was a high school graduation picture. A head shot. The guy was still wearing his mortarboard with the tassel hanging down along his cheek. The tassel was on the right side of his face, Danny noticed, so when the picture was taken, he hadn't yet graduated.

"Wow," Luke said. "He's cute." And Danny nodded. The young man really was cute. Blond, fresh-faced, with clear, clear eyes that looked so innocent one would think he had never seen anything unseemly in his whole entire life. And maybe he hadn't.

The announcer read on, still trying to sound sincerely concerned, but what he truly sounded was phony. He obviously didn't give a shit about any of it. Jesus, Danny wondered. Where do they get these guys?

"Charles Strickland has been missing since Tuesday morning. Three days ago. He was last seen at Albertson's supermarket on University Avenue, near Texas Street."

"Wow," Danny interrupted. "That's just a few blocks away."

The announcer ignored Danny, and why wouldn't he? "Mr. Strickland's vehicle was found abandoned in Albertson's parking lot. The groceries Mr. Strickland had just purchased were still in the back seat and his car door left open. Anyone with information on the man's whereabouts, please contact the San Diego Police Department immediately. Mr. Strickland was eighteen years old. He had just enlisted in the U.S. Navy and was set to report for boot camp at the Naval Training Center here in San Diego early next week. He leaves behind his parents and two brothers. He was a cherished member of the Trinity Methodist Church in North Park."

Wow, Danny thought, considering the anchorman's tagline. No wonder the guy looked so innocent. He was an honest-to-God churchgoer. And why was the anchorman talking about the guy in the past tense? Wasn't it a little cruel for the guy's family to be hearing that? Even in his youth, Danny was smart enough to know sometimes news people have no common sense.

Oddly enough, that little news bite on the evening news made quite an impression on Danny.

Somehow, seeing a real live face connected to the murder story, if it really *was* connected, made it much more tangible for him. The fact the missing guy was Danny's age and cute as hell made it even sadder than it already was. At least in Danny's eyes. Danny wondered where Charles Strickland was now. Was he still alive, being tortured and raped, or was he lying in an unmarked grave somewhere? Out in the desert, maybe, in the middle of nowhere, where he would never be found. Or maybe the guy had simply toddled down to Tijuana to get laid a few dozen times before heading off to the Navy. That option might not please his church-going parents too much, but it would certainly be better for *him.*

And if Charles Strickland was such a devoted member of the Trinity Methodist Church, why did God let such a terrible thing happen to him in the first place? That didn't seem right. The murderer should be picking off gangbangers. Or bullies. Or assholes. Leave the good people alone, for heaven's sake.

"That sucks," Luke said, still watching the TV, although the phony-ass anchorman had moved on to a house fire in the poor part of town. As if being poor wasn't bad enough, now some impoverished person didn't have a house either. Danny wasn't sure if Luke was talking about the poor guy without a house or the young guy who disappeared from Albertson's. Then Luke cleared it up by voicing his thoughts.

"The kids say they know who the killer is."

Danny moaned. "Who? DeVon and Bradley? They told you too, huh? Those kids are certifiable."

"By the way," Luke said, as if he suddenly remembered. "I met your handsome neighbor in the back. Mr. Childers. He was digging by his back fence. I heard the noise and went to investigate. Jeez, how did you stay a virgin so long living next door to that guy?"

"What do you mean?"

"He put the moves on me," Luke said. "At least I think he did. He was asking me all kinds of stuff about what I do at night and where I go."

"Naaah." Danny couldn't believe it. "You must have imagined it. The guy's a widower. His wife died a few years back."

Luke rolled his eyes and stuffed a little more pizza in his mouth. "I'm *telling* you. Pop told me we would have a gay neighbor when we moved here. I don't know how he knew. I guess he met Mr. Childers that time he came to check out the property."

Danny couldn't believe that either. "You think your dad thought Mr. Childers was gay and that's why he told you you'd have a gay neighbor?"

Luke shrugged. "Who else could he have meant? You?" He laughed. "Although it didn't take *me* long to ferret out that information, did it?"

Now it was Danny's turn to laugh. "About three minutes."

"If that." Luke slid his hand across the table and grasped Danny's index finger. He gave it a shake. "I still love you, by the way."

Danny smiled. "Me too." After a beat of silence spent gazing lovingly into each other's eyes, Danny asked, "What was he digging?"

Luke started. "Huh? Who?"

"Childers."

"Oh. Flower bed, I guess. He invited me over for Cokes and a movie some time. Seems he has a little theater set up in his den."

Danny narrowed his eyes and laid down his fork. "I didn't know that. And you're not going. Hell, no. No way. Not now, not ever. Case settled. No more movies for you. Ever. Not with Childers. Uh-uh."

Luke tilted his chair onto its back legs and folded his arms across his chest. He stared at Danny so long Danny started wiggling around in his chair, feeling guilty. Finally, Luke said, "What makes you think I wanted to? He's as old as my dad, for Christ's sake. Besides, I've got a boyfriend. You. Why would I want anybody else?"

Danny gave a weak smile. Weak because he was really touched. And turned on. "Honest?"

"Honest." And Luke let all four chair legs crash back down to the kitchen floor. Eyes wide open, he leaned across the table and laid his lips on top of Danny's. The kiss was long and hot and tasted like pizza sauce. Just the way Danny liked them.

When Luke finally dropped back into his chair, Danny stretched his long arms up above his head as far as they would go and faked a big wide yawn. He looked pretty sneaky while he was doing it. Damn, Luke's kiss had tasted good. It left Danny hungry for more.

"Welp," he said. "Time for bed, I guess."

Luke laughed and pushed his plate away. "Good idea. I suddenly seem to be really, really horny."

"I can fix that," Danny said with a grin, and arm in arm they headed for the stairs, shedding their clothes along the way. By the time they got to Danny's bedroom door, they were stark naked.

They dove onto the bed. Eighteen, naked, and madly in love.

What better way to dive onto a bed?

Two seconds later they were lost to everything but each other. They stayed that way while the night deepened around them. Later, when their passions were satisfied, at least for the time being, they lay snuggled in each other's arms. Happy and content. Just like they always did after sex.

A stranger peeking through Danny's bedroom door and seeing such happiness might have thought there was no evil in the world at all.

But how wrong he would have been.

THE moon was barely above the rooftops across the street when Danny and Luke conked out for the night. By the time Danny's eyes popped open, hours later, the moon had climbed halfway up the sky. Danny was instantly awake, certain something was wrong. Was there a fire? He took a deep breath, seeking the scent of smoke. Nothing. He craned his head around to peer at the clock. It was just short of midnight. He'd thought it was later.

Luke still lay softly snoring in his arms.

Maybe Danny had just had a bad dream. But if he had, he didn't remember it.

Then he heard Granger whimpering somewhere downstairs. Danny lifted his head to peer through the moonlight to the place where Frederick always slept. The cat was gone. Maybe Granger and Frederick were having a knock-down, drag-out battle somewhere. An interspecies Armageddon. God knows they hated each other enough.

For some reason, Danny's broken leg was really aching. Too much flinging and flopping around in the throes of passion, he supposed. Not that it wasn't worth it.

He gave Luke the softest kiss to the back of the head he could, since he didn't want to disturb him, and slowly slid his arm out from under Luke's cheek. Luke snorted but didn't wake. He rolled onto his stomach and burrowed his face in his pillow. Out for the count.

Danny took a moment to appreciate Luke's heavenly ass lying there in the moonlight just begging to be licked, then he turned away with a sigh and eased his long legs off the bed. He considered reaching for the curtain rod to try yet again to cure that goddamn itch deep inside his cast, but another round of whimpering by Granger somewhere downstairs got him heading toward the door.

Naked, he padded softly down the stairs. Softly on one foot, at least. The other foot, the one with the cast on it, made a horrible racket every time it hit a step. Sounded like a sledgehammer banging on the floor. He sure would be glad to get rid of that thing.

In the kitchen, Danny turned on the light. He quickly closed the blinds so no one could see in since he was as naked as the day he was born; then he called Granger's name.

The dog answered with another whimper. The whimper came from the service porch that separated the kitchen from the back door. Danny stepped through the kitchen door and flicked on the light. He had to blink a few times before his brain could register what he was seeing.

When it did register, a grin crept across Danny's face. He shook his head in wonder.

"Well, damn boy," he said. "You've got yourself in a pickle, haven't you?"

Granger was stuck in the cat door. His ass was lying on the service porch floor, while his forward regions were sprawled across the back stoop. At least Danny assumed they were. He'd have to swing the door open to make sure. That pet door was never meant for anything larger than a cat. Granger seemed to have found that out the hard way.

Carefully, Danny opened the door, swinging the door and Granger both out of the way. He bit back a laugh to see Granger doing some fancy sidestepping to keep up with the swinging door.

When he had the door sufficiently open, Danny stood at the edge of it so he could see both sides of the door at the same time. And both ends of Granger.

The poor dog looked up at Danny with the saddest eyes Danny had ever seen. He also appeared to be considerably embarrassed.

Danny took a minute to consider the problem. Should he push Granger's back end on out, or poke his front end back in? Hmm. Since there were teeth on the front end, and Granger was looking none too happy to say the least, Danny thought he might try pushing the back end through first.

So he did. He had to fold up Granger's back legs like a card table to do it, but once he had the legs out of the way, the rest was a cinch. He put both hands to Granger's fluffy ass and shoved. Granger, *all* of

Granger, popped out onto the back mat. It was like the miracle of birth, sort of, but without the mess and the gore and the histrionics.

The minute Granger was free, he gave himself a shake and took off across the yard, heading for the pool. No "thanks". No "appreciate the help". Nothing.

Since Danny was still naked, he couldn't very well follow the ungrateful mutt. There was a mountain of dirty laundry piled atop the clothes dryer, so Danny scrounged through it until he unearthed the cargo shorts he had worn a couple of days ago. They smelled like mildew, but what the hell. Once he tugged them on, he set out across the back lawn to retrieve Granger. Pets were sure a pain in the ass.

The grass was cold and wet on his one bare foot that wasn't encased in cement, and the backyard was dark. Even the pool lights were off, so Danny carefully edged his way around the water. The last thing he wanted to do was fall in. His cast would drag him to the bottom, gasping for air, before he knew what hit him.

Then he pulled up short. He suddenly had the feeling he was being watched. Weird. He looked up toward his bedroom window, thinking maybe Luke was staring down at him. But the window was dark and empty. No Luke.

There was some ambient light from the streetlight at the front of the house, so Danny wasn't totally blind. He watched Granger head straight for the back fence. It was dark as hell back there, what with the six-foot-tall fence and all the hibiscus plants and the looming shadow of the house blocking the streetlight out front. As luck would have it, the moon also chose that moment to duck behind a fat black cloud, making it even darker. Great.

And Danny *still* had the feeling he was being watched.

"Granger," Danny hissed. "What is it, boy? Where you going?"

Granger didn't answer. But someone else did.

A human voice in a high-pitched whisper hissed back, "Shut the hell up, dipshit! You're gonna get us caught!"

Danny squinted into the shadows, but he couldn't see a thing. He could hear Granger licking and snorting and sounding all happy though.

That eased Danny's trepidation somewhat, but he still wasn't exactly ecstatic.

What the heck was going on in his backyard, anyway?

"DeVon? Bradley? If that's you guys in the bushes there I'm going to throw your asses in the pool."

"Shut up, man! It's just me!"

That whisper belonged to Bradley. Danny recognized it now. The little shit.

"Bradley, what the hell are you doing?"

"Investigating!"

Danny was furious. "It's after midnight! I don't imagine your folks are up for Parents of the Year, huh? Why aren't you home in bed? And where is the darker half of your daring duo?"

Danny could see Bradley now. He was crawling out from under a hibiscus bush. He was pointing at the fence. "DeVon's in *there.* So be quiet. You'll get him caught. And get this dog out of my face!"

Granger was being playful, licking Bradley's nose. Licking his ears. Licking his neck. Or maybe he was just trying to get the twigs out of the kid's hair since Bradley looked like he had just crawled through a blackberry patch, snagging briers and branches and leaves along the way like he was swathed in Velcro.

And still, even with all the greenery stuck to his clothes and poking off the top of his head, there was a rope of red licorice dangling from his mouth. It was as dirty as he was. No surprise there.

"DeVon's in *where?"* Danny spat in a homicidal whisper. He didn't really need to ask that question. He had a horrible feeling he already knew the answer.

Once again, Bradley pointed at the fence behind him. "He's checking out the blood. We saw it from the tree over there." The kid pointed to an oak tree half a block away. "We wanted to get on your roof to check it out closer, but we couldn't figure out how to get up there. You don't have a ladder, do you?"

"No!" Danny snapped. "And if I did I wouldn't give it to you. What blood are you talking about?"

"The blood on Childers's driveway."

"You're nuts."

"Oh, yeah, fruit loop? What do you think of this, then?"

And reaching into his trouser pocket he pulled out something wrapped in a tissue. He waved it under Danny's nose. Bradley had a smirk on his face Danny would have given twenty bucks to slap off.

Danny wasn't about to touch whatever it was the kid was holding out to him. "What's that?" A moment later, Danny asked, "What's that smell?"

"Finger," Bradley said. "I think it's going bad."

"What do you mean, a finger? You mean, like, a *finger?*"

Since Danny looked like he had no intention whatsoever of taking the little tissue-wrapped bundle out of Bradley's hand, Bradley heaved a big put-upon sigh and unwrapped the bundle himself. When he was finished, he held something out to Danny, dangling it from his thumb and index finger.

Holding his nose, Danny leaned forward to better see it in the moonlight.

It *was* a finger. A human index finger. It still had the fingernail on it.

Danny hopped three feet back. "Holy crap! I'm gonna barf! Where the fuck did you get *that?*"

"Frederick," Bradley said.

Danny was feeling really stupid all of a sudden. "Huh? You mean my cat?"

"Yeah. He was playing with it on my back porch. Him and Childers's orange tabby. Your cat's girlfriend. I think they were going to eat it."

"But—but—where would they get something like that?"

And again, Bradley jerked his thumb at the back fence. "Over *there*. Like I told you, there's blood on Childers's driveway. Right in front of his garage. Probably from when he cut the guy's finger off."

"What guy?"

"The latest victim."

"*Who* cut the finger off?"

"Childers."

A hand came down on Danny's shoulder, and he almost had a stroke. He spun around so fast he damn near passed out. Words cannot describe how relieved he was to see Mr. Dinkens standing behind him. The man looked just as gangly and out of place as he always did. He was dressed in coveralls, like maybe he had been working on his car or something. Danny wondered if Mr. Dinkens *ever* slept.

Dinkens was about six and a half feet tall, weighed less than a jar of peanut butter, and was as ugly as a mud fence. Still, he looked friendly enough, and Danny was relieved to see it was only him and not some homicidal maniac.

"What's happening?" Mr. Dinkens asked, situating his glasses a little more firmly on his beak of a nose. "Family reunion? Neighborhood block party?" Danny guessed he was trying to be funny.

Bradley hastily stuffed the severed finger in his front pocket. "Yeah," he chirped. "That's it. Neighborhood block party. Very funny, Mr. D. You're a regular comedian. By the way, the family reunion is *next* week."

Mr. Dinkens looked down at Bradley as if he had never seen a kid before in his life. Or maybe it was all the weeds and shit that Bradley had stuck all over him that threw Mr. Dinkens for a loop. Anyway, he didn't seem too impressed.

He finally tore his gaze away from Bradley with a grunt and centered it on Danny. He stared at Danny for the longest time, taking in his bare legs and bare chest and the baggy cargo shorts barely hanging from Danny's hips. Danny was just beginning to get uncomfortable about all the staring the guy was doing when Dinkens finally focused his eyes on Danny's face. "Well, let's try to keep the racket down to a minimum, boys. Some of the neighbors might be trying to sleep."

With his civic duty apparently satisfied, Mr. Dinkens did an aboutface and sauntered off toward the front of Danny's house on his long, gangly legs, where presumably he would work his way around to the other side and go the fuck home.

Two seconds later, as Danny was just about to start interrogating Bradley again about the finger, another hand came down on his shoulder. This time Danny came really, really close to pooping his pants. Jesus. He needed to start taking tranquilizers or Kaopectate or something.

When he spun around this time, Danny found Luke there. A vast improvement over Mr. Dinkens. Luke was wearing Danny's black bathrobe. He was rubbing his eyes and fighting back a yawn like he had just woken up, which he undoubtedly had.

"What's happening?" Luke asked, looking down at Bradley. He was squinting because he hadn't put his glasses on. "We having a dipshit party?"

"Yeah," Bradley chirped. "And now that you're here, we can start. Want some finger food?"

The kid fished around in his pocket, then held up the bloody stump of the finger for Luke's benefit. Seeing as how he got a pretty good reaction earlier from his boyfriend, Danny, maybe Bradley would get a pretty good reaction from the other gay boy too. He hoped so anyway. Gay guys looked pretty funny when they were scared shitless.

"Fuck is that?" Luke asked with a shudder. He took a good long look at the finger; then he turned to Danny, then back to Bradley. The little troll.

"What the fuck's it look like?" Bradley simpered.

And then they *all* jumped three feet into the air when somebody roared on the other side of the fence. It wasn't good roaring either. It was angry roaring. Somebody was *pissed!*

"Go home!" a voice boomed in the darkness, making all three of them cringe.

Two seconds later, there was a god-awful clatter by the fence, and a moment after that, DeVon came flying over the top of the fence like he had been shot out of a catapult. Jesus, the kid was *moving.*

He landed on his feet running and didn't bother looking surprised to see Bradley and Danny and Luke all standing there watching him. He merely shagged ass right on through. In his dark face, his eyes were as big and white as Ping-Pong balls in the moonlight. He disappeared around the front of Danny's house, leaving everybody a little stunned.

"See ya," Bradley said and took off after his friend.

Left alone, Danny and Luke turned toward the fence at the back of Danny's yard, not knowing what to expect next.

What they didn't expect to hear was laughter.

It was coming from Mr. Childers's backyard.

Luke snagged Danny's hand and quietly dragged him back to the house. A moment later, Granger followed.

Remembering that creepy laugh, Luke shuddered as he locked the door behind them.

CHAPTER ELEVEN
GETTING REAL

WHEN they were safely inside the house, Luke turned to Danny. He looked almost as creeped out as DeVon had, just before the kid took off like a bat out of hell for parts unknown.

"What just happened?" Luke asked. "Was that really a finger?"

"Looked like it," Danny said. "Kid said he took it away from Frederick and Childers's cat on his back porch. It's possible. Fred is always dragging something around. The other day it was a crow on the dining room table. Bird guts everywhere. Childers's cat is probably just as bad. The two are seeing each other, you know."

"How romantic," Luke said.

"I know."

Luke thought things over for a minute. "But the kids think the finger came from the killer cutting off somebody's finger? Like— *torture?* The killer they were talking about on *TV?* The killer on the *news?*"

"Those kids are weird. No telling what they think. That finger could have come from anywhere. Somebody could just as easily have lost it in an accident. Then Frederick came along, thought it was a cocktail wienie, and took off with it."

"That's a little far-fetched," Luke said. And they both knew it was true. People don't just go around accidentally chopping off fingers left and right. And when they do, they usually pick them up and take them to the emergency room with them to be sewn back on. Gads.

Danny took a big fluttery breath. This night was a little too exciting for his taste. If he was going to have an exciting night, he'd rather have sex involved. Sex with Luke. Not disconnected body parts. Danny preferred his body parts (and Luke's) still very much connected, thank you very much. Possibly even joined together in some way or other.

"They said they saw blood on Childers's driveway. DeVon went over the fence to check it out. I wonder what he found."

Luke shrugged. "Who knows. Sounded like he got caught, though. Whatever Childers is doing, he now knows he's a suspect. At least in the eyes of the miniature detective squad. Those goofy kids are going to get themselves killed."

"Why? You think Childers is really the murderer?"

"Hell, no. I just think they could have fallen into your pool and drowned. It's dark back there. Silly twits. But if that finger was real, then I do think we should call the cops."

"No way! My dad'll get in trouble for not being in town chaperoning my sorry ass while I'm under house arrest. I've caused him enough grief. Please, Luke, don't call the police. We'll handle it some other way. Okay?"

Luke sighed. Reluctantly, he said, "Okay. But if we get murdered by a gay serial killer, it's on your head."

"Very funny. You don't really think Childers is the killer, do you?"

"Nah. Do you?"

"Nah."

Neither of them sounded entirely convinced. And although they didn't mention it out loud, they were both wondering what Childers had been chuckling about behind that fence right after DeVon took off running. He certainly *sounded* crazy enough to be a serial killer. And he sure as hell scared the shit out of DeVon too.

They needed to talk to that kid.

Danny switched off the kitchen light and pulled Luke toward the stairs. "Let's see if we can see anything from my room."

In Danny's room, they stood at the south window and gazed out over the back fence into Mr. Childers's driveway and backyard.

"He's turned his outside light off. I can't see anything."

"Me either," Luke said.

They crossed the room to look through the east window and saw Mr. Dinkens's house lit up like a Christmas tree. Every light in the place was burning. Jeez, that guy was weird. As they watched, they spotted a tiny shadow creeping along the edge of Danny's lawn, just this side of Dinkens's picket fence. It was Frederick. Still prowling around. No surprise there. Then they spotted another tiny shadow creeping along behind Frederick. Childers's cat. It must be.

In the other direction, to the west, they looked out across Danny's side lawn and the hedge separating his yard from Luke's. Luke's house was dark and quiet. Aside from the moving van parked in the driveway, it still looked vacant, Danny thought. And why shouldn't it, seeing as how its sole occupant was standing next to him in his black bathrobe, which Danny suddenly decided looked way too warm for this hot summer evening.

He reached out and gently tugged on the robe's belt until it fell undone. Then he hooked a fingertip in the collar of the robe and slipped it off Luke's shoulder; it slid down his back and fell in a heap at Luke's feet.

Luke stood beside him naked. In the moonlight, he gave Danny an amused smirk.

"Are you going somewhere with this?" Luke asked.

And awkwardly, because of his cast, Danny dropped to his knees in front of Luke and pressed his face to Luke's warm, fuzzy stomach. Luke's dick bobbed up and bumped Danny under the chin. It seemed to want attention, so Danny settled back on his haunches and ever so slowly slipped Luke's hardening cock into his mouth. By the time Danny had it halfway down his throat, it was about as hard as it was ever going to get. And that was pretty darned hard.

Luke's hands held the side of Danny's face. "Don't move," he said.

Danny did as he was asked and held his head perfectly still in Luke's hands. Except, of course, for his wandering tongue. Danny was enjoying the taste of Luke's dick too much to hold *that* still.

Slowly, Luke's hips began to move. He eased his cock from between Danny's lips almost to the very tip, then with Danny staring up at him, looking incredibly eager for anything that was about to happen, Luke slid his dick back in until his bush of red pubic hair was flush with Danny's nose.

Then he did it again. In. Out. And again. Luke could see Danny stroking his own cock while Luke fucked his face. With his other hand, Danny explored Luke's legs, easing his hand under Luke's balls, cupping them, then moving on. He burrowed his hand through Luke's trembling thighs and traced his fingertips along the crack of Luke's ass. Luke squatted the least little bit to give him better access, and Danny rested his fingertip on Luke's puckered hole. He could feel it kissing his fingertip. Flexing. Unflexing.

Danny pulled his hand back and slid it up Luke's chest as high as he could reach. Luke bent his head and took Danny's index finger into his mouth. He sucked on it, getting it good and wet, then Danny moved his hand back between Luke's legs and pressed the moist fingertip to Luke's sphincter.

Danny could feel Luke relaxing, and very gently, Danny slid his finger into Luke's opening.

Luke gasped and willed himself to relax even more. His legs were shaking as he clamped his thighs around Danny's wrist, holding Danny's hand right where he wanted it.

Danny pushed a little harder, and his finger went deeper into that delicious, hot tightness. He could feel the muscles in Luke's channel gripping him, then easing him loose, then once again drawing him deeper. All the while Luke continued to pump his cock in and out of Danny's mouth. His cock felt like iron, it was so hard. Danny had his eyes closed, relishing the sensations. The cock in his mouth. Luke's ass gripping his finger. The dripping of precome which Danny could taste now seeping from Luke's dick. His own precome making Danny's cock more responsive in his hand.

Danny stroked his own cock a little faster while he savored every inch of Luke's.

Again Luke gripped the sides of Danny's face, holding him still. He pulled his cock free and Danny pleaded softly, "No," when he felt it go.

"Wait," Luke whispered, then he turned around and placed his ass in Danny's face. He bent over with his hands on the windowsill, opening himself up to Danny completely.

Eyes wide and eager, Danny moistened his finger again, this time with his own saliva, and slid it into that perfect opening. Luke said, "Oh," and reached around and pulled Danny's hand nearer. He spread his legs wider and Danny eased a second finger into Luke's ass.

"Oh, God," Luke sighed. "Oh, God, Danny. Fuck me. Fuck me *now*. I can't wait any longer."

Danny pressed his lips to Luke's opening next to his two buried fingers, and when he pulled the fingers free he replaced them with his lips. His tongue slid into Luke's ass, and Luke gasped like a fish out of water. "Oh, Lord, Danny. Stop playing around. *Fuck me*."

Danny rose to his feet behind Luke and slid an arm around Luke's chest, holding him tight.

With Luke still bent forward, resting his forearms on the windowsill, Danny spit on his own long cock and smeared his juices across the head. His knees were shaking when he pressed the head of his dick to Luke's sphincter. It was his turn to gasp when Luke reached between his legs to cup Danny's balls, and with his fingertips, he helped guide Danny's cock to where he wanted it to go.

For the very first time in his life, Danny felt the incredible heat and closeness of a man's ass envelop his cock as he eased himself past the tight ring of muscle that protected Luke's very core.

"Don't stop," Luke hissed. "All the way. Put it all the way in."

Danny gripped his arm around Luke and held him hard against him as he pushed his hips forward. His long, fat cock slid all the way in. The heat of Luke's ass enveloped him. They both had their eyes closed, savoring the sensations. The piercer and the pierced.

"Oh, man, Luke. You are so beautiful." Danny could barely speak now, he was trembling so hard. His breath was coming in desperate little puffs of air. His lips were pressed to the back of Luke's neck and Luke still reached underneath himself to cup Danny's balls with his free hand as he leaned against the windowsill, legs spread wide, eyes squeezed shut.

"Let me get used to you," Luke stammered. Oh, God, Danny's cock felt heavenly inside him. Luke forced his sphincter to relax even more, and finally, when he thought he was ready, he said, "Okay, Danny. Fuck me. Fuck me, baby."

And Danny slowly drew his cock away from that ring of muscle until only the head remained inside. Then, holding Luke as tightly as he could against him, Danny slid his cock back in. The sensations were so intense Danny had to close his eyes. Luke's fingertips cupping his balls, the muscles in Luke's ass stroking his cock, holding it in, letting it go.

Danny forced himself to open his eyes and look out the window over Luke's shoulder, just so he wouldn't come too fast. He didn't want this to end. Ever.

He thought of his dad, he thought of his car, he thought of those two damned kids crawling around in the wet grass by the back fence. He thought of everything he could think of, just so he wouldn't think about how wonderful Luke's ass felt sliding around his dick. Gripping it. Releasing it. Gripping it again.

They were both trembling so uncontrollably now they could barely stand up. Danny was no longer trying to ease himself in and out of Luke. He was fucking him for all he was worth. He couldn't have stopped if he wanted to. His hips, coated with sweat, slapped against Luke's ass cheeks as he drove his cock repeatedly into that eager opening. Luke was crying out and pulling Danny closer, taking that long cock as deep inside himself as he could get it.

Danny was biting at the back of Luke's neck now. He wasn't sure, but he thought he might even be tasting blood. Christ, had he bitten him? If he had, Luke didn't seem to mind.

"I'm gonna come," Luke cried out.

And Danny felt Luke's ass clench onto his cock as the come erupted from Luke's cock, splattering the wall, splattering the windowsill. Danny reached around and grabbed the spurting cock in his fist. Luke had come without touching himself at all, Danny realized. Just the sensation of his own cock sliding in and out of Luke's velvet ass had been enough to make Luke erupt in orgasm. That was the sexiest thing Danny could ever imagine.

Feeling the hot come on his fist as he reached around to pump Luke's cock, still seeping all over his hand, Danny knew he couldn't stop his own moment of ejaculation. He was about to explode, whether he wanted to or not.

"Oh, Christ," Luke stammered, "your cock is so big now. Come inside me, Danny. Come inside me."

Danny cried out. His whole body thrumming like a tuning fork, he rose up onto his tiptoes when the sperm tore from his cock, filling Luke's insides. Danny continued to pump his cock into that gorgeous hot ass as his come kept surging out. Danny was sweating bullets, now, his wide-open mouth pressed hungrily to the back of Luke's neck, his dick buried as deep as it would go inside that heavenly wet hole, and Danny just let himself come and come and come.

When the spurting stopped, Danny still refused to pull away. He felt his cock, ever so slowly, begin to soften inside Luke's ass.

With a groan, Luke pushed himself away from the windowsill and stood upright. He reached around behind him and continued to hold Danny next to him. Continued to hold Danny *inside* him.

He turned his head to find Danny's lips. With Danny's cock still softly buried deep inside his core, Luke kissed Danny's lips as if he had never tasted him before. Both their hearts were pounding, an echoing thunder reverberating in the moonlight. Danny's tongue shot into Luke's mouth, and Luke smiled to feel his mouth and his ass both invaded with Danny's presence. It was an incredible sensation. For Danny too. Danny's senses were so overloaded, he didn't know *how* to feel. He only knew he had loved every single nanosecond of what had just happened.

Neither wanted the feelings to end, but gradually, Danny's softening cock began to ease its way free.

Luke shuddered when the head of Danny's cock slipped through his anal ring completely, signaling an end to all they had just experienced. He felt empty. Deserted. Only Danny's lips against his own made him still feel whole. Still feel loved.

Slowly, they both opened their eyes to the moonlit night surrounding them. They found each other's faces in the darkness. Again, their lips came together.

Danny took Luke's hand and tugged him toward the bed. "Let me hold you," he said.

And Luke followed him to Danny's bed, where they collapsed in each other's arms.

With the afterglow of their lovemaking still blocking all other thoughts, except those of love and lingering hunger, they let their bodies and minds relax as they lay together face to face. Groin to groin.

"I'm never letting you go," Danny whispered. "Never."

"Good," Luke whispered back.

It had been a long day. They were tired. Even the memory of the incredible closeness they had just experienced could not keep them awake long. With their lips still brushing together in one lingeringly gentle good-night kiss, they slowly let the day slip into memory. They fell asleep inhaling the scent of each other's breath, all the troubles in the world, for a while, forgotten.

Neither had seen the binoculars trained on them as they stood at the window making love. If they had, they might have been more careful in the hours to come.

But as it was, they simply slept. And while they slept, their dreams were kind.

Their awakening would be considerably less so.

HOURS later, in the stillest part of the night, Luke eased himself from Danny's arms and trudged toward the bathroom to pee. He softly cursed when he stumbled over Granger, who was lying by the bathroom door. Luke stood still for a second listening for the sounds of Danny waking up, but when he didn't hear anything but Danny's gentle breathing, he headed on into the bathroom and did his business.

For some reason, Luke felt wide awake. He was hungry, but rather than go downstairs and forage around for something to eat, he decided he could live without food until morning. But food wasn't the only thing he was hungry for. He was hungry for Danny too, but that could also wait until morning. Maybe.

To take his mind off his cravings, Luke padded naked through the darkness to each of Danny's three windows, one after the other, gazing out at the night. At San Diego. His new home. Granger trailed along beside him, periodically pressing his snout to Luke's leg, begging to be petted, begging for attention. Luke willingly obeyed, reaching down to pat Granger's neck or twiddle his ear. At every touch from his beloved human, Granger's tail swept happily back and forth, stirring the shadows behind him.

At the first window, Luke stared down at glimmering sparks of moonlight reflected off the water in the swimming pool. The outside lights were still off. The underwater lights too. The yard was pitch-black, the pool an empty black rectangle. No moving shadows passed across it. Just those tiny patches of reflected light, like shards of glass, glittering on the surface of the water. The neighborhood beyond Danny's yard looked peaceful and still. There was no traffic on the street. Luke thought he must be the only person awake for blocks around.

He could not have been more wrong.

At the second window, Luke looked out at the opposite view of the city. Rooftops, chimneys, palm trees outlined against the star-spattered sky. A tiny red light blinked atop a tall antenna miles away, barely discernible in the nighttime haze. Closer in, there were porch lights burning here and there. Luke smelled wood smoke. Could someone really have set a fire in their fireplace in this god-awful summer heat? Maybe for romantic purposes? Luke smiled at the thought. He turned and looked at Danny, still splayed out sound asleep on the bed behind him. His bare skin shone like ivory in the moonlight coming through the window. Luke closed his eyes for the briefest of moments and remembered the taste of that skin against his tongue. His dick shifted at the memory. He stared at Danny for the longest time, then forced himself to turn away and let Danny sleep.

Reluctant now, since he had other things on his mind, sex being the most pressing, Luke moved to the third and last window in Danny's bedroom. Holding the curtain aside with his hand, he looked out at the house he and his dad now called home. The house was shadowy and angular and looked kind of creepy sitting there all hunched over in the darkness without a light burning anywhere. Luke supposed he should have left a porch light on at least, but it was too late to worry about that now. He could see his own bedroom window across the way. The curtains were open and he could just make out the corner of his bed, the white bedspread catching the moonlight coming through the window.

As he stared at it, a shadow passed in front of his bed. Just—the smallest of shadows. Had a bird flown between the window and the moon? An owl, maybe?

Since Danny's window was wide open, Luke leaned out on the sill, wishing he had a pair of binoculars. Then he remembered Danny spying on him from this very window just days before. *And Danny had been watching Luke through a pair of binoculars.*

Luke turned from the window and squinted around the room, trying to find the binoculars Danny had used. He looked down at his feet, and damned if they weren't there. On the floor. Right beneath the window.

Luke scooped them up, stuck his head outside as he leaned across the sill, and adjusted the lenses until his bedroom window came into focus.

The shadow inside his room was still moving. And it was a *human* shadow! Luke could see it standing farther from the window now. Farther from the bed. It looked like whoever it was, was going through his dresser drawers.

Holy shit! It was a burglar! He must have left a door unlocked!

He had to call 911! Luke grabbed for his phone, which was conveniently right in front of him, perched on the windowsill like a potted plant. Then he remembered the severed finger. Luke had promised Danny he wouldn't call the cops about *that,* so he supposed he damn well shouldn't call the cops about *this.* Granted, the burglar was in the house next door to Danny's, but the cops would ask questions: "Where were you at the time of the break-in? Why weren't you home at this late hour? How did you see the intruder in your bedroom when you say you weren't even in the house?"

All those questions would lead the cops right to Danny. And once they got to Danny, they would realize Danny's father was nowhere around. And that would spell trouble. Trouble even for Luke, since he would be the one who got his lover's dad in dutch with the cops. The last thing he wanted to do was piss off Danny. Jesus! He wanted to *marry* Danny, not piss him off.

So what was he supposed to do? Just let the burglar burgle around and take whatever the hell he wanted. Uh-uh. That wasn't about to happen.

Luke shuffled around the room in the dark, grabbing his shorts off the floor. He snagged a baseball bat standing in the corner which, unbeknownst to him, was left over from Danny's thirteenth summer visiting his dad. That was the summer Danny had taken a shot at joining Little League. He was so skinny and gangly that summer, he was next to worthless on the ball field. The only thing Danny could really accomplish with any sense of continuity was falling down. He fell down a lot. So he gave up on baseball after two games. But he kept the bat. It had been standing untouched in the corner of his bedroom ever since. Until tonight, when Luke grabbed it like a knight grabbing his trusty mace.

Luke stood there in the darkness for a few seconds, hefting the bat, gauging its weight. It felt good and solid in his hands. Should dent a burglar's skull quite handily, thank you very much. If Luke didn't chicken out. Or if the fucker didn't have a gun.

That thought stopped him. But not for long. He had to do *something.* He had money in one of those dresser drawers.

Bat in hand, Luke turned to wake Danny and tell him where he was going. He quickly realized that was a really bad idea. Danny would insist on going with him. And that would set off his ankle monitor. Or he would insist that, rather than put himself in harm's way, Luke should call the cops and forget about what Danny's dad had said about not getting the police over here. That would get his dad in trouble.

Luke stood there beside the bed looking down at Danny's gorgeous naked body laid out beneath him. The guy was still softly snoring. Apparently, he could sleep through anything.

Luke chewed his lip, deciding what to do.

When, behind him, Granger put his front paws on the open windowsill and softly growled at the intruder across the way, Luke knew he had to act. And he had to act alone.

He kissed his fingertip and gently pressed the kiss to Danny's forehead. Danny didn't stir.

"Come on, boy," Luke whispered, clutching the bat, the very weight of it giving him courage.

Granger perked up his ears and followed Luke through the bedroom door.

Shit just got real, Luke thought, as he stepped out into the moonlit night with Granger at his heels. *Shit just got really, really real.*

He had no idea how real it was about to get.

AS QUIETLY as he could, Luke stuck the key in the back door and eased his way across the threshold. He had the oddest impression *he* was the intruder in this strange, dark house. After all, he had only spent one or two nights here before he found Danny and started sleeping over there. This house was barely broken in. Luke didn't feel like he was stepping into his own home at all. Actually, it felt like he had stumbled through a doorway into a place he had never been before in his life. But that wasn't true. In the shadowy kitchen, barely lit by the distant light of the streetlamp half a block away, he could see the mess he had made there just that afternoon. Kitchen crap everywhere. Boxes scattered to hell and back. Kitchen chairs piled on the kitchen table just to get them out of the way while he unpacked box after box after box of junk he and his dad didn't really need but had dragged halfway across the country with them anyway.

The house was dead silent, but for his own heartbeat pounding inside his head. It was beating so hard, it sounded like the thumper they used in the movie *Dune* to attract the worms. *Thump thump thump thump.* Spooky. His own heartbeat was giving him the heebie-jeebies. What the hell was that about? And then there were Granger's toenails clackety-clacking across the tile floor. That was spooky too.

Hell, the whole fucking house was spooky.

Luke stood stark still, head tipped to the side, and just listened, trying to catch a sound from the intruder upstairs. He must still be up there. Luke didn't think the guy could have left without him knowing, although he supposed it was possible. Going barefoot, Luke's footsteps were silent. And he didn't think the burglar could hear his heartbeat. It wasn't pounding *that* loud. He crossed the kitchen like a drifting shadow and stepped through the dining room door.

This part of the house was even darker than the kitchen. Bushes outside the windows blocked the streetlight off in the distance completely. And the moon was straight up in the sky now, ducking in and out of a passing bank of clouds, so it wasn't much help either.

Luke's house had a banistered staircase, not unlike Danny's. Thank God, this part of the house was carpeted so Granger's toenails were silenced.

Luke took a firmer grip on the baseball bat with his right hand. With his other hand, he grasped the newel post and cast his eyes toward the well of shadows leading up to the second floor. If this was a horror movie, it would be at this point right here when Luke would scream from the back row, "Don't go up there, asshole!" And then he would watch as the idiot on the screen went up there anyway.

Just like he was doing. Boy, people never learn.

Luke took it slow. One step at a time. Granger wasn't being much help, lurking at Luke's back the way he was doing, the chicken. Next time Luke got a dog, he'd get something butch. Like a Rottweiler. Or a pit bull. Something with balls and an attitude. Well, maybe he wouldn't. He sort of liked Granger the way he was, even if he wasn't the bravest thing on four legs.

Luke heard a sound that stopped him cold. Just the tiniest sound. Metallic. Then he placed it. It was the rattle of a venetian blind and it was coming from *behind him.* Downstairs! With his heart doing a real tap dance now, Luke turned on the stair. He was about halfway up. Granger was two steps below him. Granger didn't seem to have heard the sound at all since he was still looking up instead of back the way they had come.

Now Luke didn't know what to think. Had he heard a sound or not? Should he go back down, or keep going up? Before he could decide, he heard another sound. It was the sound of a floorboard creaking. Just one little creak. Like a hesitant footfall. And this time it was definitely above him.

Oh, man.

Luke wiped a dribble of sweat off his forehead, straightened his glasses, regripped the baseball bat, and kept climbing up. Granger followed along behind him, occasionally bumping the back of Luke's bare leg with his ice-cold nose and making Luke jump every time he did it.

With one more step to go, Luke suddenly felt the air and light change around him. A sound like thunder rumbled toward him. Footsteps. Pounding footsteps. They were headed right for him!

Granger started barking. It startled Luke so badly he almost fainted.

Luke raised the bat in front of his face to ward off whatever was coming at him. He felt Granger rush between his legs with a growl, then a pair of hands came out of the shadows and gave Luke a shove. Luke windmilled his arms for a second, teetering, trying to regain his balance, but he didn't manage it very well. The next thing he knew, he was falling backward down the stairs, *sailing* actually, and he was hitting every single step along the way. With his head. With his ass. With his elbow. The bat went flying out of his hands and clattered across the floor below. Luke had just enough presence of mind as he tumbled down the stairs to tear his glasses from his face and clutch them in his fist to protect them.

He hit the foyer floor with a *whump* that knocked every whiff of air out of his lungs. He lay there for a second, taking stock. Flexing his fingers. Wiggling his toes. Nothing seemed to be broken. "Ouch," he whispered, not because he was hurting so much, but more because he just wanted to see if he could still talk. That way he'd know he was alive.

He was just about to pull himself to his feet when the thundering footsteps returned. A tall shadow came flying down the staircase right at him once again. And once again, Luke crossed his arms in front of his face to ward off the danger. A pair of long legs sailed over him where he lay all crumpled up on the bottom step. A second later, another shadow sailed over him. A smaller shadow. It was Granger. He was really barking up a storm now. Snapping, snarling, growling. Acting all protective and gutsy now that the bad guy was on the run.

In the distance, Luke heard a door bang against the wall, and footsteps clattered down the back steps. Granger's bark grew more distant, then it stopped altogether.

"Fuck," Luke murmured, dragging himself to his feet. He slipped his glasses back on and immediately took them off again and wiped them on his T-shirt. They were smudged from having been held in his sweaty hands while he cartwheeled backward down the stupid stairs.

Standing, Luke took stock of his injuries. There weren't many. His elbow was skinned, as was his knee. He had a kink in his neck where he'd landed on his head at some point as he tumbled down the stairs. And his ear hurt like a mother. When he touched it, it felt wet. Blood. Must have taken some skin off there too.

It took Luke a minute to realize that maybe he really wasn't out of danger after all. The guy could come back. Or there could be someone else inside the house. He squinted through the shadows until he located the baseball bat. He scooped it off the floor with a groan, and hearing a new sound directly behind him, he whirled around with a good tight grip on the bat, holding it at eleven o'clock, ready for bear, when he saw it was only Granger grinning up at him.

"Well, shit, boy," Luke said. "Scare me to death, why don't you?"

He squatted to take Granger's head between his hands and listened to the darkness around him, not sure what to expect. Judging by Granger's attitude, the danger was gone. But Granger wasn't exactly combat-ready, so Luke thought he'd do better to trust his own instincts rather than the dog's.

Bat still poised to take off the first head that came along, Luke stalked back the way he had come, down the hallway and through the kitchen to the back door. It was standing wide open, but there was no one there, and no one anywhere in sight. The driveway was clear of all humanity and the yard was empty.

Luke pulled the door closed and locked himself inside the house. Then he thought maybe that might not be too good an idea, so he unlocked the door again and left it ajar, in case he had to beat a hasty retreat.

Then he switched on the kitchen light and headed back to the staircase, flicking every light switch he came across along the way.

The first floor looked okay, so he put one shaky foot on the first step of the staircase, then another shaky foot, and finally just said "Fuck it," and raced up the stairs with a war whoop, hoping to scare any intruder away if there still happened to be one around.

He peeked around the edge of his bedroom door, switched on the ceiling light, and heaved a sigh of relief. The room was empty.

Someone had certainly been there, though. No two ways around that. The room was a mess. Even more than usual.

The first thing that caught Luke's eye was the dresser drawers. They had all been pulled open, his underwear yanked out by the handfuls and scattered across the floor and over the bed. Luke stepped closer, and once again, he removed his glasses and wiped them clean with the tail of his shirt because he really couldn't believe he was seeing what he thought he was seeing. Then he bent over his bed and looked closer.

When he suddenly figured it out, he jerked upright and felt a chill creep up his back like an icy finger being scraped along his spine.

The underwear the intruder had flung across Luke's bed was splashed with semen. Jism city.

Jesus, Luke thought. *What a fucking pervert.*

His fear and his stress and his raggedy, jangled nerves suddenly got the better of him. He made a mad dash for the bathroom and landed on his knees in front of the commode like a base runner sliding into home plate.

Hugging the toilet bowl like it was his new best friend, Luke barfed up everything in his stomach.

Granger sat patiently at his side, whimpering, until he was finished.

Finally, Luke lifted his head and blinked back tears. Christ! Grabbing at the toilet paper, he peeled off a fistful and wiped his mouth. When he was finished, he glanced in the bowl.

Man, he thought, *twenty dollars' worth of pizza looks a whole lot better going in than it does coming out.*

Then he barfed again.

CHAPTER TWELVE
BATTLE PLANS

LUKE hissed. That alcohol *burned.*

"Sorry," Danny said. "Almost done. Bear with me."

Luke watched as Danny finished wiping the crud and blood and carpet lint off of Luke's skinned knee with a humongous wad of alcohol-soaked cotton. Danny was sitting cross-legged on the kitchen floor in front of him, and Luke was parked in the dining room chair sipping at one of Danny's dad's beers to calm his nerves. Danny had already finished treating Luke's skinned elbow and his poor scraped ear. Now that the excitement was winding down, Luke thought Danny actually looked more scared than *he* did. Somehow that realization made Luke love the guy all the more.

They were both in wrinkled shorts. Nothing else. T-shirts had been totally forgotten what with the drama and all.

"You couldn't see who it was?" Danny asked for the third time, oh so carefully plucking a strand of cotton away from Luke's wounded knee with his fingertips. "You couldn't see his face at all?"

"Nope." Luke pushed the beer away. He didn't like the taste, and he was afraid it would make him barf again. Danny watched him, then reached up and grabbed the bottle for himself. He poured what was left of the beer right down his throat. Watching him, Luke almost smiled.

Danny's eyes were as big as silver dollars. Luke supposed his were too. Wow. What a night.

Danny stopped what he was doing and cupped both hands behind Luke's calves, loving the fuzzy warm feel of them in his hands. He also loved the way Luke looked down at him with a gentle smile when he did it.

"I'll call the cops if you want," Danny said. "Maybe now we should. Dad will just have to understand."

Luke reached out with a fingertip and pushed a tress of Danny's long hair away from his eyes. That movement caused Danny to lean forward and kiss Luke's knee, the uninjured one, before sitting back on his haunches and once again looking up into Luke's face.

"No," Luke said. "What are they going to do? A DNA test on the sperm? Those tests take weeks. That's if they'll do them at all. DNA testing is expensive as hell and police forces are always hard up for money. I watch *CSI*. I know how cops think. No, we'll just keep our eyes open for a few more days. When our dads get back, we'll tell them what happened and let them decide what to do. I don't want to get you or your dad into any trouble. And it's not like the guy really hurt anything. A box of laundry soap and about a dozen cans of spray disinfectant will fix it right up. My come-splattered underwear will be as good as new. And it's not like it hasn't been splattered with come before. Tee hee."

"Yeah, but that was yours! *This* is just so damned *sick*. And how did he get in, Luke? You locked the doors, right?"

Luke shrugged. "I thought I did, but who the hell knows? My brains have been so centered on your dick lately, I don't know *what* I'm doing half the time. Not that I mind, you understand. It's just the way things are."

"Thanks," Danny said with a grateful smirk. "Knowing you're thinking about my dick makes it better. As long as you don't walk into a bus or anything while you're thinking about it."

Luke grinned, then the grin turned to a grimace when he flexed his leg to work the kinks out of his injured knee. It would be sore for a couple of days. At least until the skin healed. His elbow and ear too.

Overall, however, Luke figured he had got off pretty easy. The night's adventures could have resulted in considerably worse injuries.

Danny was still stroking Luke's calves and thinking out loud. "I couldn't believe it when you woke me up and told me what happened. I didn't even hear you leave the house. I guess it's just as well. I couldn't have gone with you anyway."

"No," Luke said, "but I wish I *had* woken you up. Maybe if you had been watching from the bedroom window, you could have seen who it was that ran out my back door after knocking me ass-over-teakettle down the stairs."

"Yeah," Danny conceded. "Maybe."

Silence fell around them as they thought about all that had happened. Granger snoozed in the corner, worn out from all the excitement. Frederick was God-knows-where. The kitchen clock was ticking away the seconds on the wall above the Mr. Coffee machine, sounding really loud in the wee small hours of the morning when the rest of the world was pretty much conked out. Except for them and the pervert, of course. They were still up. Luke supposed it had been quite a night for all three of them.

Finally, Luke asked the question that had been preying on both their minds. The question they had managed to avoid, so far, but couldn't avoid any longer. He figured it was time somebody asked it, and it might as well be him. Get all the bad shit out in the open: that was his motto. Or it seemed to be.

"Danny, do you think this has anything to do with the killings? Do you think those kids are right? About the killer living in the neighborhood, I mean. Or was this just some sicko numbnuts pervert out on a mission to whack off on somebody else's Fruit of the Looms?"

Danny didn't answer. Not directly. But he did ask the second question they had both been avoiding. "So—what do you think? Was it Childers?"

Luke had been considering that very question. It was all tangled up in his mind. It was like someone had tossed snippets of memory from all the night's events into a hat and stirred them up. Tumbling down the stairs bass-ackwards. Hearing the baseball bat clatter on the landing below after it went flying out of his grip. Hearing Granger growl like an enraged wolf when he was really just a pussycat and even the bad guy probably knew it. Listening to his own brains bounce around inside his brainpan after hitting that last step as hard as he did with the back of his head.

Luke tried to sift through all those memory bytes to get to what really mattered. He saw again the two hands shooting out of the shadows to shove him down the stairs. He saw long legs flying over him as he lay twisted in a pile at the foot of the stairs, stunned. He heard someone gasping for breath and muttering curses as they threw themselves through the back door.

Was it Childers? Could it have been him? Luke wasn't sure.

Luke was hesitant when he spoke, still trying to sort it all out in his mind. "I have an impression in my head that the guy was taller than Childers. But I was on my ass at the bottom of a flight of stairs, so maybe that's why the guy looked taller. I don't know, Danny. If you were a cop and you were asking me if I could identify the intruder in a police line-up, I'd have to say—no. Not in a million years. It could have been Childers. It could have been you. It could have been Santa Claus. I just don't know." After a moment, Luke added, "Well, maybe not Santa Claus. This guy wasn't fat."

A third question suddenly popped into Danny's head. It stopped him cold. It was a question which had not occurred to Danny until this very second. He didn't like this question at all, but he had to ask it. So he did, although it made his blood run cold just to hear the words coming out of his mouth.

"Luke, if it was really the killer who was in your house tonight, do you think that means he's after you now? Do you think you're his next intended victim?"

Luke gazed down at the seriousness on Danny's face. A deadly fear burned in Danny's eyes as he looked up at Luke from where he was still squatting on the kitchen floor between Luke's legs. Danny's big gentle hands were still cupping Luke's thighs, and Luke loved feeling them there against his skin.

"I love you so much," Luke said, unable to stop the words from pouring out. "And—I don't know the answer to what you're asking me.

I hope the hell not. I don't want to be *anybody's* next victim. What do you think?"

Danny stroked the back of Luke's legs as he spoke. His words were so softly uttered Luke could barely hear them. They were softly uttered because Danny didn't want to say them. But he knew he had to. There was no getting around it.

"I think you look a little like that blond guy on the news. The one that's missing. I think if this asshole has a thing for young guys, he would sure as hell come after you because you are without a doubt the most gorgeous young guy I've ever seen in my life. I also think we have to assume he is coming after you, just to be on the safe side. I think we should barricade ourselves inside this house until our dads get back. That's what I think. That's exactly what I think."

Luke opened his mouth to say—what? For one of the few times in his life he found himself truly speechless. His brain was sure in hyperdrive, though, for all the good it was doing him.

A tentative tap at the back door made them both whirl around. That wasn't the sound of Frederick bumping his way through the pet door. That sound was made by a human hand.

In tandem, Luke and Danny gazed back into each other's faces with wide, startled eyes. Then they turned toward the clock to see what time it was. It was almost three in the morning. Who the hell would knock on their door at three in the morning?

Danny's first instinct was to turn the lights out and hide. His second instinct was the one he decided to run with. He took a deep breath, grabbed the baseball bat from the kitchen table where Luke had left it, and strode bravely to the back door on his clompy-ass cast and flung the damn thing open.

It took Danny exactly four seconds to do all that. While he did, Luke didn't move from the kitchen table, although he did catch himself looking around for another weapon, just in case.

But he didn't find one. Not before he heard Danny say, "Oh! It's you! I—I—well, shit, oh, excuse me, didn't mean to say shit. Well, please, don't just stand out there in the dark. Come on in."

And Luke found himself rising to his feet. He had always been taught to rise to his feet when a lady entered a room. Even at three in the morning. And even if the lady was wearing fluffy pink house slippers with fluffy pink rabbit ears poking up off the toes.

And even if the lady looked as terrified as this one.

DANNY had never seen his neighbor, Mrs. Trumball, this up close and personal. It was a little disconcerting, to tell the truth. He was more used to seeing her from three houses away, in the dark, dumping old gin bottles in the trash when she thought no one was watching. And she *certainly* didn't think anyone was watching her through *binoculars*, as Danny always did. Danny didn't figure she would be too thrilled if she knew about *that*.

This close, Mrs. Trumball was a sight to behold. She truly was. Her hair was dyed a horrific DayGlo red, but not lately, it seemed, since a good inch of gray regrowth could be seen snuggled up to her scalp. The rest of her hair, which looked as dry as toast, was wrapped around wire hair rollers with a nasty looking plastic pin that was a good four inches long stabbing each one into place like a rapier. One lone roller, somewhere at the crown of her head, had disappeared entirely, and a perfect red *S* of foot-long hair flapped around every time she moved. There were split ends *all over* that flapping red *S* of hair. Danny was sorely tempted to recommend a conditioner. Then he thought, *How gay is that?*

Mrs. Trumball's age was pretty much indeterminable. She could have been forty. She could have been eighty. The wrinkles in her face were etched deep by several layers of make-up, which seemed to have been continually reapplied but never actually removed. Talk about clogged pores. Her eyes were as gray as the roots of her hair. And just as sad. Her lipstick was a screamingly bright red and came remarkably close to matching her hair. It had bled at the corners of her mouth, making her look a little like the Joker in the latest Batman movie.

The woman's housecoat was pink and faded and had little roses all over it, along with a goodly crop of lint nubbins. Her slippers, as previously noted, were pink and faded and had big fat rabbit ears sticking off the toes, limp with age. There was also a little rabbit nose perched on the end of one of the woman's slippers with two felt rabbit teeth hanging underneath it. The nose on the other foot seemed to have disappeared along with the hair roller, although the two felt rabbit teeth were still sewn on, making that rabbit look a little incomplete. Like the Cheshire cat on his way out.

Years of guzzling gin had taken a toll. Overall, the impression Mrs. Trumball would probably convey at first glance was one of abject uncertainty. Shy. Battered down. Inconsequential. And that of a raging alcoholic.

But not tonight. Tonight she looked damn near sober. Terrified people usually do.

The first words out of her mouth made Danny question that assessment. Maybe she wasn't sober after all, seeing as how she wasn't making much sense. She was certainly terrified, however. Nothing would change Danny's mind about that.

"Evil," she said, in a breathless little whisper. "It's here." She cast her eyes at the kitchen windows, one after the other, obviously expecting to see satanic faces peeking in. She aimed her gray, terrified eyes back to Danny, then to Luke, who was still standing by the table, too surprised to move.

Finally, Luke snatched up a fleck of civility and pulled out another chair. "Here," he said. "Have a seat."

The woman ignored the offer. She turned her eyes back to Danny.

"The boys are gone. I saw them sneaking around earlier but now they're gone. DeVon and Bradley." A tiny smile wrinkled the corners of her eyes. "They come by for cupcakes sometimes. I make them the way boys like them, with lots and lots of icing. And a cherry sometimes, stuck on the top. A *maraschino* cherry. Just for fun, you know? The boys are my friends. But now they're gone. I tried to call the police and tell them, but they won't listen to me anymore. They shoo me away like I'm nuts. I've been trying to tell them about the evil for weeks and weeks, you know? The evil living right here in the neighborhood. But they just won't listen. I guess I've called them too many times. Now I'm just a pest." She looked down at her hands, turning them over and over in front of her like she had never seen them before in her life. Her hands looked fragile, Danny noted. Fragile and pale and small. Then she dropped them back to her sides and gazed again at Danny's face. "I might be a pest, but I'm not nuts. I'm scared. Scared for my friends."

"What happened to them?" Danny asked, although he thought maybe he already knew. God, he hoped not.

"The evil man took them. I knew he would. I tried to tell the boys not to run around the neighborhood like they do at all hours of the night. Sneaking out of their houses. Playing at being detectives. They wouldn't listen. *Nobody* listens to me." Then she jerked her head to the side, startled at seeing Granger for the first time as he stood there staring at her. She studied Granger for a couple of heartbeats, and now seemed to find it necessary to explain things to *him*. "I'm really not nuts. I'm just—not well. And I'm not stupid either. It's the police that are stupid. I've called them a hundred times. They won't even take my calls anymore."

She narrowed her eyes and muttered something that Danny thought might not be appropriate to mutter over crumpets at high tea. Mrs. Trumball seemed to have a very low opinion indeed of the San Diego Police Department. Glancing down at the police monitor on his ankle, Danny had to face the fact he pretty much shared the same opinion.

It was Luke who cut to the chase. "What do you want us to do?" he asked.

Mrs. Trumball gazed on Luke's face the way Danny sometimes did. Appreciative of its beauty. Touched by its sweetness.

She stepped forward and took Luke's hand in both of hers. Her eyes bored so deeply into Luke's, he almost flinched at the intensity of them.

"Find them," Mrs. Trumball said. "Find them and take them home. The boys. Find them."

"We don't know where they live," Luke said.

She expelled an impatient puff of air. "Then bring them to me, and *I'll* take them home."

Danny stepped forward and laid a hand on Luke's shoulder. Mrs. Trumball smiled shyly when he did. *She knows*, Danny thought. *She knows we're lovers.*

Together, Danny and Luke faced this odd woman with the haunted eyes, but it was Luke who finally asked the pertinent question.

"Where are they?" he asked. "Who took them?"

Mrs. Trumball laid a pale hand to her breast. It fluttered there like a dying bird. Danny could smell the fear on the woman even from where he stood. Fear, perfume, and gin. The three scents did not mix well.

"You *know* who took them," she said in a fierce whisper, reaching out and laying cold fingertips to Luke's cheek. "You saw him tonight yourself. He was in your house. I saw him run away." She slid her fingers along Luke's jawline until they brushed his injured ear. "He hurt you. I'm sorry."

Luke stepped back just enough to remove her cold fingers from his face. They felt awful. Damp and icy. And his ear was too damned sore to be sympathized with. Plus, there was something about the smell of the woman Luke did not like. Something *feral*. Like maybe, on top of everything else, she was a little lax in the feminine hygiene department.

Luke scraped his palm along his cheek to erase the feel of her touch. "Don't you think it would be better to let the police handle it? It's their job and—and besides, why should we risk our lives just because the police are too stupid to listen to you?"

The smile she suddenly aimed at Luke was as cold as her fingertips. She looked like a poker player holding four aces and suddenly not afraid for everyone to know it.

She gave a tiny shrug, as if to say Luke should be able to figure that out for himself.

"But why should *we* do this?" Danny insisted, starting to get mad. Starting to feel a little put-upon here.

Mrs. Trumball merely studied his angry expression, like an entomologist might study a bug. "Because they're your friends too.

And because it's the right thing to do. And you boys know it is. And also because you two are the only ones who know I'm not crazy."

Danny and Luke shared a look, and somehow they both knew what the woman had said was true. They *would* have to help those kids. If the cops wouldn't do it, it might as well be them. They still weren't convinced she wasn't crazy though. They'd have to get back to her on that one.

"*And,*" Mrs. Trumball added, still staring at Danny's glower as if she enjoyed seeing someone else mad for a change besides herself. "Because he's coming after your boyfriend next. I think you know that too."

On that happy note she turned and headed for the door. Just before walking through it, she turned one last time. "But don't worry *too* much," she whispered, hands cupped to the sides of her mouth as if the night outside had ears. "Help is on the way."

And with that, she split. The door closed behind her with a teeny tiny click.

Danny imagined the woman standing just outside his door, tugging a flask out of her housecoat pocket and taking a bracing slug of gin before scurrying home through the shadows like a rat.

Jesus. What a woman.

"WHAT the hell did she mean when she said help is on the way? What help?" Luke asked, looking powerfully confused. This whole damn night had sucked all the way through from beginning to end. Well, except for the part where Danny was writhing beneath him and coming like Old Faithful. That part was great. "And do you really think I'm going to be the next victim like she said? You don't believe that, do you, Danny?"

Danny pulled Luke into his arms and snuggled his neck for a minute.

"No," he said. "I don't believe it. I don't believe it because we're not going to let it happen. But yeah, Luke. I do think the guy that squirted jism all over your underwear is the killer. And I think he's got the hots for you. And I think that to have the hots for you, he must have met you face-to-face. And the only person in the neighborhood I can think of that you've met face-to-face is—"

"Childers," Luke said.

Danny nodded. "Childers."

Luke kissed the tender skin under Danny's ear. He could feel Danny shiver when he did it.

"So I guess maybe the kids have been right all along about the guy." Luke said the words like it really pissed him off to have to admit it. All he wanted to do was hop into bed with the man he loved and fool around and then get some sleep and get up and fool around some more. Chasing serial killers wasn't part of his game plan. Not now. Not ever.

But those two kids were in danger now. *Real* danger. He had to *try* to rescue them.

Danny could see the wheels turning in Luke's head. He knew what Luke was thinking, because he was thinking the same thing.

"Let's go, then," Danny said.

"No," Luke said, shaking his head like he meant it. "You can't go. You'll get yourself in trouble and your dad too. I can sneak over there better on my own anyway. I can sneak over there and look around. If I find the kids, I'll raise a holy ruckus until the cops come. If I don't find the kids, I'll sneak back over here and drag your beautiful body back to bed and stick my tongue up your ass. Deal?"

"No," Danny hissed, sounding fiercely determined. "You're not going anywhere without me. I won't let you. Now help me get this damn thing off my ankle." He bent down and took a grip on the ankle monitor, trying to figure out how it attached. Then he looked back up at Luke looking down at him. "Although I like your idea about sticking your tongue in my ass. Maybe we can keep those plans on hold for later."

"You're nuts," Luke said.

Danny grinned. "Yeah, well, so are you. And if we pull this rescue off, we'll be heroes. Just think of the stories we'll have to tell our grandchildren."

Luke rolled his eyes. "We're gay. We won't have any grandchildren."

"Oh, yeah."

At that very moment, they heard the bang and rattle of the pet door swinging open on the service porch.

"Fucking cat," Danny said.

Luke made a face. "That's an awful lot of noise for a cat. Cats are quiet and sneaky. That sounds more like a rhinoceros."

They pushed open the door leading to the service porch to check it out. Danny flicked on the overhead light and they just stood there staring. Speechless. Both of them.

DeVon's head and shoulders were poking through the pet door. "Howdy," he said, when he saw he had an audience. "How about a hand? I think I'm just about stuck in this fucking thing."

Danny stepped forward, grabbed DeVon's paw and pulled him on through, nearly scraping off the kid's pants in the process.

While DeVon pulled his trousers back up, dusted himself off, and looked proud as punch for some unfathomable reason, Bradley stuck *his* head through the pet flap right behind him. This time Danny waved him back out and opened the back door for him instead. Just to simplify matters.

"Thanks," Bradley said. "That pet door is a nuisance. It's too damn little."

"It's for a *cat!*" Danny growled. He started tapping his foot, the one without the cast, just like his mother used to do when she was getting good and fed up with his shenanigans. Danny stopped the foot tapping the minute he realized he was copying the woman. But that didn't mean he still couldn't be sarcastic. "And why the hell aren't you guys being held captive like you're supposed to be. Mrs. Trumball said the killer had your asses in lockup, and we had to rescue you. We were just about to do that. Pretty soon. When we got around to it. Eventually."

DeVon could be sarcastic too. "Pretty soon? Eventually? My black ass. We could have been dead by now."

"Yeah," Bradley echoed. "Dead. My ass is white, by the way."

DeVon giggled and punched him in the ribs.

Luke bent forward and aimed a finger at Bradley's sternum. "Why aren't you kids home in bed where you belong?"

Bradley yanked a lint-covered licorice whip from his back pocket and stuffed it in his mouth. "My folks think I'm sleeping over at DeVon's."

"Yeah," DeVon added. "And my folks think I'm sleeping over at Bradley's."

Luke grabbed both kids' shirtfronts and pulled them close. "Not the brightest parents in the world, are they?"

"Nope," Bradley said.

"And that's the way we like it," DeVon chipped in with a grin.

"Guess I would too," Luke said, releasing them with a friendly poke in both their bellies.

Danny grabbed Luke's arm to get his attention. His face was lit up like someone had just hit it with the high beams. "Now we don't have to go. Now we can do what you said earlier. You know." And he stuck his tongue out and wiggled it around.

Luke grinned. But his grin died a pretty quick death when Bradley kicked the door out of sheer peevishness, or so it appeared.

"None of that homo shit, boys. We got work to do. The rescue is still on, you know. Nothing has changed. It's just that the rescuee is different than who you thought it was going to be."

"Why?" Danny asked. "You're both here. We're both here. Who the hell else is there left to rescue?"

"Charlie," DeVon said. "I think he's still alive. Charlie Strickland. Remember him?"

"Shit," Luke said. "The guy on the news. The cute blond."

"Yeah," DeVon snorted. "Thought that would get your attention."

"So where is he?" Danny asked.

Bradley shrugged. "Don't know."

Luke leaned in and stuck his finger in Bradley's chest. This time he didn't do it quite so nicely. "What do you mean you don't know?

How are we supposed to rescue somebody if we don't know where he's at?"

"He's close," DeVon explained. "We just don't know exactly where Childers has him stashed. But the guy's in trouble. We heard him cry out again about an hour ago. So he's close. And he's hurting. Don't forget he's already lost a finger." He started slapping his pants pockets. "I've still got it here somewhere."

Danny held his hand in the air like a traffic cop. "Spare us. I've already seen the damn thing. That was a day ago, and it was ripe then."

This time Bradley's face lit up. "Yeah, well, you should smell it now. I had to spray it with Glade to keep the smell down."

Danny glared at the kid as if he couldn't believe what he was hearing. "That's sick. That's just sick."

While Bradley merely shrugged, DeVon jumped into the fray. "So you guys ready? Or would you maybe want to get dressed first? This isn't a gay pride parade, you know. It's a rescue mission. And put some shoes on. God knows where we'll end up."

Danny snickered at the parade remark while Luke just looked pissed. Without saying a word, they both turned to the pile of dirty laundry on top the dryer and sifted through it until they found a couple of T-shirts. Dirty, wrinkled, mildewy T-shirts. They slipped them over their heads. They ignored the suggestion about the shoes. Luke didn't know where his were, and Danny only needed one anyway.

Danny grabbed the baseball bat, and Luke said, "That's mine."

Danny rolled his eyes. "Fine." He opened a junk drawer and pulled out a hammer.

"No, I want *that*," Luke said.

Danny laughed and handed him the hammer while Luke surrendered the baseball bat.

It was DeVon's turn to tap his foot. "Whenever you girls are finished swapping weapons and sorting through the laundry, we'll just be going then, okay?"

Luke hefted the hammer like he couldn't wait to try it out on somebody's head. Maybe DeVon's. "Let's rumble," he said, hoping he sounded butch, but apparently he hadn't.

As soon as DeVon and Bradley were finished doubling up and laughing at his "rumble" remark, and not very charitably either, the kids ushered Luke and Danny out the back door. Since stealth would be required, poor Granger was left behind to whimper in the kitchen. He couldn't be trusted to remain silent in a pinch. Most dogs can't, and everybody there knew it.

On the back stoop, Danny and Luke lagged behind long enough to discuss one more pressing matter left hanging. The ankle monitor.

They stood looking down at it like maybe it was going to explode or something. The little flashing green light was annoying as hell. Unfortunately, they both knew that a flashing *red* light would be even more annoying.

"I can get past the back fence with it, no problem," Danny said. "I just don't know how far it will let me go once I get there."

"Let's leave it on until it goes red, then rip it off and run like rabbits."

"Blithely irrational. Without a lick of sense. Falls apart under pressure. Cuter than a bug's ear. I guess that's why I love you."

"Can the cops track you with it on?"

"Sure," Danny said. "But not if we rip it off. Of course, if we *do* rip it off, that'll bring the cops here in a red-hot minute."

"Maybe it will let you go farther past the fence than you think."

"Maybe."

"Or we can remove it now and take our chances. What do you think?"

Danny stood there looking down at his foot like it was the first time he had ever noticed he had one. He hemmed and hawed around for about ten seconds, then finally made a decision. If you want to call it that. "Let's leave it on and hope for the best. No, let's don't. Yeah, let's do. No, let's not. Oh, God, let me think."

Luke nodded, like he expected nothing less. "Fanatically indecisive. Unwaveringly irresolute. Has a really big dick. Guess that's why I love *you.*"

"The big dick doesn't really help us much in the current circumstances though, does it?"

"No," Luke said. "But it'll certainly come in handy later."

"If we survive."

"Well, yeah. If we survive."

Luke finally made the decision for both of them. "Fuck it. Let's just go. Leave the damn monitor alone for now. If it goes red, *then* we'll decide what to do about it."

Danny locked the door behind them, slid the jangly house keys into his pocket, and got a good grip on the baseball bat. Like Babe Ruth climbing into the batter's box.

"Oy. God help us all," Danny mumbled.

"And a bigass amen to that," Luke mumbled right back, knowing he looked ridiculous lugging a hammer around like some insane carpenter.

And after all that, the rescue mission finally got underway. Such as it was.

CHAPTER THIRTEEN
BLOOD IN THE POOL

IT WAS no surprise to anybody when DeVon led his little troop of amateur ninjas straight into the backyard, around the edge of Danny's pool, and right up to the back fence separating Danny's yard from Mr. Childers's property. Having purposely left the outside lights off, it was so damn dark Danny couldn't see his hand flapping around in front of his face. The wind was up too. It felt like rain, of all things. Danny squinted up at the sky and saw—nothing. No moon. No stars. Nothing. The heavens were buried in clouds. Big fat black ones. No wonder it felt like rain. One never really expects that in San Diego.

Of course, one never really expects to find a serial killer chopping people up on the other side of their back fence either. The world was packed *full* of surprises. Sort of like a piñata.

"I feel like an idiot," Luke groused.

"You'll get used to it," Bradley chirped. "We did."

Following DeVon and Bradley, with Luke sticking close to his side, Danny reluctantly ducked under the hibiscus plants, dragging his cast along behind him like an anchor. The plants were tall and fat and gave good cover. Under the bushes, it was even darker than it was *out* from under the bushes. And it was pretty dark out there. Once they were huddled in a group in the shadows, the only light they could see anywhere was the tiny green light blinking on Danny's ankle. At least it was still green. Just the thought of that little light blinking red made Danny's heart skip a beat. But the thought of what Charles Strickland might be going through at the hands of a homicidal maniac gave Danny the courage to keep going. That cute guy. Jeez, he'd already lost a finger. What other horrors had he been subjected to?

Danny was shocked back to reality by the feel of a hand sliding into his back pocket. Taking stock of his own appendages, he realized it wasn't his. It was Luke, making contact, being there for him, drawing strength from Danny's presence and giving back some of his own. Danny couldn't hold back the smile that spread across his face. Even with all the creepy shit going on, he was really enjoying the heck out of being in love. He pulled Luke's hand from his back pocket and pressed it to his lips. Then he stuffed it back into his pocket like a wallet. He liked feeling it there.

"Don't worry," Luke whispered, "I've got your back."

"Oh, please," Bradley hissed in the darkness, and DeVon giggled. "If you've got his back, can I have a wing?"

"I'm a breast man myself," DeVon chimed in in a vicious little whisper. "Got any of those, Danielle?"

Good lord, Danny thought. DeVon and Bradley were already assholes and they were barely eleven years old. What would they be like when they were adults? Assuming they lived that long. And judging by tonight's adventures, that was assuming a lot.

Then Danny wondered about more pressing matters. Like just how the four of them were going to quietly get over this six-foot-high fence. Especially when one of them had a broken leg.

"Everybody stay right here," DeVon ordered, and the next thing Danny knew, the kid was gone. Just gone.

"Where the hell did he go?" Luke asked.

"Loose boards," Bradley whispered, and Danny and Luke could see him in the darkness raising and lowering a three-board section of the fence for their benefit. Jeez, they had their own trapdoor into the viper's nest. How disturbing was that? "Cool, huh?" Bradley grinned. "We'll follow DeVon in as soon as he gives us an all-clear."

"Can't wait," Luke droned.

Danny wanted to ask Bradley who died and made him boss, but he was afraid the little shit would snicker at him again. God, what a brat.

Before any of them had time to do any more worrying, the trapdoor in the fence popped up with a squeak and DeVon stuck his head through. He had to lie on his belly in the dirt to do it. It was so dark under the bushes, the only thing Danny could see of the kid's dark-skinned face was the whites of his eyes and the flash of some really nice-looking choppers. "Coast is clear," DeVon whispered. "Childers ain't home and his car's gone. We have to hurry if we're going to search the place. God knows when he'll be back." He pulled his head back like a turtle and disappeared. The boards banged shut.

"Oh man," Bradley groaned. "Oh man, oh man, oh man." He sounded like he had lost his winning lottery ticket or his favorite grandmother had just kicked the bucket or he had suddenly found a syphilis canker on the end of his dingdong.

"What's wrong?" Luke hissed. "What are you 'oh manning' about?"

Bradley grabbed Luke by the front of his T-shirt and pulled him close so his voice wouldn't carry. "What if we're too late? What if Childers already killed the poor guy and now he's taking him somewhere to bury him? What if the finger in my pocket is the only part of Charlie Strickland anybody will ever see again? We'll have to turn the finger over to his parents for burial. Holy shit. How they gonna like that, huh? And how are they gonna feel about the fact that I sprayed the only remaining chunk of their son with Glade so he wouldn't stink up my pocket? Huh? How they gonna like that?"

"Well, we'll deal with your concerns when the time comes," Luke hissed right back, fighting the urge to roll his eyes. Or laugh. Or puke. He wasn't sure which. Danny seemed to be rendered speechless by what Bradley had just said, and who could blame him, Luke thought. Luke's hand was still in Danny's back pocket so he gave Danny's ass a squeeze for reassurance. Felt nice. They both thought so. "Let's just do it, okay?" Luke said, "Let's just do it and get it over with. Strickland is fine, and we're going to rescue him, just like we said we'd do. But DeVon is right too. Childers could come back any second, and I for one don't want to be caught inside his house when he does."

"At least you won't be beating off in his underwear drawer," Danny offered.

"True," Luke agreed, leaning in and speaking so softly only Danny could hear. "But I'm damned sure going to beat off all over you later."

That seemed to perk Danny right up. He whispered right back, "Ooh. You promise?"

"I don't know what you guys just said but I still think you're both deeply disturbed," Bradley commented drily, and then he dove under the loose boards and disappeared. Alice down the rabbit hole. The last they saw of Bradley was his nasty-ass tennis shoes sliding under the fence.

Danny looked at Luke in the dark. He couldn't really see him, but he knew he was there because his hand was still in his pocket. "You ready?" he asked.

"Yeah. I'll go first so you won't kick me in the head with your cast. I'm beat up enough already." His skinned ear and skinned elbow and skinned knee were all stinging like crazy, but he didn't think now was the time to whine about it. "And don't forget. Mrs. Trumball said help was on the way. I still don't know what she meant by that."

"Me neither. Maybe it was the gin talking. Or wishful thinking."

"I hope not," Luke said. He sounded like he meant it.

"Okay," Danny said, giving Luke a quick kiss. He was aiming for his lips but in the dark he hit his nose. Close enough. "See you on the other side."

"Okay. I love you."

"I love you too."

And fifteen seconds later there wasn't a soul in Danny's backyard. In fact, the only pair of eyes in attendance were the ones staring out through Danny's kitchen window. It was Granger, sitting with his ass in the kitchen sink, trying to see where everyone had gone.

He was looking pretty desperate too, because he really, *really* had to pee.

Stupid humans.

THIS was the first time Danny had ever been on Mr. Childers's property. It was a big lot, nicely maintained, with a ranch style house in the front, a two-car garage set at an angle behind the house, and a lot of southwestern style landscaping: sandy ground, succulents everywhere, wagon wheels propped up here and there, a terra cotta Mexican peasant snoozing under a ceramic sombrero that doubled as a bird bath. Tacky. There was also a cactus around every corner. And they were big.

"Yeeouch! Luke hissed. "Watch out for the cactus!"

Mr. Childers's backyard was almost as dark as Danny's, but not quite. The sandy soil was a lighter color than Danny's grass, and even without moonlight, they could pretty well see where they were going.

Luke and Danny found DeVon and Bradley waiting for them at the corner of the garage.

"Jesus," DeVon growled. "You finally decided to show up, huh? What were you doing? Smooching and declaring your undying love for each other under the fucking bushes?"

Bradley giggled. Luke and Danny ignored them both. Mostly because smooching and declaring their undying love for each other was *exactly* what they had been doing.

Danny looked down to make sure his ankle monitor was still green. It was. He knew he couldn't go much farther before it switched to red and every cop in San Diego would be chasing after his ass.

DeVon pointed a finger toward the concrete apron leading into the garage. There was a big stain right in the middle of it which stood out clearly against the pale color of the driveway.

"See that? That's blood," DeVon whispered. "Childers didn't even try to clean it up, the dumb shit. DNA evidence for the cops."

Danny wasn't convinced. If Childers was a serial killer and he chopped off some guy's finger in the middle of his driveway, Danny couldn't imagine the guy not hosing away the evidence pronto, or more to the point, doing the dastardly deed in a more secluded location to begin with. "Probably antifreeze," he said.

And DeVon grumped, "Think what you like. I know better."

Luke had been studying the terrain. The house was small and neat. One story. Every light in the place was off. Even the yard lights. The garage doors were closed up tight.

"How do you know his car is gone?" Luke asked.

DeVon pulled a small flashlight from his pants pocket. He grabbed Luke by his shirttail and dragged him toward a window in the side of the garage. As he shined the light through the glass, all four of them stuck their heads together and looked inside. The garage was empty except for the usual crap stored around the edges. Tools, boxes, washer and dryer. An old chifforobe. On the far side of the garage, in the space designed for a second car, Childers had set up a gym, with a Nautilus machine, a treadmill, a Bosu ball, and an old TV perched on an orange crate that he presumably used to watch exercise videos while he worked out.

No wonder the guy was such a hunk, both Danny and Luke thought. But they had the good sense not to say it in front of the kids or they'd never hear the end of it.

"See?" DeVon said. "No car."

"And no cute blond kidnappee chained to the wall either," Danny huffed with exasperation.

"Maybe he's in the house," Bradley said. He was chewing on a licorice stick again. Danny could smell it, and he could hear the kid gnawing on it like a cow ripping at a bale of hay.

"Or maybe he really is dead and Childers carted him off to get rid of the body," Danny muttered.

Luke couldn't believe his ears. "You're not buying into all this, are you?" He turned on DeVon and demanded point blank, "If you don't show me some real evidence in the next five seconds, I'm leaving, and I'm taking my easily hornswoggled lover with me."

"Wow," Bradley breathed, turning to DeVon. "They really are gay. Lovers, no less. You were right. I owe you fifty cents."

They all jumped straight up into the air when the garage door suddenly started clattering up into the ceiling: squeaking, rattling, groaning. It sounded like it hadn't been oiled for, like, eighty or ninety years.

As soon as the four of them finished executing their tandem leap of fear, they hunkered down against the wall of the garage and prayed to God they wouldn't be discovered by whoever it was who had just opened that damned door. Except for the garage, there was nothing nearby to hide behind. If whoever it was decided to walk around the corner, there was no way they wouldn't be spotted.

They waited for the sound of footsteps. Nothing. Then suddenly headlights swept across the fence behind them as a car turned in off the street. It rumbled straight up the driveway and steered into the garage while the four of them hunkered even lower. The radio was blasting disco music. Must be an oldie station, Danny thought. Disco music to Danny was somewhat akin to a guy in a powdered wig playing minuets on a clavichord. Ancient.

The motor and the radio went dead at the same moment. Two car doors squeaked open and they heard two pair of feet hitting the garage floor. One set of footfalls had a solid thump to them. The other set was kind of clicky and clacky. All four of them knew what that clicky-clacky sound meant. Whoever, the second person was, she was female, and she was wearing high heel shoes.

Their suspicions were confirmed when they heard a woman's high-pitched squeal of laughter.

"Ooh, Mike," the woman tittered. "You have a Bosu ball!" Danny didn't think she sounded like a card-carrying member of Mensa. "Oh, and a medicine ball too! You must work out a *lot*." And she tittered again. Bimbo city, Danny thought. He could feel Luke silently giggling beside him and flapping his wrist around in the air making fun of the poor broad.

They heard the boom of Mike Childers's masculine voice crooning right back at her. "Let's go in the house and I'll give you a tour of the rest of my balls."

The woman tittered again, and Danny couldn't blame her. He wouldn't mind taking that tour himself. Beside him, Luke was laughing so hard he was practically peeing in his pants. His face was so red from trying to do it silently that Danny wondered if he was about to have a stroke.

Bradley was holding his hands over his mouth trying not to laugh too. DeVon was just looking mad. This turn of events was not one he expected at all. If Childers was straight, then how the hell could he be a gay serial killer?

Danny gathered up his courage and peeked through the garage window. He saw Mr. Childers with his arm around a petite little thing in a miniskirt and stiletto heels, and from Danny's viewpoint, it didn't look like either one of them could keep their hands off the other.

Childers steered the woman through the garage door, hit a button on the wall as he passed, and the garage door started sliding back down behind them, still squeaking, rattling, and groaning, just like it had when it went up. As soon as the door banged shut, the garage light went out.

The four of them held their breath, still afraid Childers might for some ungodly reason peek around the corner of the garage and catch them lurking in the shadows. But their fears were for naught. The footsteps clattered up the walk to the back door of the house, mixed with the sounds of a few more feminine giggles and some sexy masculine cooing. It seemed Mr. Childers had some moves when it came to members of the opposite sex. They heard a tinkle of keys, the squeak of a door opening, and a second later the squeak and bang of a door closing.

The lovebirds were inside.

DeVon, Bradley, Danny, and Luke took that as a cue to breathe again.

But Luke was furious.

"I'm out of here. So is Danny. This guy isn't a killer. And he never *was* one."

Bradley scratched his head. "I'm not sure that sentence makes a whole lot of sense."

Luke grabbed Danny's arm and dragged him toward the back fence.

At that moment, they heard a cry that stopped them dead in their tracks. The cry did not come from inside Childers's house. It didn't come from his garage either. It came from somewhere else. All four of them seemed to be looking in different directions, trying to decide where the sound had actually originated.

A moment later, a sob could be heard. Just one short sob, then silence. Danny thought that truncated sob was absolutely the saddest sound he had ever heard in his life. Full of pain. Full of anguish. Full of terror. The way Luke's arm came out to pull him close, he figured it must have had the same effect on Luke. Danny ignored the shivers skittering up his back like mice with little cold feet. The truth hit him like a 2-by-4 to the back of the head.

"We're in the wrong place!" Danny hissed at Luke. "We've got the *wrong house!*"

"Holy shit!" DeVon said. "You're right. But whose house was it? Where did the crying *come* from?"

"I think it was over there," Bradley whispered, pointing north toward Luke's place.

"No," DeVon hissed. "It came from over there!" He pointed east.

"I thought it came from across the street," Luke interjected, not sounding too sure of himself even while he said it.

Then another scream tore through the night. Not a muffled sob this time. This time it was a scream guaranteed to wake the dead. It sounded like the screeching wail of a banshee on the Irish moors, and it made every hair on Danny's body stand up and do the Watusi. Holy heebie-jeebies! He could feel Luke flinch away from the sound as if he had been struck.

This time all four of them knew exactly where the scream came from. It came from Danny's backyard. Not more than ten feet away. Just on the other side of the fence!

They took one hesitant step toward the echo of that horrible screaming shriek when they heard the splash. It sounded like someone had dropped an anvil in Danny's swimming pool.

That woke them up. They ran straight for the hole in the fence. DeVon was the first to dive through. Then Bradley, then Luke. Danny struggled under the fence dead last, grunting, groaning, and cursing the damn cast on his leg with every move he made.

And then it started to rain.

AFTER crawling under the fence, Danny staggered to his feet, slapped his way through the bushes, and shook himself off. He froze when he heard a rumble in the sky. He looked up and blinked back the spattering of raindrops that hit his face. They were cold, but they actually felt pretty good. Bracing. It wasn't raining hard yet, but it felt like it wanted to. Thunder rumbled over their heads again. It sounded like a bowling ball ambling its weary way toward the pins after being dropped by a grunting six-year-old. Immediately afterward, a couple of sharper claps of thunder tore across the sky like distant artillery fire.

"Holy shit," DeVon said. "What now? We at war with Mexico?"

Luke answered while he gave Danny a hand dusting himself off. "That wasn't gunfire, you moron, it was thunder."

"Wow," DeVon said. "I don't think I've ever heard thunder before."

Danny shook his head and tsked. "Californians."

"Fuck the weather updates," Bradley said, "Where did that scream come from? DeVon, flash your light on the pool. Let's see what splashed. I heard something splash."

"Yeah," Luke said. "Me too."

Above the storm and the rain and the ever-increasing wind, they heard a hullabaloo taking place inside Danny's house. It was Granger, and he was barking with such ferocious energy he sounded like *six* dogs. Six *pissed off* dogs. He wanted the hell out! Now!

"Listen to Granger!" Danny said. "He's going batshit. I'm too slow with this cast. Here Bradley, take the house key and open the back door for Granger so he'll shut up."

For a change, Bradley did as he was told with a minimum of grousing. He was back in less than a minute with Granger hot on his heels. Granger pranced around the four of them, happy as a clam, bouncing and hopping, his tail going a mile a minute. The dog said hello to each of them in turn then returned to his master and hiked up his leg to pee on a rose bush while Luke patted his head. He peed for about a minute. He really had to go. When his business with the rose bush was finished, Granger went prancing around saying hello to everybody again. One happy dog.

The rain was coming down harder now. It felt like icy pinpricks against Danny's skin, and it was starting to plaster his long hair to the back of his neck. It wasn't bracing any more either. He was starting to shiver. Then Luke snuggled up beside him, stroking his arm, making his presence known, making Danny feel safe. And Danny forgot about the rain. Sometimes his love for Luke just filled him up so much nothing else could seem to get inside.

A flash of lightning illuminated the pool, and all four of them froze in horror. Even Granger stopped what he was doing and blinked. Danny leaned in closer to get a better look at the water, but by the time he did the lightning had blinked out and the pool was swallowed in shadow.

"Did you see that?" Bradley hissed. "Did you see the water? Did you see it?"

Luke sounded confused, his voice a stunned hush. "We saw it. At least I think we saw it."

"Go on, DeVon," Bradley urged. "Shine your flashlight at the pool. Shine it in the water. I wanna see it again."

"What a snot," DeVon muttered, but he did as he was asked. He shone the flashlight into the pool.

Into the pink, pink water of the pool.

Lightning flashed. Thunder grumbled across the sky once again. Granger cowered closer to the ground, trying to get away from the sound. No one was paying any attention to the sky *or* the dog. They were all staring at the water.

"Is that water—*pink*?" Bradley asked, whipping out another licorice whip and mindlessly stuffing it in his mouth. He couldn't take his eyes off the water. He was waiting for the lightning to flash again. He was *willing* the lightning to flash again. Just so he could see.

Danny opted for a more hands-on approach. He awkwardly clomped across the soggy lawn to an electrical box located by the back door. He opened it, found the proper button by memory since the outside lights were still off, and flicked the switch. The underwater pool lights came to life. Everyone stared at the water. The surface was speckled with raindrops. But it was the water *under* the surface that drew everyone's attention. For it was *under* the surface where the water was pinkest.

It was *there* where the water was mixed with blood.

It was no great mystery where the blood came from either. It came from the small still creature settling slowly and silently to the bottom of the pool. Lifeless. Eyes open and unblinking. Orange coat, lush and thick in life, swaying with the motion of the water as it sank into the depths. Long, elegant tail, unnervingly still. Four little feet, unmoving.

They were all watching when the animal came to rest at the bottom of the pool with a tiny jerk. Almost an audible, muted thud. It just lay there then, on the floor of the pool under six feet of water. Motionless, but for its lush coat still shifting and flowing with the stir of the currents surrounding it.

Luke was the first to find his voice. "My God, is that— Frederick?"

"No," Danny said, squatting at the edge of the water, easing his weight off his broken leg. It was aching again. Either from the damp or too much running around. He peered through the rain-spattered surface of the swimming pool to get a better look at the lifeless body resting on the bottom. "I think it's Frederick's girlfriend. Mr. Childers's cat. I don't know her name. Poor thing."

"Somebody threw her in," DeVon said. "And look at her neck. Somebody cut her throat first. They cut her throat then threw her into the pool."

It was true. Even as they watched, they could see a trickle of red still streaming into the pink water from the horrific gash under the creature's chin. That trickle of red made the water a little bit pinker, made it a little bit more—horrible.

Bradley echoed Danny. "Poor thing." He looked around the yard. He seemed to be paying extra close attention to the stand of hibiscus bushes by the back fence. They provided the only decent hiding place in the whole yard. If someone was there, that's where they would have to be, lurking in the shadows, watching them. Watching them.

Bradley shivered, and it wasn't the icy rain that made him shiver either. For the first time tonight, it was real fear.

"Let's turn the pool lights off," he whispered, hugging himself against the rain.

"He's right," Luke said. "We're too exposed out here."

So Danny sloshed a clumsy path back across the wet grass and flicked the pool lights off. The four of them were once again sheathed in darkness. This time the darkness felt like an ally. They found themselves dreading the flashes of lightning which exposed them every time they streaked across the sky above their heads.

Luke was watching the fence now too. Just like Bradley. But not the fence in the back. And not the shorter picket fence that abutted the west side of the yard where his own house stood either. His attention was centered solely on the east fence. It was picketed just like the one by his house. Waist-high. There was a hedge on this side of it, also just like the hedge on the opposite side of the yard. These were the hedges Danny had just trimmed. The east fence, the one Luke was now staring at, was the closest to the pool. Someone could have easily hurled the cat over the fence and into the pool. They wouldn't have had to set foot in Danny's yard at all.

Luke gripped Danny's arm. With his other hand he pointed to the house beyond the fence. "Who lives over there?"

"Dinkens," Danny said. "Dinkens and his wife. Why? You think they might have heard something?"

"No," Luke said in a jittery voice that got everyone's attention. Even Bradley and DeVon tore their eyes away from the pool and gazed at Luke for a change. Then they followed his gaze to the fence and the house beyond.

"That's where creepoid lives," DeVon said in a whisper. "He ran us off once. Remember, Brad?"

"Yeah. He's got a big fat wife. She's really nice, but I haven't seen her lately."

Danny blinked. Come to think of it, he hadn't seen the woman lately either. Didn't mean much, he supposed. But still. It was curious.

"Maybe we should go have a word with Mr. Dinkens." It was Danny who said the words.

"Think he's up?" Luke asked.

In a hushed voice, Danny said, "That's the funny thing. Mr. Dinkens is *always* up."

He and Luke shared a look. Then they shared another look.

"Where's your hammer?" Danny asked.

Luke looked down at himself. He patted his pockets. "I don't know. I guess I lost it."

He looked at Danny. "Where's your bat?"

Danny stared at his two empty hands like they were the strangest things he had ever seen in his life. Good grief. He must have lost the bat when he went under the fence.

He looked back at Luke. "Well, aren't we a couple of nimrods."

"Pretty much," Bradley mumbled.

At that very moment, there came a silent hush between thunderclaps. Again they could hear the gentle patter of raindrops hitting the pool. And just as Danny was wiping the rain from his eyes and brushing the sodden hair away from his face, they heard the sob again.

They all heard it. Every one of them.

It was just a weak, weak sob, as if whoever had let it out had just about used up their very last ounce of strength. Once again, Danny thought it was the saddest sound he had ever heard. It was so sad he thought he felt his heart crack open just a little bit to hear it.

This time there was no question where the sound came from. It came from the east.

It came from Mr. Dinkens's house.

Granger froze at the side of the pool, and slowly, step by eerie step, he approached the east fence. His hackles were standing straight up and he moved like a zombie. In slow motion. Stalking. Careful. Tense yet fearless. His fangs were bared. His sodden tail hung straight down to the ground. For a dog who had been happy as hell just a few minutes earlier, he was now dead serious. You could see it in his stance. Granger wasn't fooling around.

"Someone's there," Luke said. "Just on the other side of the fence. I heard a footstep on gravel."

All four of them ducked, crouching at the edge of the pool. They were glad now that Danny had turned the pool lights off. Really glad. Because this time they knew there was really something out there to fear.

And this time they were pretty sure they knew where to find it.

It was then that Frederick came tearing through the hedge with a caterwauling screech. Four hearts almost stopped dead when the cat tore between their legs, dashed across the yard, and flew through Danny's pet door with a bang.

In the shocked hush, it was DeVon who spoke first.

"Damn, I think I just had me a heart attack."

CHAPTER FOURTEEN
BREAKING IN

DINKENS'S house was dark. If there was a light burning anywhere, it didn't show from the outside. It was a ramshackle, two-story monstrosity that must have been the height of architectural chic a century or so ago, but it was pretty much an eyesore now. Unkempt. Bedraggled. It had not seen a new coat of paint for decades. The shingles on the roof, what could be seen of them two floors up, were twisted and brittle from their never-ending exposure to the hot California sun. When lightning streaked across the sky behind the roof, Danny thought those poor blistered roofing shingles looked like ragged curls of shaved chocolate strewn across a butt-ugly cake. He wondered if they still repelled water, or was Dinkens inside right now, frantically positioning pots and pans under a thousand leaks, trying to stay afloat in the storm? Looming into view every now and then in those intermittent flashes of lightning, the house bore an amazing resemblance to Norman Bates's childhood home on the hill behind his nasty little motel.

Staring at the house as he squinted through the rain, Danny was surprised he had never noticed the resemblance before. Jeez, the joint was creepy as hell.

And there was no doubt whatsoever the sob they heard before the damn cat came tearing between their legs scaring them all to death had come from that house. It must have.

"Should we call the cops?" Bradley asked in a quivery voice. The rain was really cold now. It was making the kid's teeth chatter, although he was putting on a brave face about it so no one would think he was a wuss.

Luke was the first to answer, thinking of Danny and Danny's dad. Worried about them above all else. "No. Not yet. Let's do some snooping first." He spoke in a whisper. The four of them were kneeling at the edge of the pool between a couple of lawn chairs. Trying to stay low. Trying not to be visible in those sparks of lightning that seemed to light up the whole world every now and then. The rain helped hide them. And the darkness too. But still, whoever had flung the dead cat into the pool not more than two minutes ago couldn't be very far away. No point making their presence known if they didn't have to.

Luke brushed his fingers along Danny's cheek to get his attention. Even with the rain and the storm and the fear and the rattled nerves, he felt desire blossom up at the feel of Danny's skin. Damn, he'd be glad when they were back in bed cuddling. Or maybe doing more than cuddling. "Babe, we need to check the place out. Dinkens's place. I want you to stay here."

"No," Danny said, trying to balance himself on his one good knee while the leg with the cast stuck straight out in front of him. He waited until he was sure Luke was looking at him. They were both dripping wet and shivering, but Danny wanted Luke to know how determined he was. He needed Luke to understand that if either of them went anywhere, they were *both* going. "I want to help the Strickland guy, too, but I also want to make sure you stay safe. I'm coming with you. Don't bother arguing, because I'm coming. I don't care what you say."

"Well, poop," Luke said, fighting a grin. "Guess you're coming." He couldn't honestly say he was sorry.

Danny stood up with a groan and took one clumsy step toward the hedge. He stumbled to a stop when he heard a door click quietly closed somewhere inside Dinkens's creepyass house. He couldn't really tell if it was an inside door or an outside door, but somehow the sound of that unseen door snapping closed brought Danny's father to mind. Danny could see his dad's earnest face hovering in front of him in the shadows. "Stay out of trouble, Son. Don't do anything to make me ashamed."

His father had never really said those words, not exactly, but they were implied. They were most certainly implied. Maybe Danny imagined those words because of the guilt he felt over the trouble he had *already* caused his dad. Would Danny's actions on this night be like the snapping closed of a door between him and his dad? Was he about to irreparably sever their budding relationship just as it was getting good and started? That's the last thing Danny wanted. The very last.

For the hundredth time in the last two weeks, he stared down at the ankle monitor and the little green light blinking in the middle of it.

"What is it?" Luke asked. "I thought you were coming." He was ushering the kids together, trying to get them both moving in the right direction. He pointed to where he wanted them to go, and they went. It was funny how well they took orders when they were scared shitless.

"I—don't know," Danny stammered. He sounded angry. Angry with himself more than anything, and suddenly uncertain about what he should do.

In a strobe of lightning he saw everyone waiting for him. DeVon and Bradley were hunkered down beside the hedge now, ten or fifteen feet away. They were soaking wet and miserable and huddled as close to each other as they could get without maybe embarrassing themselves. Danny was pretty sure they didn't want any gay innuendoes thrown in *their* direction, although they certainly didn't hesitate to toss them around at other people. They were looking back at Danny and Luke now where they squatted on the wet grass, wondering what the hell was taking them so long, but they didn't want to yell. They didn't want to make any noise. After all, there was a serial killer (maybe) just on the other side of this hedge. No point giving the bastard a heads-up that he was about to run headlong into his worst nightmare. Them.

Yeah, right. Bradley couldn't even *think* that thought with a straight face. If anybody was scared here, it was *them,* not Dinkens. And Bradley damn well knew it. Just because he was only eleven years old didn't mean he was stupid.

Luke needed windshield wipers on his glasses. He couldn't see anything. That wouldn't do. He yanked them off his face and stuffed them in the pocket of his shorts. He wasn't doing needlepoint here. He just needed to see trees and houses and serial killers and stuff.

He pulled Danny into his arms. It was easier to speak softly that way. And also because he simply liked having Danny in his arms.

"You don't have to leave the yard, Danny. I'll be okay. I'll scream like a foghorn if I need you. I promise. And no matter what happens, we won't call the cops until we know for sure Strickland is in there and Dinkens is holding him hostage. We're just going to look around. No confrontations. Deal? Oh, and if it's the kids you're worried about, don't. I'll watch them too. God knows somebody needs to. Their parents don't seem to be up to the task."

Danny laughed, but it was just for show. He didn't really *feel* like laughing. What he felt like doing was grabbing Luke's hand and pulling him as far away from this place as he could. Back into the house, back to bed, back to the place where he could have him just the way he wanted him. Naked, eager, trembling with desire; not frightened and dripping wet and shivering from the cold. Danny just wanted them both to forget about it all. The killings; everything.

But that was impossible. The blond kid was in that house. Maybe. Charles Strickland. That decaying human finger Bradley carried around in his back pocket came from someone. The odds of it being anyone *other* than Charles Strickland were pretty slim. If Childers wasn't holding the guy hostage, and it was certainly starting to look like he wasn't, then who was? Dinkens? Was that possible? Childers sure as hell didn't kill his own cat and throw it in Danny's pool. Besides, they had just watched him go into his house with the bimbo in the high heels only minutes before it happened.

But Dinkens was home. Dinkens was close. And Dinkens was a creep. That should be enough evidence for anybody, Danny thought. It was beginning to be enough for him.

That's why he didn't want Luke anywhere near the guy. Especially not without Danny there to look after him.

But Danny had his dad to think about too. And their future together, him and his dad.

Crap. Moral dilemmas were a pain in the butt.

Granger gave himself a shake to remove some of the rainwater from his coat. He shook it all over Danny and Luke, getting them wetter than they already were, if that were even possible. It got them moving too.

"Okay," Danny said. "I'll wait here. I'll give you ten minutes. No more."

Luke grinned. "You're not wearing a watch."

Danny harrumphed. "Fine. I'll count off the seconds in my head. Then I'll go in the house and use your phone to call the cops. I can't call out on my phone. Judge's orders."

"You don't really have to call the cops, Danny. You can just stick your foot over the hedge and they'll be here before you know it. Every cop in town."

"True." Danny took a deep breath, shivered from the cold, pulled Luke tight into his arms, and said, "If you see Strickland, come right back out. We'll let the cops handle it. If you get stuck, or if Dinkens starts anything, scream as loud as you can, and I'll get the police's attention one way or another." Then he frowned. It was a really pitiful frown, what with his shivering and with all the rain dribbling down his face and his long wet hair slathered to his cheeks and forehead. "I feel like a coward not going with you."

Luke kissed Danny's frown to see if it would go away. It didn't. Not entirely. "You're not a coward, babe. You're backup. If this were a movie, you'd be the guy watching Bruce Willis's ass."

A dreamy look crossed Danny's face. "Well, *that* puts it all in a pleasantly new perspective." And when Luke shook a warning fist in Danny's face with a grin, Danny hastily added, "Of course, I'd rather be watching *your* ass. Not that Bruce doesn't have a fine posterior and all. For an old guy."

"That's better," Luke said, leering and waggling his eyebrows in a blink of lightning. Then he gave Danny a quick kiss. Before Danny knew what was happening, Luke was gone from his side, duck-walking across the wet grass, keeping low so he couldn't be seen from the other side of the hedge. He joined Bradley and DeVon at the edge of the lawn, and Danny had to grin at the two kids when they pulled out of each other's arms just before Luke got there. Danny supposed at their age it was better to suffer hypothermia than be thought a fruit loop.

Well, they'd grow out of that one day. Maybe. Danny certainly did.

THE picket fence that abutted Danny's east hedge was only three feet high. So was the hedge. There was no gate, but Luke figured they wouldn't need one.

Three heads peeked over the hedge. Luke, Bradley, DeVon. They all three wiped the rain out of their eyes at the same time, almost as if their movements were choreographed.

"See anything?" Luke hissed.

"Just rain," DeVon hissed back.

"And one ugly-ass house," hissed Bradley. They all three giggled.

"Come on then," Luke said, assuming the mantle of leadership whether the kids wanted him to or not. Age carried a few rewards with it. So did height.

Luke was the first to fight his way through the hedge and straddle the fence. Once that was accomplished, he offered a helping hand to Bradley and DeVon. They seemed grateful for the help. While the fence was only three feet tall, that's a pretty good straddle for an eleven-year-old. And the points on the picket fence were sharp as hell. Neither of the boys wanted to slip in the mud and find *those* things crammed up their butts.

Safely across the fence, they once again hunkered low and waited for the lightning to show them which way to go.

They didn't have to wait long. The lightning struck so hard and so near, they almost all keeled over in a dead faint. Thunder boomed out in a horrendous crash about two seconds later.

"That was *close*," Luke hissed when the sky finally stopped grumbling.

"Look," DeVon said, pointing toward the corner of Dinkens's house where a downspout was shooting water across the yard like a water cannon. "There's a little back porch back there. Let's get in out of the rain."

"Okay," Luke said. Reaching out he took both boys' hands. Stooping low they ran across the gravel driveway, which made way too much noise under their feet, and then they sloshed through a lawn of mud since there wasn't any grass on it. The porch was about two feet off the ground. There was no railing, but it did have a roof. They carefully stepped up out of the rain, praying to God the boards beneath their feet wouldn't squeak. They did, but not much. The roar of the storm would surely cover the sound.

By this time, Luke was sorely regretting not donning shoes like the kids had told him to. His bare feet were freezing, and the gravel in the driveway had felt like chunks of glass underfoot.

It was nice being out of the rain for a change, although it didn't warm them up much. The wind swept around the back of the house like it had just blown off a glacier. The porch was covered with a tin roof and the rain struck it with such force, and made so much noise doing it, the three didn't even try to talk to each other. They just cowered together against the back of the house as far from the door as they could get and considered their options.

Thankfully, Dinkens didn't have any exterior lights on. There was a fixture for a porch light stuck on the wall above where Luke was cowering, and looking up at it now, Luke saw there wasn't even a light bulb in it. Well, good. That made their job a little easier.

An unlatched screen door was hung over the back door, and it banged and rattled in the wind. There was a window onto the porch, but a heavy curtain was drawn across it. No light could be seen coming from the inside. If anyone tried to look out, Luke would see the curtain move. Adversely, the damn curtain prevented them from peeking into the interior of the house to see what was going on in there, if anything. There was no window in the door.

Luke regretted not asking Danny before they split up if Dinkens had a dog they should be worried about. He figured he'd try to ask the kids, if they ever got far enough away from that rattling screen door and thundering tin roof where they could carry on a conversation without having to yell.

It dawned on Luke that if Charles Strickland sobbed now, they would never be able to hear it. Hell, the guy could scream bloody murder ten feet away and they might never hear a thing.

They had to get inside the house.

While Bradley and DeVon watched with wide, frightened eyes, Luke slowly peeled open the unlatched screen door and ever so gently tested the door knob on the back door. He could almost hear the kids breathe a sigh of relief when Luke learned it was locked.

Luke looked out into the rain with the kids crowded up behind him.

They would just have to find a different way in.

DANNY watched Luke and the boys wade through the hedge and hop the fence, then he limped up to the hedge at the same spot where they had just been and peered across into Dinkens's yard. He just glimpsed the tail end of the three of them running for the back of Dinkens's house. After they rounded the corner, Danny couldn't see them anymore. He was holding onto Granger's collar, and the dog wasn't too happy about it. Danny couldn't tell if Granger wanted to follow Luke or if he just wanted to get out of the rain. Funny that those were pretty much the only two things Danny wanted right then as well.

Unfortunately, the poor dog would just have to forget it. Danny needed Granger there with him. For moral support if nothing else. Plus the dog couldn't be trusted not to bark at the wrong time and expose Luke and the kids to danger. They were dealing with a serial killer after all. This wasn't a church picnic.

Danny's broken leg was really killing him now. It was all the moisture in the air, he supposed. Plus his cast was soaked. It felt kind of funky inside. Danny wondered if it was about to disintegrate in the rain. Surely it was sturdier than that. His monitor was still blinking green. Apparently a little rain didn't affect that thing much. The monitor felt cold and clammy against his skin, like someone had snatched a dead fish out of the fridge and wrapped it around his ankle.

Danny pulled the wet dog closer, and they huddled together against the lashing rain with their faces in the hedge, waiting to see what would happen next. He would hate to do it to his father, but if things went bad on the other side of the fence, Danny was bound and determined to jump the fucking thing and help Luke out. Screw the cops and screw the consequences.

Luke was his lover. If anything happened to Luke, Danny wasn't sure he'd have the strength to go on. He had never really known before how powerful love can be, but lordy, he knew it now.

"It'll be okay, boy," he crooned into Granger's wet ear. "Luke'll be back soon. He'll be back soon."

And the two of them, man and dog, settled in to wait. They ignored the rain as best they could.

Danny thought about fetching an umbrella, but he didn't want to leave the hedge even for two seconds in case Luke called for help.

He'd just have to do without it.

On the bright side, Danny figured if the four of them actually solved the killer case for the cops, then surely that would go a long way to making the judge a little more forgiving when it came to Danny breaking house arrest and making that little red light go off.

At least he hoped it would. You never knew with judges.

BACK in the rain, Luke and the kids shivered and groused and tried not to break their necks as they traversed the alien landscape of Dinkens's backyard. Luke figured the guy must never have thrown anything away in his life. There were more derelicts back here than there were on skid row. A derelict washing machine, the old ringer type, with weeds growing out of the tub. A derelict pickup truck propped up on concrete blocks that looked like it hadn't seen the highway in thirty years. There were three or four derelict TVs scattered around, and more chairs and tables with broken legs tossed here and there than you could shake a stick at. The guy was hard on his furniture.

DeVon cussed when he got tripped up in a tangle of chicken wire and landed on his hands and knees in the mud. Two seconds later, Luke cussed another blue streak when he stubbed his bare toe on the tipped-over base of a concrete birdbath, which didn't budge an inch when he banged it. The bowl of the birdbath was nowhere in sight. Luke was pretty sure his toe hit high *C* on impact.

Dinkens had a garage back here that was about to topple over. It didn't look like he ever used it since he had so much crap piled up in front of the door.

Moving closer to the house, hopefully to get a little out of the rain, they wormed their way along a back wall, trying to see where they were going in the scattered flashes of lightning. DeVon had lost his flashlight at some point during the proceedings. When a particularly extended stretch of darkness left them blind a little longer than usual, Luke once again stubbed his toe on something big and flat and laid out directly in his path right beside the house.

He fell forward in the blackness, expecting to feel his hands hit the mud, but what he hit was something wooden. He hissed with pain when his already skinned knee came down on it hard. He quickly scrambled around trying to get himself back up since he didn't understand what it was he had landed on.

Then a streak of lightning solved the mystery.

It was the trapdoor into what must be a basement or a fruit cellar. It sat at an angle against the side of the house. The boards were twisted and warped, the paint all flaky from a century of sun and the two doors clattered and banged when Luke landed on them like they were barely holding themselves together.

"Wow," DeVon whispered, once he got a good look at it. "Is that thing locked?"

And peering closer, Danny saw it was. An old Yale combination lock was stuck through a rusty hasp. The hasp was nailed into the wood with a couple of huge staples that had worked themselves about halfway out over the years. It didn't look as if the trapdoor was ever used, since it was buried under a mound of old flower pots and crap.

Looking up at the windows of the house to make sure no curtains were moving and no one was watching, Luke gave the lock a tug, and damned if it didn't come off in his hand, hasp and all.

DeVon and Bradley immediately started clearing the top of the trapdoor of all the junk piled on it as quietly as they could. In less than a minute, they were done.

It was a double door. Each side swung up and out of the way. Carefully, Luke gripped the edge of the side closest to him and lifted. With a squeak, the door opened up. And as soon as it did, the three of them gave a gasp of surprise. Quickly, Luke lowered the door back down.

They gazed at each other in the rain.

"There was a light on," Bradley hissed.

"Yeah," DeVon said. "You think the dude's in there?"

There had been a light in the basement indeed. A dim one, but a light. Luke had just caught a glimpse of muddy concrete steps leading down to a dirty landing before he decided to shut the trapdoor again and think things over before proceeding.

So that's what he did. And while he was doing it, he was trying not to drown in the rain. They were positioned directly under a break in the rain gutter two floors up on the eave of the house. It was a little like standing under Angel Falls in South America without a fucking umbrella.

Luke tried to listen. Were there any noises coming from inside the house? Then he realized he was being ridiculous. In the first place, if Dinkens had heard them at the trapdoor, he would be here by now raising hell. Then Luke realized the man could be in there with a jack hammer digging a trap for them in the concrete floor of the basement, and they probably wouldn't be able to hear it.

Dinkens must be in some other part of the house. Luke wasn't sure why Dinkens would leave a light burning in the basement if he wasn't going to be down there, but then he thought, *Yes, maybe I do.* And that thought made a shiver go up his spine.

"Stay behind me," Luke said to the boys, and their nerves were so jangled by now they did what Luke asked without even making faces about it.

Luke could feel one of the boys, he thought maybe it was DeVon, holding onto the tail of his shirt as he bent over one more time and lifted the trapdoor far enough for them to sneak underneath it. When they were all three hunkered down on the concrete steps, five feet below ground level, Luke eased the trapdoor closed over their heads.

They were in the house. And it smelled terrible.

CHAPTER FIFTEEN
WHO'S RESCUING WHOM?

DANNY squinted through the rain and saw a light blink on in an upstairs window of Dinkens's house. Just as quickly, it blinked back off again. Maybe Dinkens had fetched something from upstairs.

Danny figured it would be getting light soon. It must be four thirty in the morning. It looked like it was going to be one of those days when the rain never stops. He was surprised Bradley or DeVon's folks hadn't called out the National Guard by now, trying to find their two recalcitrant offspring and drag them home to have their heinies tanned. Danny supposed the kids had simply hoodwinked their parents into thinking they were all innocent and cuddly, sleeping over at their best friend's house, safely tucked away in their best friend's bed. God, parents are dim.

Danny's leg was hurting so badly now, he simply had to sit his ass down in the cold, wet grass and stick the cast straight out in front of him. It didn't help much, but it did ease the pain a bit. The problem was, from here he couldn't see over the hedge.

He wormed his way into a place where the hedge was sparse and sidled up to the picket fence. He was freezing, and his ass was in the mud, but it did keep a little of the rain off his head, being buried in the hedge like he was. An added bonus was that now he could stick his face up to the slats in the fence and look out over Dinkens's shithole of a lawn without any danger of being seen.

Granger squeezed in alongside him and laid himself out across Danny's lap, as if Danny wasn't uncomfortable enough.

Still, it was good to have a little company.

He stroked Granger's wet coat and twiddled his wet ears and wondered what Luke was doing while Granger washed Danny's face with a friendly tongue.

He and Granger both flinched when a really close crash of lightning scared the bejesus out of them.

"Come on, Luke. Come on, come on, come on."

Danny closed his eyes, suffered the rain, barely tolerated the lightning, and waited, glad Granger was there beside him. But wishing it was Luke instead.

And praying to God that Luke was still safe.

LUKE and the two boys cowered on the concrete steps with the big old trapdoor looming over their heads. The trapdoor shut out some of the racket from the storm pummeling the world outside, but not all of it. They could still hear the water gushing from the broken rain gutter two stories up at the top of the house, and they still cringed at the occasional boom of thunder rattling across the heavens. At least they were out of the rain and wind. Or most of it. A few drops of ice-cold drizzle still dribbled through the cracks in the door, landing on their heads. Luke decided Dinkens's house needed a hell of a lot more than weather stripping to get it up to snuff. It needed some major renovation. The place was a wreck.

Luke shook himself off as best he could and looked around.

A few steps down was a doorway, which presumably led into the basement. And it was exactly that. A doorway. An opening. There was no door in it. There was a glow of ambient light coming from somewhere inside. It illuminated a carpet of dirt and leaves and twigs which coated the stairs going down, all the detritus that had sifted through the ratty trapdoors over the years and come to rest on the concrete steps beneath.

Luke held his finger to his lips to let everyone know to be quiet, as if that was really necessary. He slowly descended the steps with DeVon and Bradley scrunched up behind him, trying to see over his shoulders. They both had hold of his shirttail now. Luke felt like a mother possum lugging her offspring around on her back.

Before stepping through the doorway, Luke peeked around in both directions. Satisfied there were no murderers waiting to jump him just inside, he stepped on through. He was so tense he had to remind himself to breathe.

There was just enough light to navigate by.

The basement looked like a million other basements. Concrete floor, unfinished brick walls, little rectangular windows high on the walls, unglassed but screened over, letting the cold air inside. Crap was stacked everywhere. Boxes, furniture, old bicycles, trunks, cedar chests, clothing simply thrown in jumbled, mildewy piles. There were enough cobwebs hanging from the ceiling to knit a couple of sweaters.

The place smelled musty and fetid, like damp soil and mouse droppings and food left out to rot. It was an unwholesome reek that made Luke's toes curl. A stench, really. Luke found himself breathing through his mouth so he wouldn't have to smell it. The air was cold too. Those little open windows high in the wall, and the concrete floor and brick walls, made the place feel like a dungeon in some old Errol Flynn movie: a place where screams might be heard at all times of the day and night, and tortured souls were offered up to Jesus on a regular basis. A bad place. A place where nobody in their right mind would ever want to spend any time.

In one corner of the dank, dim basement, an ancient furnace stood guard. It was silent and dead. A mute, looming presence, like a stone stele in a forgotten Mayan temple, unseen by man for hundreds of years but still spooky as hell. Luke got the impression the furnace had been turned off a long time ago and the pilot light never relit. He wondered what Dinkens used for heat. Space heaters, he supposed. He also wondered how many rats were using the furnace for a condo. Dozens, probably.

The area around the furnace was the only floor space that wasn't buried in trash and piled high with junk. It looked as if someone had tried to keep the area clear. Looking closer, Luke saw the dust on the floor had been disturbed, as if a thousand footsteps had wandered through it in the very same spot. It reminded him of a path. Or a game trail. And the moment Luke thought *those* words, another shiver shot up his spine.

Game trail.

The light that dimly illuminated the broad, sprawling basement was shining from somewhere behind the ancient furnace. And the moment Luke realized that, he also heard the moan.

That, too, came from behind the furnace. He suddenly found his heart stuck up in his throat like a rag in a tailpipe. He could barely breathe. And oddly enough, there was also a tiny tingle of exhilaration strumming away at his nerve endings. My God, he thought, maybe we've really done it. Maybe we've really found the poor blond guy who was snatched from a supermarket parking lot and never seen again by anyone who meant to do him any good. My God. Maybe they were actually going to succeed in saving the life of a young man named Charles Strickland. They'd be heroes.

If they survived.

"Wait here," Luke whispered to the boys, his voice little more than a croak.

"Fuck that," both boys whispered right back.

So the three of them headed for the furnace on stealthy feet, not sure what they would find on the other side, but each and every one of them had an idea of what they *might* find. And they were not looking forward to the discovery. Or maybe they were.

Halfway there, Bradley tugged on Luke's shirt to make him stop. When he did, Luke saw what Bradley was pointing at. There was a staircase climbing the wall to the right, way off in the shadows at the other end of the basement. It was obviously the way to the upper part of the house. If Dinkens were to catch them down here, that was the way he would have to come.

"Keep your eyes on it," Luke whispered.

The boys nodded. Words unnecessary.

Again, they approached the old furnace. The closer they came to it, the brighter grew the ambient light behind it. And the stronger the stench of rot and filth grew as well.

Whatever they were about to discover behind that damn furnace, it wouldn't be good. They all knew that as well as they knew their own names.

They took another step forward. Luke was just about to reach out and steady himself on the side of the cold furnace before walking around to see what was behind it, when DeVon gave a gasp that almost scared Luke to death. Bradley suddenly flung his arms around Luke's waist and held on for dear life. Whatever had startled DeVon had startled the crap out of Bradley too.

Luke turned. "What is it?" His voice was a mere breath of sound in the dusty old basement. He couldn't have spoken any louder if he wanted to. Fear seemed to be holding his vocal cords in a tight little fist, letting nothing out of his mouth but an occasional squeak. *"What is it?"* he hissed again.

DeVon and Bradley both pointed to something huddled by the wall off to their left. Whatever it was, it was dumped inside an old metal bathtub, the oblong kind. There was a frayed and mildewed bath towel, filled with holes, flung over the top of the pile, but it seemed to have slipped to the side, exposing what was underneath.

It took Luke about two seconds to realize this was where the majority of the stench emanated from.

Without his glasses on, Luke had to step closer to see what it was.

He fumbled for his glasses in his pocket, and no sooner had he slipped them over his nose than Bradley went apeshit.

His voice was more high-pitched than Luke had ever heard it. The kid sounded like a rat squealing in terror. "Holy shit, it's her! It's her! Mrs. Dinkens! It's her!"

The kid was trying to run back the way they had just come, but Luke held onto him. He was more afraid of what might happen to Bradley off on his own in this creepy damn house than he was afraid of whatever it was that was staring him in the face from that rusty old washtub.

DeVon was strangely quiet. Luke looked down at him. The kid was gripping Luke's arm and his eyeballs were as big as dinner plates. He was staring at whatever was piled up under that bath towel like he had locked eyes with Medusa. He couldn't have looked away if he wanted to.

Luke decided since both kids seemed to know what this pile of mysterious crap was, or *who* it was, then maybe he should figure it out too. So he leaned in close. When his eyes focused, he sucked in a great gulp of air and stumbled backward.

It *was* a woman. An obese woman. She was sitting nude in rolls of fat, squeezed into that old tub like three pounds of butter in a one-pound container. She had a sprinkling of snow or sugar or flour sprinkled all over her that looked kind of silly at first. Then Luke realized what it was. And it wasn't a raggedy bath towel over her head and shoulders.

It was lime. A coating of lime.

She was being decomposed. Set there to rot and disappear forever.

DeVon's words seemed to come crawling out of his mouth unbidden. Luke had never seen a more stunned look on a human face before in his life.

"It *is* Mrs. Dinkens. She used to make us cookies." And after a moment of silence when Luke could hear nothing but his own heart clamoring around inside his chest, DeVon added softly, "He's killed her too."

Luke felt bile crawl up into his throat, and now it was his turn to fight the urge to run, but before he could form a rational enough thought to battle the urge, a trembling voice spoke out from behind the furnace. The voice was barely audible. A male voice. It was how Luke imagined a voice would sound if it had screamed the very vocal cords out of its throat after hours, days, weeks, of torture and pain.

The voice spoke two simple words.

"Help me."

Now Luke *had* to grab the side of the furnace just to prevent himself from toppling over. His legs were jelly. The power of gravity seemed to have suddenly increased because the two boys had such a grip on him it felt like they were dragging him down through a hole in the floor, never to be seen again.

When Luke was just beginning to think maybe it was a good idea for the three of them to run after all, a rattling cough stayed Luke's feet. It came from behind the furnace. The cough was so filled with pain, so infused with *horror,* that it made Luke's eyes water in sympathy just to hear it. It also rooted him to the floor where he stood.

It took Luke a minute to get a grip on his fear, but when he did, he put his arms around both boys and pulled them close. That gave him courage. And it gave the boys courage too. Together they stepped determinedly around the rusty old furnace. And then, together, they drew in a collective gasp.

There was a little room back there. New concrete blocks had been laid to the ceiling in a square about ten feet by ten feet. There was a door into this tiny room, but it was flung wide at the moment.

The room was a cage.

Charles Strickland lay naked, handcuffed by one hand to a large iron ring buried in the concrete wall. He was filthy and looked nothing like the handsome young man Luke had seen on the news that night in his cap and gown, with the sparkle of a bright future glimmering in his eyes. This guy wasn't anything like that guy. This guy had been through hell. Clearly. He had a filthy, bloody bandage loosely wrapped around one hand, and he cradled that hand close to his chest. The pain of his missing finger, his mutilated hand, was etched across his face.

Luke could see the ribs poking through the skin of his chest. He looked like he hadn't eaten anything in a month. But that was impossible. He had only disappeared a few days ago.

The young man sat on the cold stone floor, his bare buttocks resting in a smear of blood.

As Luke stared at him, speechless, Charles Strickland stretched out a filthy hand and said, "Water. Please. I'm so thirsty."

Then Strickland stared at the two boys still clinging to Luke like they were hanging from a cliff. Strickland seemed to have never seen such interesting creatures in his life. Luke found himself wondering if the young man was still sane.

"I was expecting a SWAT team," Strickland croaked in his pain-addled voice, "not a fourth grade field trip." The sound of his voice was almost lost beneath the raging of the storm.

"Hey!" DeVon countered, offended to the core. "We're in the *fifth* grade."

"Hush," Luke said. He dropped to his knees in front of Strickland and the young man turned his wide, emotionless eyes to him as Luke tried to figure out how to extract his hand from the manacle.

"Where's the key?" Luke gently asked, cupping Strickland's chin in his fingers, trying to keep him focused, trying to make him understand. "If you tell me where the key is, I can get you out of here."

And behind them, at the base of the stairs, a voice echoed loud and strong through the fetid air of the musty old basement.

"I assume you're talking about *this* key."

And amid a jangle of metal, Luke and the two boys spun to face the voice.

And the man who had uttered the words.

EVEN being cold and miserable and aching and hungry and worried to death about Luke's safety, Danny somehow still managed to doze off as he sat there under the hedge. The storm raged around him; the ice-cold rain continually pelted his head; and Granger was spread out across his lap like a wet carpet, but none of it mattered. Danny was sound asleep. Only when his subconscious mind thought of Luke, out there somewhere, maybe facing danger, did Danny snap to attention and wake the hell up.

The minute he did, he peeked through the slats of the picket fence into Dinkens's yard, and saw a shadow flitting along in front of the tumbledown garage in the back. And it was only because of a lucky flash of lightning at exactly the right moment he saw even *that*.

Granger woke up when he sensed Danny grow tense beneath him. He crawled off Danny's lap and Danny groaned as the blood shot back into his cramped legs.

"Holy shit, Granger! You've crippled me!"

He rubbed his legs and looked once again through the picket fence.

The shadow was gone.

Danny looked around to make sure no one was watching, and with another groan, he grabbed the fence and pulled himself to his feet. As the blood dribbled down into his blood-starved arteries, Danny thought he had never felt such pain in his life. Even breaking his leg didn't compare to it.

Finally, after a couple of minutes, the pain turned to relief and he was able to stand it. The pins and needles went away a couple of minutes after that.

He gazed around. First at his yard, then at Dinkens's yard, then toward the street out front. He saw no one. Not a soul.

He awkwardly flung his broken leg across the picket fence first, then he followed it with his good leg. Then he reached back over the fence and scooped his arms under Granger and lifted him over to set him at his feet.

"Stay!" Danny commanded, and Granger stood by his side, although he was trembling in his eagerness to run. Danny had never realized until that moment just how well trained Luke's dog really was. Well, good. It would make things easier.

"Heel, boy," Danny whispered, and together they moved as quietly as they could through the storm, hugging the fence, staying low, heading for Dinkens's backyard.

Danny was really limping now. He couldn't help wondering if he had done permanent damage to his broken leg. Not to mention the fact his bare feet were killing him too. Christ, sometimes he had no sense at all, coming out here barefoot and all.

He stuck his head around the corner of Dinkens's house and saw the back porch. He headed for it without even thinking, wanting to get out of the rain. At least for a couple of minutes. The lightning was still flashing and the thunder was still banging around up in the sky, but Danny thought maybe the storm was beginning to taper off.

He stepped up onto the porch with a grunt and Granger hopped up beside him, limber as a fox.

Granger immediately crossed the porch and stood staring off the other side.

Danny tilted his head and listened. He wasn't sure, but he thought he could hear someone banging around over there in the shadows. He wondered how close he could get to them before he was spotted and all hell broke loose.

The thing was, that shadow he had seen crossing in front of Dinkens's garage earlier, well, that wasn't Luke. No way. And it wasn't either of the kids either. Danny was sure it wasn't.

But the funny thing was—it was too short to be Dinkens too.

So just who the hell was it stumbling around in the dark out here with the rest of them?

And why did Danny have a really bad feeling gnawing away at his guts about the way this whole damn night was turning out?

He carefully stepped off the far side of the porch, with Granger following, and approached the sounds he could still hear in the shadows ahead. He bent and picked up a goodly sized rock that struck his poor toe when his toe wasn't looking. He didn't know who the enemy was up ahead, but at least now he had a weapon to defend himself with.

And then it hit him. Almost like a bolt of lightning.

He looked down. His ankle monitor was flashing *red!*

MR. DINKENS didn't look anything like he had the first time Luke saw him. He wasn't properly dressed for one thing. He was wrapped up in a ratty old plaid bathrobe, his bare feet, under white hairless ankles, were stuffed in an old pair of house slippers that had most certainly seen better days. There was a towel draped around his shoulders, and his hair was wet. He had obviously just been outside not more than a few minutes earlier, and everyone in the room knew what he had been doing.

There were scratches up and down Dinkens's shins like he'd been savaged by a dog. He saw Luke staring at them.

"Fucker likes to kick," Dinkens said, tilting his head at Strickland.

"Water," Strickland said.

And Dinkens smiled a nasty little smile.

To Luke's surprise it was Bradley who seemed really pissed about the whole thing. "You killed your wife."

Dinkens looked down at the kid as he stepped off the stairs and moved closer. "And your point is—?"

"She made us cookies. She was nice."

"She was a pig, kid. She looks like four hundred pounds of bread dough in that damn tub. Didn't you see her? Besides she was getting suspicious about my little hobby. Had to get rid of her. Not to mention the fact that it was costing a fortune to feed her. That woman could *eat*."

DeVon took a crack at the bastard. "You killed the cat too. Why'd you kill the cat?"

"Hate cats," he said, and left it at that. "Hate kids, too, so watch your mouth."

Then, with a blink of his eyes, he dismissed both Bradley and DeVon and turned to Luke.

"I was coming after you next, kiddo. I had no intention of playing the game with anyone so close to home, but you're just too tempting not to have a taste of. Fooling around with the kid next door, aren't you? Maybe I'll take both of you at once. Make you perform. That might be interesting." He looked back at the kids. "But first these little fuckers have to go."

Luke dragged the boys behind him. He stepped in front of them, wondering how he would protect them if, God forbid, Dinkens pulled out a gun.

But before he could find out *what* Dinkens had in mind, a gust of wind swept through the basement, scattering leaves and dust bunnies at their feet. The sound of the storm outside was suddenly a lot nearer, a lot louder.

Someone had opened the trapdoor.

Dinkens seemed to have been expecting it. "And here's your boyfriend, right on cue," he said with a lazy smile.

With Luke and the boys standing in front of the little light burning inside Strickland's cage, the basement was a lot darker than it had been before. All four of them heard footsteps descending the concrete steps beneath the trapdoor, shuffling footsteps, but they couldn't see who it was.

Luke was praying to God it wasn't Danny. But praying or not, he was really surprised to learn that it actually *wasn't* Danny.

"Arthur, you always were an asshole. Let those kids go."

Luke couldn't believe it. It was Mrs. Trumball.

She stepped out of the stairway and placed herself in the light for all to see. She was still in her faded housecoat and bunny slippers, and if anything, Luke thought her makeup looked worse than it had when they saw her earlier, probably thanks to the rain. She was clutching a gin bottle in her hand.

She was sopping wet.

Luke had never been so happy to see anyone in his life.

Dinkens seemed to feel differently about it. "Lord, Ruth, don't you ever take your hair out of those fucking rollers," and with that, Dinkens raised his hand. In it he held a revolver.

"Put that gun down!" a male voice bellowed from the staircase Dinkens had just come down. Dinkens whirled around and took a pot shot at whoever the hell was back there, but he knew he'd missed. Then he swung around and fired a shot at Mrs. Trumball.

He blew one of her rollers clean off her head. And most of the hair along with it.

"Aaarrgghh!" Outraged, Mrs. Trumball bellowed like a bull. She hauled back and flung the half-full bottle of gin across the basement with such force, and with such deadly accuracy, that when it hit Dinkens in the head, his dentures went flying out of his mouth and landed at Luke's feet.

"Yuk," DeVon said. "Teeth."

Bradley pointed to the stairs leading up to the house, and the two men standing on it.

"Who the heck are *they?*"

AT THE sound of the first gunshot, Danny went stumbling across Dinkens's backyard, swinging his cast back and forth like a wrecking ball trying to keep it out of his way as he blinked away the rain and tried to locate where the sound came from. He knew it was a shot. He just didn't know who was shooting. Or exactly where it came from. Or who was the target. He just prayed to God it wasn't Luke.

He snagged his cast on a pile of rusty metal fence posts and went flying. He landed on the posts, causing one holy hell of a racket. All of the fence posts had sharp edges at one end, and they took most of the skin from Danny's palms when he hit them.

He hardly noticed. He was back on his feet, still running full out on his long, gangly legs, or as full out as the cast would allow. He was still trying to locate the source of the gunshot. Panic was setting in. Where was Luke?

In a flash of lightning that came about two seconds too late, Danny saw the flung open trapdoor materialize beneath his feet at about the very same moment he plunged through the opening with a scream. He hit the concrete steps at an angle, and in a puff of plaster dust, his cast burst open like a piñata. Danny screamed again because that motherfucker *hurt.*

He grabbed his broken leg which was now barely protected by the shattered remnants of the cast. He tried desperately to shield it from more injury as he went tumbling down the remaining steps like a rag doll. At the bottom, he hit Mrs. Trumball full in the back and sent them both sprawling. Luckily, they landed in a pile of discarded clothing. The only truly disturbing aspect of their landing was the fact about twenty rats went running for their lives from beneath the pile of clothes where they had apparently been holding an Alanon meeting or something.

"Look," DeVon screeched happily. "Rats!"

"Ooh," Mrs. Trumball snarked. "Vermin!"

"Please get off my leg," Danny requested of her as politely as he could. Then he passed out.

Across the room, Dinkens clawed his way to his feet. He still had the gun in his hand, but before he could lift it and aim it and take another pot shot at somebody, Luke made a running tackle and took him down again. The two of them wrestled across the basement floor, Luke trying to get the gun away, Dinkens trying to shoot him with it. It was about then the two strangers Bradley had never seen before came tromping all the way down the staircase from inside the house and jumped into the fray.

One of the men was tall and dark and handsome, and the other was shorter and redheaded and *just* as handsome. It was a funny thing, Bradley had time to think, but they looked a lot like Danny and Luke.

The taller man must have played football in school. When he kicked Mr. Dinkens in the head, it was all Bradley could do not to throw his arms in the air and scream, "Field goal!"

And when the redheaded guy kicked Dinkens in the head from the *other* side, it was all Bradley could do not to scream "Penalty. Unnecessary roughness! But that's okay. Go ahead and do it anyway!"

Those two kicks in the head pretty much knocked the poop juice out of Mr. Dinkens. If he was awake after the second kick, he sure didn't show it. In fact, he never moved again.

"Danny!" Luke screamed. He ran to the pile of cast-off clothes and dropped to his knees at Danny's side.

It was about then Danny opened his eyes and said, "Hi, baby."

Luke smiled down at him and kissed him on the lips. Then he kissed him a few more times. He showered Danny's face with so many kisses even Mrs. Trumball began to look a little surprised.

But not nearly as surprised as the two men who'd kicked Dinkens in the head.

They ran to the pile of discarded clothing right behind Luke. By then Luke was finished smothering Danny with kisses. He was now cradling Danny's head in his arms and urging him not to move so he wouldn't hurt his leg any more than it was already hurt. While he did that, the tall man with the dark hair bent over Danny and gave him a hug.

"Whoa there, buddy!" Luke cried. "Why are you hugging my boyfriend?"

The man gazed into Luke's face and Luke recognized the guy in the zoo picture on the wall in Danny's kitchen. "Oh. Mr. Shay. My God. I mean, I'm sorry. I mean—uh—my God. It's a real pleasure to meet you. Yessiree. A real pleasure indeed."

Luke finally stopped stammering and shut the hell up.

"Hi, Dad," Danny said.

Danny's father's eyebrow shot up, but he didn't speak. Even in his confusion, he looked like he was trying not to smile.

The redheaded man came up behind Danny's dad and slipped an arm around him to help him to his feet. When they stood, their hands came together in a clench and stayed there.

Danny looked at the other man. The shorter man. The man with reddish hair. The man holding his father's hand. "You're Luke's dad. You must be. You look just like him."

Danny and Luke just stared at their two fathers clasping hands, while the two fathers stood there looking down at them. Danny brought Luke's fingers up to his face and gave each one a kiss. Danny's father did the same with the man's hand he was holding. Then the four men understood everything.

"I think I see what your business trips were all about," Danny finally said.

His father grinned. "And I think I see what you wanted to have a heart-to-heart talk about. Are you okay?"

"Yeah," Danny said, "I'm—" and then he turned toward the tiny room behind the furnace, groaning when he twisted his leg. "My God, Luke! Strickland! We have to take care of Strickland!"

It was then they all heard the cooing going on. It was Mrs. Trumball and the two boys. Mrs. Trumball was holding a glass of water to Strickland's parched lips, helping him drink, cooing words of comfort into his ear, telling him everything would be all right. Bradley had rummaged through the pile of cast-off clothing to find an old shirt to cover Strickland's nakedness. DeVon was still in the process of rooting through the pockets in Dinkens's bathrobe. Finally, he pulled out a key and held it up in the air for everyone to see. "Aha!" he cried. "Freedom!"

He quickly slipped the key into the rusty old manacle holding Strickland's hand to the ring in the wall, and with a clank and a sigh, Strickland lowered his arm for the first time in three days.

Then he wept, and the boys and Mrs. Trumball wrapped their arms around the young man and wept with him.

It was right then, a day late and a dollar short, that sixteen cops from the San Diego Police Department, each and every one of them looking smug and self-important, came barreling through both basement doors and stomping down both flights of stairs like a herd of blue-clad bison.

"Danny Shay!" Somebody screamed through a bullhorn. "Your light turned red, Bucko. You're under arrest!"

Luke and Danny could only laugh. It was just too ridiculous. Then their dads laughed. Then Mrs. Trumball laughed, but that was only because DeVon had returned her unbroken bottle of gin from where he found it under the stairs where it rolled after she bonked Dinkens in the head with it, knocking his teeth halfway across the basement.

"Stupid cops," Mrs. Trumball groused. "Never around when you *need* them, but boy, the moment you *don't* need them, they show up in droves." She took a healthy slug of gin to calm her nerves, not caring what anybody thought about it. In fact, maybe her days of *hiding* and drinking were over. Maybe from now on she would simply *drink.* She was tired of slinking around. Maybe there would be even more exciting nights like this in her future, if she just got out of the house a little more often.

She tossed back a second slug of gin and mulled it over while she went back to comforting Strickland. The poor boy.

Dinkens gave a snort now and then, but he never woke up through all the ensuing commotion. When he did wake up, Danny figured he would be in for quite a surprise.

Danny tried not to grimace and fidget around while Luke ever so gently wrapped a folded blanket around his broken leg and shattered cast and secured it with his belt to keep the bone in place until the EMTs arrived. Danny stared up at his dad, who was still holding hands with Luke's dad. The two of them were looking down at Danny and Luke and smiling proudly. Neither of them seemed particularly surprised to find their two sons so affectionate with each other. But as far as surprises went, Danny didn't figure anybody had received a bigger surprise than *he* had.

It was amazing. His dad looked almost as happy as Danny felt.

And apparently he was gayer than a goose, just like Danny. Danny supposed that was what he had wanted to talk about when he got back from Tucson. That and the fact he was dragging a lover back home with him, and Danny's new mom was actually going to be another dad.

Good Lord, now he and his dad were both with the men they loved.

Who in the world would ever have seen *that* surprise coming?

Meanwhile the sixteen cops milled around looking mightily confused, obviously wondering whom to arrest first.

CHAPTER SIXTEEN
HOUSING CONSIDERATIONS

DANNY was in his room, sprawled out in his recliner, staring down at the brand new cast on his leg. If anything, he hated this cast more than the last one. This one was tighter. It hurt more. Or maybe his leg was still sore from the night before. He tilted his head just a smidgeon to the right and considered his other leg, which was now blessedly monitor free. And what a relief *that* was. The left leg might be miserable as hell, but the right leg was happy as a clam. Then Danny shifted his eyes to the middle and stared at Luke's gorgeous face. He was squatting on the floor at Danny's feet with his chin on the footrest of the recliner, looking lovingly up at Danny's face. Luke had his fingers tucked inside the top of Danny's cast, just below the knee, because Danny said it made it hurt less when he did. With his other hand, Luke was stroking Danny's warm thigh and getting lascivious thoughts. Luke suspected Danny was getting the same thoughts he was.

They were both in their daily uniform of baggy shorts and T-shirts. The sun was climbing up the morning sky outside Danny's bedroom window, and the storm was happily over. It probably wouldn't rain again for six months. But that's San Diego for you.

Courtesy of their fathers, Luke and Danny were holding celebratory beers in their hands and taking a sip now and then while they talked. Neither of them was too crazy about the taste.

They were sure as hell crazy about each other, though.

Luke held his beer up in a toast. "Here's to the judge for releasing you from house arrest and stripping you of that goddamn ankle monitor and commending you for your selfless act of bravery in helping to rescue poor Charlie. You're a hero, Danny. Who'd have thunk it, huh?"

Danny laughed while they clinked their bottles together. "You're a hero too. The judge said so. And while we're thanking our friend the judge, let's also thank him for having second thoughts and deciding to have the D.A.'s office investigate my old boss for siphoning money from his employees' paychecks. The bastard."

"The bastard," Luke agreed, hoisting his beer.

Again they clinked their bottles together.

And one more toast. "Here's to Mrs. Trumball," Danny said. "The woman came through like the trooper she truly is. She promised help would be forthcoming, and by golly help forthcame. Or however you say it." As an afterthought, he added, "And here's to hoping that someday soon she'll learn how to remove her makeup at night so it won't keep accumulating like a bazillion coats of paint."

Luke giggled.

They had learned only that morning it was Mrs. Trumball who contacted Danny's dad the evening before and told him to get his ass home because the neighborhood was going to hell in a handbasket and his son was in the middle of it. So when she told the boys help was on the way, she knew of what she spoke.

They also learned that after the escapade in Dinkens's basement, Mrs. Trumball had ratted out DeVon and Bradley to their parents about roaming the neighborhood at all hours of the day and night. Now, Mrs. Trumball reported, the two boys were under their own form of house arrest, grounded until somewhere in the vicinity of their thirtieth birthdays. Danny and Luke figured they were going to miss seeing the boys around. But maybe not much. The little shits.

"To Mrs. Trumball," Luke said. "God bless her gin-soaked tattling heart." And again their bottles clinked.

At the sound of paper tearing, they looked over to the bookcase by the window where Frederick was mangling a copy of *The Wind in the Willows*. Having grown tired of Mark Twain, he had apparently decided to see what damage he could do in the world of children's literature. Judging by the scraps of paper scattered all over the carpet beneath him, the damage was turning out to be considerable. Mr. Toad was having a rough day indeed.

Granger was licking his balls by the door. And that is pretty much all that needs to be said about that.

"Why do you think he did it?" Danny asked. "Dinkens, I mean. Just why the heck did he do it? Take all those lives. Hurt all those people."

Luke gave his head a sad little shake. "Who knows? Sick. Mean. Just plain nuts. Who knows? At least Strickland's going to be okay. He lost his finger but he kept his life. That's something."

"Physically, he'll be all right," Danny said, "but who knows what the ordeal did to his head. He'll probably need to do some healing inside. I think I would. The other victims weren't so lucky."

Luke sadly gazed through the open window. "No. They weren't."

Behind them, Danny's bedroom doorknob rattled. But then it stopped. Silence reigned for a good ten seconds while they heard hushed voices in the hall. Eventually, there came a gentle rapping on the door.

"Can we come in?" a voice called out.

Danny grinned. It was his dad. Probably afraid of walking in on some sort of horrible new gay sex rite only homosexuals under the age of nineteen know about. At least Danny had his dad trained not to just walk on in like he used to back in the days when Danny only had sex with himself. That was a step in the right direction. And by the way, boy was Danny glad *those* days were over.

"Come on in!" Danny yelled. To Luke, he muttered, "You stay exactly where you are."

Luke gave him a mock salute and kissed his toe. "I intend to," he said. "They'll have to get used to it sooner or later."

The door opened and both fathers walked into the room. They were in matching bathrobes Danny had never seen before. They weren't holding hands at the moment, but Danny thought their cheeks were suspiciously rosy. He wondered just exactly what they might have been doing to make them look like that. Then he decided maybe he didn't want to know.

They sat side by side at the edge of the bed, hips touching, staring at their two sons in front of them. Luke's hand was still resting on Danny's thigh, the fingers of his other hand were still tucked inside the top of Danny's cast, and he wasn't about to move either of them. He seemed slightly surprised when no one asked him to.

Danny studied Luke's dad. The guy really was handsome. He looked a lot like Luke. Ginger hair, shorter than Danny's dad, but like Luke, better built. Danny's father smiled gently at Danny as Danny scoped out the man beside him.

"His name is Jeff. Jeff Jamison," his father said. "Jeff, this is my son, Danny. You met Mr. Jamison last night, Danny, but maybe you don't remember, what with all the excitement and everything."

"Hello, Danny," Luke's dad said. "Call me Jeff." His voice was as soft as butter. He had an easy smile Danny suspected rarely left his face. Danny liked the man immediately. And he was thrilled for his dad too. He really was. They looked happy together, and Danny was glad his father had found someone.

Was Danny shocked to have learned his father was gay? No, he decided. Not at all. It was just the way some people are. What they did in their bedrooms didn't matter. What mattered was what they felt in their hearts. How they treated the people around them. How they lived the lives that were given them. That's what mattered.

Danny's father was a good man. Gay or straight, he would always be a good man.

Luke tilted his head at Danny's dad, but he spoke to his own father. "I take it this is the gay neighbor you said we would be living next to when we moved to San Diego."

"That's the one," his dad said proudly. "But I'm afraid there's been a change of plans. We aren't going to be neighbors after all."

Luke and Danny both tensed up. Worried looks shot across their faces. It was Luke who spoke first. "You mean we're not buying the house?" His voice was two octaves higher than usual.

Danny watched as the two older men's hands just sort of *found* each other and their fingers intertwined. Neither his dad nor Luke's dad seemed to have made an effort to seek the other out. It just happened.

Luke's dad said, "Don't worry. We're still buying the house. I transferred money for a down payment this morning. It's a done deal."

Luke looked confused. "Then why do you say we won't be neighbors? If you move somewhere else, I'm not going. I want to be with Danny."

Danny laid his hand over Luke's, but he didn't say anything. He still looked worried, though. His eyes were burning holes in his father, waiting to hear what the hell the two men were beating around the bush about.

It was Danny's father who tried to explain. "We're not going to be neighbors, boys, because Jeff and I want to live together. We're assuming you guys want to live together too."

"Well, *duh!*" Danny snapped. And just as quickly, he said, "Sorry. Didn't mean to say that, Pop. I just don't understand what's going on. Just give it to us in plain English, okay? You're scaring the heck out of us."

Both men grinned.

"Don't be afraid, Danny. Dan and I have a proposition for you both." It was Luke's father speaking. He still held Danny's father's hand. If anything, he seemed to have scooted a little closer to the man he was in love with. "We've decided to help you boys get started. We know what it's like to be gay, and we know what it's like to be in love. We also, believe it or not, remember what it's like to be young and broke. We don't want you guys to struggle like we did when we were your age."

A little line formed between Danny's eyebrows. He was confused. "I wish one of you would just spit it out. What are you trying to say exactly?"

Luke's dad took a deep breath and laid things out in the open. "We want you boys to take the new house. I mean, not *legally,* but just to live in. Rent free. For as long as you need it."

Luke and Danny sprang to attention, grins creeping across their faces. Luke's face snuggled up to Danny's foot, the one without the cast, and stayed there. Occasionally he planted a kiss on Danny's newly monitor-free ankle.

"With a few caveats," Danny's dad interjected. "We'll expect you to both either start working or start some sort of schooling as soon as you can. We would prefer schooling, but we'll leave it up to you. We just want you to find something to do that you can be happy doing for the rest of your life. And that doesn't mean flipping burgers and destroying ice machines for the next forty years."

Danny laughed. His father didn't.

It was Jeff's turn. "As soon as you're on your feet, moneywise, Dan and I expect the two of you to pay the utilities on the house. Lights, water, the works. We expect you to keep the property in good shape and we expect you to say good morning when you see either one of us across the hedge."

"What if it's afternoon?" Luke asked.

"Don't be a wiseass," his father said.

Danny's dad leaned forward and stared more closely at Danny's face. He waited until his son was staring back and paying full attention.

"Danny, I kind of think you boys are too young to be lovers. But Jeff feels differently. What do *you* think, Son? Are you honestly ready to commit to one person? To always be there with them when they want you there, and maybe take a hike now and then when they need to be alone? Are you ready for that kind of commitment? It isn't always easy being gay, Son. And it really isn't easy being lovers. It takes work."

Danny didn't hesitate. He held Luke's hand while he spoke. "Being gay is something I have no control over. I am what I am. Just like you are. Just like all four of us are. But I do know I want to be with Luke. I'll do whatever it takes to make him happy. And I don't doubt for a minute that he'll do the same for me. We *have* to be lovers, Pop. It isn't even a matter of choice. We *need* to be together."

Danny's dad smiled at the earnestness on his son's face. He turned to Luke. "And you?" he asked softly. "What do you think of all this?"

Even while he spoke, Luke did not lift his cheek from Danny's foot. "I think I loved your son the first minute I saw him. Tell me, sir. Do you believe in love at first sight?"

Danny's father dragged his eyes to the man beside him. "Yes," he said. "I've believed in it ever since I met your dad. It's like—it's like—"

Luke finished the thought for him. "It's like a bolt of lightning. A bolt of lightning that crashes right into your heart. Don't you think? Don't you think that's what it's like?"

Danny's father nodded. There was a sparkle in his eyes that hadn't been there before. A new huskiness in his voice. "That's exactly what it's like," he said. "Lightning. Right to the heart."

"I'm crazy nuts about your son, sir. I'll be good to him. I will." Luke's eyes were open, honest, sincere.

"I'm not worried about that, Luke."

"And I'll be good to *your* son," Danny said to the ginger-haired man in love with his father.

Jeff smiled another gentle smile when Danny spoke the words that so clearly came from the boy's heart. "And I'm not worried about *that,* Danny."

Without realizing he was even doing it, Danny's father lifted Jeff's hand to his face and held it to his cheek while he spoke. "So this is definitely what you both want."

"Yes, sir," Luke said. His blue eyes were crystal clear. Filled with love. Filled with determination.

"We'll never be happy any other way," Danny said. "Just like the two of you, I think."

"Yes," Jeff said. "Just like the two of us."

Luke's father laid his head on his new lover's shoulder. Together, the two men simply sat there and stared at the two boys they had raised half a country apart from each other. But somehow their boys had come together. Just like they had. A happiness lit up both men's eyes and Danny felt his own eyes tear up to see it there.

Danny's dad cleared his throat. "Danny. Luke. If you're sure this is who you are, and if you're sure this is what you want, then you have our full blessing. All we ask is that you give us your blessing in return."

"Gladly," Danny said.

"Happily," Luke said, at the very same moment.

"Meow," Frederick said from the bookcase, and all four laughed.

"On *that* note," Jeff announced, pulling himself to his feet and tightening the belt on his bathrobe, "I'm going to go start breakfast. Breakfast for everybody. You boys come down when you're ready. Or when you smell the house burning down around you. I'm not much of a cook."

"Don't worry." Danny's father grinned. "I am. I'll give you a hand."

They headed for the door. They both seemed a little relieved that the conversation was over. Danny supposed this was a bit like the gay version of the "birds and the bees" speech. Every parent is always glad to see that end, too, or so Danny had heard. He couldn't imagine why.

Well, maybe he could.

Danny's father turned back at the door. With a wink to both Luke and his son, he said, "You boys come on downstairs, okay? You had a hell of a night. You need some food in you." With a grin threatening to turn up the corners of his mouth, he added, "I don't imagine we'll see you again for the rest of the day after breakfast is over. Right? You'll be sleeping in, I guess. Spending the day in bed, what with your being so exhausted from your adventures, and then your stint in the emergency room getting a new cast put on and all."

Danny laughed, clutching Luke's hand just a little bit tighter. "Right as rain, Pop. Really exhausted. Worn out completely. Both of us. We'll probably sleep for maybe a couple of days."

At his feet, Luke merely smiled, although he blushed when he did it. Inside his head, he was agreeing all over the place. He had all *kinds* of things he wanted to do with Danny after breakfast, and it might indeed take two full days to get them all done. Sleeping in wasn't exactly involved, but the bed certainly was. And Danny's strong arms and long lean legs and everything to be found between those arms and legs was most *certainly* involved.

With a shake of their heads, as if maybe they knew exactly what their sons were thinking, and they probably did, the two fathers closed the door quietly behind them, leaving the boys alone.

Danny gazed at Luke's face. In Luke's perfect cornflower-blue eyes, he saw not a glimmer of doubt that Danny was everything Luke wanted. Danny hoped Luke could see the same truth, the same certainty, in his own eyes. Because it was there. He knew it was. This was just the way Danny always dreamed love would be. There was not a doubt between the two of them. They both knew exactly what they wanted.

They wanted each other. Period.

But first, a little breakfast.

Danny grunted his way to his feet. He pulled Luke up from the floor. Then he couldn't hold it in another minute.

"We've got a house!" Danny screamed.

"All to ourselves!" Luke screamed right back.

Still grinning and jumping around, stunned by their good fortune, they headed through the door.

Halfway down the stairs a tornado flew past. It was Frederick, and Granger was hot on his heels. They were both madder than hell. Between the two of them, they sounded like *forty* dogs and cats and a couple of Tasmanian devils.

"Aw, pets," Luke sighed happily.

Danny pulled Luke close to use him as a crutch, and Luke was more than happy to be used. Together they headed for the kitchen and the smell of bacon frying in a skillet. It smelled heavenly. Danny suddenly realized how hungry he was.

Somebody dropped a pot lid on the kitchen floor, and his father's laughter rang out. Luke's dad joined in. They sounded like a couple of kids.

Danny smiled, listening to them.

"You love me," Luke whispered in his ear.

"You love me too," Danny said, opening his eyes and savoring the sound of Luke's voice, savoring the sight of Luke's perfect face. Savoring the warmth of Luke's arms holding him tight.

Then they laughed, because they simply had to. And, still laughing, they joined their dads in the kitchen.

JOHN INMAN has been writing fiction since he was old enough to hold a pencil. He and his partner live in beautiful San Diego, California. Together, they share a passion for theater, books, hiking and biking along the trails and canyons of San Diego or, if the mood strikes, simply kicking back with a beer and a movie. John's advice for anyone who wishes to be a writer? "Set time aside to write every day and do it. Don't be afraid to share what you've written. Feedback is important. When a rejection slip comes in, just tear it up and try again. Keep mailing stuff out. Keep writing and rewriting and then rewrite one more time. Every minute of the struggle is worth it in the end, so don't give up. Ever. Remember that publishers are a lot like lovers. Sometimes you have to look a long time to find the one that's right for you."

You can contact John at john492@att.net, on Facebook: http://www.facebook.com/john.inman.79, or on his website: http://www.johninmanauthor.com/

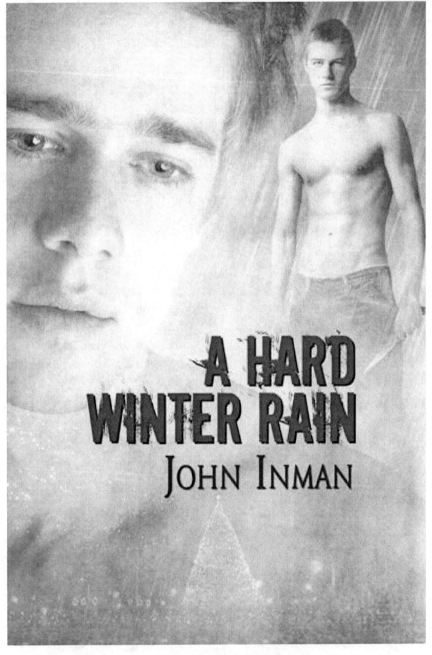

A HARD WINTER RAIN

JOHN INMAN

Also from JOHN INMAN

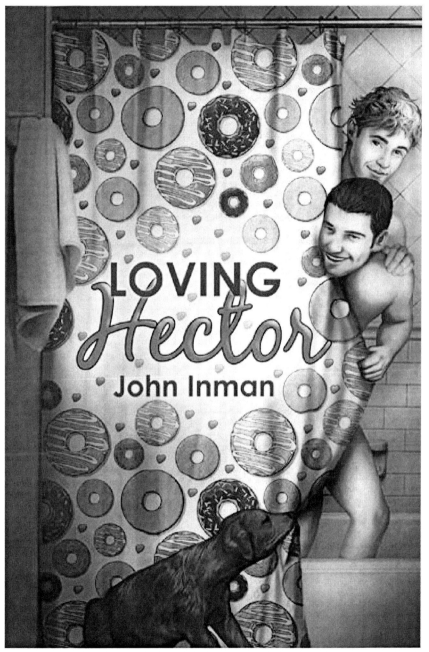

LOVING Hector

John Inman

http://www.dreamspinnerpress.com

Also from JOHN INMAN

http://www.dreamspinnerpress.com

Roots And Wings

D.W. MARCHWELL

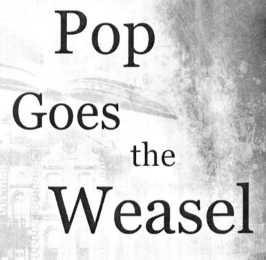

Pop
Goes
the
Weasel

Stephen Osborne

CPSIA information can be obtained
at www.ICGtesting.com
Printed in the USA
FFOW02n1623170516
24157FF